BECKA'S SONG

Frankie J. Jones

Bella
BOOKS

2008

Bella Books, Inc.
P.O. Box 10543
Tallahassee, FL 32302

Printed in the United States of America on acid-free paper
First Edition

Editor: Christi Cassidy
Cover Designer: Stephanie Solomon-Lopez

ISBN 10: 1-59493-138-0
ISBN 13: 978-1-59493-138-3

DEDICATION
To Martha and our next round of adventures

ACKNOWLEDGMENTS

Martha Cabrera—Thanks for putting up with me, Megan and the multitude of characters who wander through our lives. If there is a hereafter, it must have a special place set aside for the spouses of writers.

Peggy Herring—Thanks for helping make it possible. Enjoy your weekends!

Carol Poynor—nitpicker extraordinaire. Thanks for everything you do. With you around I'll never feel "really badly."

Christi Cassidy—Thanks for all your hard work and attention to detail. I appreciate your honesty and strong sense of professionalism. Happy birding.

A SPECIAL NOTE OF THANKS
TO MY READERS

When I first entertained the notion of trying to get a manuscript published, I envisioned one book. Never in my wildest dreams did I imagine fifteen. I definitely would have laughed at the idea that those books would be written in less than twelve years, but here it is—number fifteen.

To everyone who has ever read one of my books and especially to all those wonderful women in San Antonio who were always there to help in any way they could, I thank you for making my dream come true.

ABOUT THE AUTHOR

Frankie is an award-winning artist and freelance nature photographer. In her spare time she likes to rummage through flea markets and junk shops in search of broken treasure in need of repair. Her hobbies include woodworking, metal detecting and genealogy.

Authors love to hear from their readers. You may contact Frankie by e-mail at <u>FrankieJJones@aol.com</u>.

Writing as Frankie J. Jones
The Road Home
Voices of the Heart
For Every Season
Survival of Love
Midas Touch
Room for Love
Captive Heart
Whispers in the Wind
Rhythm Tide

Writing as Megan Carter
Midnight Melodies
Please Forgive Me
Passionate Kisses
When Love Finds a Home
On the Wings of Love

CHAPTER ONE

Lee moved through the gauzy darkness of pre-dawn without the aid of a flashlight. She had traveled the well-worn path many times over the past ten years. This was her sanctuary. She stopped and took a deep breath to savor the earthy aroma of the autumn air. From the slight burn in her calves, she knew she had topped the hill and was within a quarter mile of her destination. From here on the terrain would be more level. She zipped her lightweight jacket against a slight chill that warned of the colder days to come. Overhead the sky grew lighter and sounds of movement were starting to whisper through the woods. In the distance, a mockingbird tested a few notes on the morning air.

These small details reminded her that she needed to keep moving. As she settled into a comfortable pace, her rhythmic footsteps played counterpoint to the ever-broadening spectrum of melodies from the mockingbird perched somewhere high above. Vague shapes became discernible as the morning sun raced toward the horizon. Determined to beat the sun, she increased her speed. Soon the twittering of birds and the soft rustle of the small creatures of the forest would fill the air. Before that occurred, she would be securely hidden away in the blind. On this cool, crisp late-September morning, Lee Dresher sought a bigger prize. In her eagerness to reach her goal, she had to fight the urge to run. Every fiber of her being screamed that today was the day. Today the twelve-point buck would return.

She rolled her shoulders and smiled at the comfortable weight of the specially designed backpack that held her camera gear. Nearly three weeks had passed since she'd first spotted the magnificent buck from the blind that she had constructed years earlier. The blind was nothing more than a tight bower of living limbs and vines that she kept carefully trimmed and woven together to provide her a comfortable four-foot-by-six-foot space. It was located in a small clearing with a pristine creek that was icy cold year-round. The clearing provided her with the perfect site to shoot wildlife photos as the animals and birds came in for water. To ensure she never frightened them away from the life-sustaining stream, she always arrived prior to daybreak. She was vigilant about making as little impact as possible when she left.

Three weeks ago when she had spotted the buck at the edge of the clearing, he blended in so perfectly with the landscape that she'd nearly overlooked him. Despite all her mental coaxing, he had stubbornly refused to leave the safety of the woods. Since then she had rolled out of bed every morning at five and made the mile-long trek to the blind so that she could have her tripod and camera set up in case he returned. She sat in the blind each morning until nine. Then she raced home for a hot shower before driving into town to the art gallery she owned.

This morning, some inner sense told her today was the day he would return. She hadn't even taken time to make coffee before grabbing her gear and heading out.

When she arrived at the blind, she took a moment to listen to the gentle gurgling of the creek before she pulled a small flashlight from the multi-pocketed photographer's vest that she wore over her jacket. This was the only time she allowed anything to announce her presence in the forest, but she was afraid of snakes. She wouldn't feel comfortable in the blind until she checked it thoroughly to make sure some wandering timber rattler or one of a variety of other slithery serpents hadn't taken up residence. She flashed the light around the small enclosure. When she was satisfied the blind was empty of everything except the old, metal folding chair she kept there, she switched off the light, stepped inside and carefully pulled the limbs back together behind her. There was less light inside the blind, but she didn't need to see in order to set up her equipment. She slipped off the pack and placed it on the chair. Within a matter of a few moments, she had the tripod adjusted to the desired height. She ignored the chair and settled into a comfortable position on the ground. Then she removed her trusty Pentax K1000 from the case. She owned a pro digital camera with scads of bells and whistles and two other film cameras, but she found herself going back to her old reliable Pentax whenever she was after that perfect shot. Maybe it was simply her imagination or an ingrained sense of comfort with the older camera, but her shots with it always seemed sharper and more vibrant.

With practiced assurance, she attached a medium-length zoom lens to the camera, joined the quick-release attachment on the camera to its mate on the tripod and screwed on the cable release mechanism. She adjusted the tripod's location until the camera's lens poked through one of the carefully trimmed holes in the blind. With great care she slowly reached out and removed the lens cap. She patted the pockets of her photographer's vest. It was a nervous habit rather than an actual search. She knew there were three rolls of high-speed film and two of a slower speed. She also had an extra battery for the camera and even one for the flash that she used almost exclusively for floral or still life shots. In that same pocket she carried a shower cap in case she was ever caught in a sudden rainstorm and needed to protect the camera. The rest of the contents in the vest consisted of a compass, a small first-aid kit that included a tiny magnifying glass and a pair of tweezers that were great for removing thorns, a notepad, a mechanical pencil, a cell phone that she turned off before leaving the house, a bag of trail mix, a bottle of water and a soft brush with a squeeze bulb to clean the camera lens. The large pocket on the back of the vest held a small sketchpad. Satisfied that all was in order, she settled down for the hardest part—waiting. Too anxious to sit still she pulled the notepad and pencil from her pocket. Then with the flashlight beneath her jacket so that only the faintest light was visible, she started making a list of things she needed to take care of. The most important one was to call Barry Masters and have him come out to refill her propane tank before the cold weather kicked in.

The sky grew lighter. Individual trees and rocks slowly came into focus. Lee put away the pad and flashlight. She moved her head slowly to peer out the various peepholes she'd made in the blind. If the buck was coming, he would be there soon.

She twisted the drawstring on her jacket hood around her finger and waited. Rays of sunlight began to filter through the trees and paint bright patches of light onto the ground. With the sun came the first inkling of doubt that maybe this wasn't to be the day after all.

Squirrels began to chatter as they rushed about frantically collecting their winter food supply. More and more birds were belting out their morning repertoire and fluttering about. A cottontail hopped from the brush less than six feet from Lee. The sun cast a rosy glow through the thin skin of his ears. Her fingers itched to pull the sketchpad from her pocket and draw it, but she made herself wait. The distraction might make her slow in spotting the buck or, worse yet, miss him entirely. She turned her attention back to the forest surrounding the small clearing. Her eyes scanned the brush, looking for even the slightest bit of movement. Suddenly she froze as she caught a glimpse of antlers.

Lee held her breath as the twelve-point buck took a tentative step forward. Adrenaline surged through her, making it difficult for her to move slowly. Just a few more steps, she begged silently as she eased her hand over and took hold of the cable release. Her thumb caressed the button that would trigger the shutter as she stared through the viewfinder. The soft twitter of birds harmonized with the gentle babbling of the creek. A few more steps would place the buck in the glade where the early morning sunlight would sidelight him perfectly. The stream and dazzling display of fall colors from the trees beyond it would provide the perfect backdrop.

The buck blew softly and stamped his feet. His breath fogged in the brisk morning air. Lee's finger itched to snap off a few headshots, but she made herself wait. She needed the full-body shot. She told herself not to stare directly at him. She had heard plenty of tales from old-time hunters who swore animals could sense when they were being watched, and years of her own experience seemed to validate the claim. She shifted her gaze to the top of the viewfinder and focused on his antlers instead.

Seconds ticked away. A trickle of sweat made its way down her neck. Her body began to warm from the core. She fought to ignore it. Now was not the time for a hot flash. Her thumb quivered with anticipation.

His head held high, the buck took a cautious step forward and then another.

Lee's hand began to shake. She risked another quick glance at the settings on the camera. Then as if by magic, the buck stepped completely into the clearing, and raised his head as though he were posing just for her. He seemed to be staring straight at her, waiting. Lee sent a silent word of thanks to Veronica, the patron saint of photographers, as she inhaled and slowly released the breath. Her thumb began to apply steady pressure to the cable release button. Just before it clicked, a loud crashing in the brush beside her snapped her eye from the camera. Her hand jerked. She didn't have to look down to know the movement had caused the camera to shake. She watched, dumbfounded, as a woman wearing a bright red sweater and jeans pushed out of the brush and made her way toward the stream.

By the time Lee's brain registered what was happening, the buck was long gone. Stunned, she could only stare over her camera as the woman moved past her and took a seat on a large boulder by the stream.

As realization hit her, Lee jumped up. Normally she wouldn't have minded anyone walking across her land, but she intended to give this stranger a thorough lecture on trespassing. She turned to make her way out of the blind when through one of the peepholes in the side she saw the woman lower her face into her hands and start sobbing. Not the quiet tears-rolling-down-the-face sobs of merely having a good cry, but rather one of those deep-down tear-at-your-soul cries. Lee could only watch as the woman wailed. The depth of the anguish quickly extinguished her anger.

A cold chill ran down her back as she recalled the old ghost story about the wailing woman who wandered along creeks looking for her drowned children. She shoved the thought away. She wasn't in the Girl Scouts anymore and she'd never heard of any ghost who stumbled out of the woods in a bright red sweater. Especially sweaters that looked that good. She slapped herself on the forehead. She was supposed to be giving this stranger a piece of her mind about trespassing, not staring at her breasts, which were hard to ignore. She hesitated. She should just walk over there and confront the woman, but she couldn't. The moment was too intimate. She knew how mortified she herself would be if someone saw her in such a vulnerable position.

Lee sat down and simply watched. The woman was petite but much too thin. She wore her light brown hair short, but it looked professionally styled. Her jeans and boots showed very little sign of use. Everything about her style of dress suggested she wasn't from the area. Here, women tended to lean toward clothes that were both comfortable and durable.

The woman's misery touched Lee's heart. She knew what it was like to feel so unhappy. For her it had been her struggle with her sexuality and a failed marriage.

It began in her junior year of high school when she started dating Brandon Dresher. She fell in love with his enchanted dream of sailing around the world while writing the great American novel. For months, images of breathtaking sunsets in faraway places and soft sea breezes carried her through the monotony of school and working in her father's jewelry store. With Brandon there to fill her dreams with wonderful distant shorelines, her life was close to perfect until the day that a new student, Jean Braddock, walked into her life. Jean was everything that Lee's world wasn't. Jean smoked cigarettes, cut classes and wore ripped jeans and jump boots. Lee tried to stay away from the newcomer, but when Jean looked at her, a fire would catch hold in Lee and leave her shaking and weak. A cat-and-mouse game quickly developed, and Jean was definitely the cat. For the next several months, Lee managed to avoid being alone with her, but then two weeks before graduation she found herself alone in the girls' restroom with Jean. Even now, she wasn't sure exactly how it happened. All she could remember was Jean walking toward her and the next thing she knew, they were in a stall, her pants were around her ankles and Jean's hand was between her legs. The most frightening aspect of the episode was how much she enjoyed it, and how much she had wanted it to happen again. The incident threw her world completely off balance. It took her three days to convince Brandon to elope.

Lee tensed as the woman finally raised her head. She couldn't help but smile when the stranger removed a large blue bandanna from her pocket and loudly blew her nose. As the woman dried her eyes, Lee was able to get a good look at her face. She knew all of her neighbors and had better than fair knowledge of nearly everyone in the area. Some she didn't know by name, but she recognized their faces. This woman was a complete stranger.

The northern boundary of Lee's property bordered the Ouachita National Forest, but it was rare that hikers ever ventured this far away from the trails. The closest house, the old Peterson place, was about two miles down the road, but if you cut through the woods, it would be a lot closer. Lee had been keeping an eye on the property in case it went on the market. Mr. Peterson had died nearly three years ago. Since then the house and its adjoining sixty acres had stood empty. None of the three Peterson children seemed interested in moving back, so she felt certain they would eventually sell. Lee owned two hundred and fifty acres but intended to snap up any reasonably priced land that became available around her. The last thing she wanted was a subdivision of tract houses spoiling her tiny piece of paradise.

Lee's back had started to ache from sitting on the hard ground before the woman finally stood up and disappeared into the woods. Lee struggled to her feet and rubbed her butt. Maybe it was time to add a small cushion to her little hideout. She carefully broke down the camera setup and packed everything away. After she had the tripod securely fastened to the bottom of the pack, she slipped the straps over her arms and pushed it around until the weight settled comfortably on her back. She stepped out of the blind and carefully pushed the limbs back together before giving one last look toward the area the buck had been standing. He probably wouldn't return for several days, but just in case, she would start her vigil again the following morning.

CHAPTER TWO

Lee parked her twelve-year-old blue and white Ford pickup in the alley behind the Dresher Gallery of Fine Arts. The truck looked like hell, and despite having over a hundred and twenty-two thousand miles on it, the motor was still sound. She loved everything about it. She used her key to enter through the back door. The gallery opened at nine, but her assistant, Gladys Downing, usually arrived at eight thirty.

Lee hung her jacket on a hook in the back room and slipped her lunch into the small refrigerator. There were several cardboard boxes stacked along the wall. They contained prints and postcards of Lee's artwork. She had placed the orders for the extra stock several weeks ago in preparation for the upcoming holiday rush. In addition to her own paintings and photographs, the gallery also carried the work of eight other artists who resided in Christmas or the surrounding area. From her own paintings, she provided both originals and Giclée prints, plus less expensive paper prints in a range of sizes all the way down to postcards. She had quickly discovered that it was much easier to sell a twenty-five-dollar print than it was a two-thousand-dollar original.

"I was beginning to wonder if that old clunker of yours had finally left you on the side of the road," Gladys called out as she joined Lee. "I don't know why you don't buy yourself a decent vehicle."

As always, Gladys looked as though she had dressed to step into a boardroom with some high-powered executives. Today she wore a sharp-looking burgundy skirt and jacket with a black blouse. Her heels matched the skirt and jacket. A thin woven silver chain necklace with a matching bracelet and small silver loop earrings completed her ensemble. Gladys loved clothes. She could spot and name designer labels as easily as Lee could determine hues of paint.

"I had the strangest experience this morning," Lee said, ignoring the comments about her truck. It might look like a disreputable heap, but she loved it and intended to drive it as long as possible.

Gladys looked up from the papers she had been reviewing. "Oh, don't tell me Melinda Thayer finally caught you."

Lee rolled her eyes. "I'm perfectly happy being single. Melinda Thayer isn't ever going to catch me." Melinda was a sketch artist who moved to Christmas nearly two years ago. Lee loved Melinda's work and agreed to show some of her pieces at the gallery. It wasn't long before Lee realized that Melinda's interest seemed more directed toward the gallery owner than the business itself.

"Be careful, girl—never say never." Gladys waggled at finger at her. "I once said I'd never leave Chicago and now look at me living out here in the middle of the boonies." She gave Lee a knowing look. "I'm married to Smokey the Bear and have two grown cubs. Lawd, if my poor mama could see me now," she drawled in an exaggerated tone, "she'd be wonderin' how her poor black child ended up in this lily-white Hooterville."

"Oh, stop it. You're not the only African-American family in Christmas and you told me yourself that your mother grew up in a small Illinois farming community just outside Chicago. As for you being a poor child, I distinctively remember you telling me that your mother was a doctor on staff at Rush University Medical Center Hospital." Lee shook her head as she thought about Gladys's husband, Dewayne, a ranger at Ouachita National Forest. "If I could find someone as sweet as Dewayne, maybe I'd settle down."

"You settle down. Now there's something I'd like to see. But you're right about Dewayne. He is a handsome devil, if I do say so myself."

At forty-five, Dewayne Downing was six-feet-four with the body of a linebacker. He and Gladys had met in college. They had moved to Christmas about eight years ago after he was assigned to the Ouachita site. Gladys had walked into the gallery one hot afternoon to look around and the two women started talking. Lee took an instant liking to the woman who loved to brag about her twin boys who had, with the aid of scholarships, years of summer jobs, family support and determination, graduated from Harvard. Lee had been thinking about hiring an assistant and Gladys more than filled all the requirements she was looking for. Now she was an integral part of the business. Gladys had an uncanny sense for business and was completely at ease with the customers. She was such an important part of the gallery that Lee had been thinking about offering her a partnership in the business.

"What was the strange experience?" Gladys asked. "And don't you dare start talking about UFOs or Bigfoot."

Lee smiled. Every few months a new set of stories about UFOs or Bigfoot seemed to sprout up like weeds around the area. Maybe it was due to the remoteness of the town, which was practically surrounded by the million-acre Ouachita National Forest, or maybe people were just bored with the doldrums of everyday life. "I was at the blind."

"That's not news."

"Let me finish. I was sitting there and the buck came up. I

was just about to snap the photo when this woman walks right out of the forest."

Gladys looked at her over the top of her reading glasses. "Who was she?"

"I don't know. I've never seen her before. But get this. Just as I was getting ready to climb out of the blind and read her the riot act on trespassing, she sits down by the creek and bursts into tears."

"What did you do?"

Lee took a coffee cup from a small cabinet. "I waited until she left and then I left. Do you want some coffee?"

"No. I've already had two cups. Any more and I'll be bouncing off the ceiling." She watched as Lee poured the coffee. "So you didn't say anything to this woman?"

"No. I was too shocked at first and then it was embarrassing. How could I step out and tell her that I had been sitting there watching her cry?"

"What did she look like?"

Lee sipped her coffee before replying. "About my age, I guess. She had short, light brown hair and was wearing a red sweater, jeans and boots."

Gladys shook her head. "That could describe almost every woman in town."

"What else can I say? I told you I don't know her."

"Well, if she's living around here, she'll show up in town eventually." Gladys waved the sheaf of papers she'd brought with her. "Clarissa Jenkins dropped these off a few minutes ago."

"What is it?"

"It's the schedule for Decoration Days."

On the last Saturday of September, the town virtually shut down for a two-day frenzy in which practically every able-bodied member of the community arrived to help decorate the town to kick off the holiday season. These next three months were what kept most of the businesses afloat. The remainder of Lee's year depended on the sporadic art-lovers' dollars. The campers and hikers who visited the national forest didn't contribute much to her sales. This year had been a mediocre one. The local merchants were praying that the holiday season would be vigorous enough to carry them through the lean winter months until business picked up again in the spring.

"What are we responsible for?" Lee asked as she wrapped her hands around her coffee cup.

"Lucky us. We're painting signs."

"It could be worse. Remember the year we had to help braid the horses' manes?"

Gladys wrinkled her nose. "You're right. At least we only have to paint the signs once."

"Where are we working?"

Gladys flipped one of the pages over. "We're supposed to be at the VFW Hall at six a.m. next Saturday morning."

Lee tried not to groan. This event was the lifeblood of the town, but it was also a lot of hard work. She grabbed a yogurt from the refrigerator. "I guess I should get to work." She took a spoon from the drawer and headed to her studio. As she entered the room and closed the door, she took a deep breath and slowly relaxed. She loved this room because of all the natural light the windows allowed. After purchasing the building, which had originally been an old five-and-dime store, along with the large lot where it sat, she hired a contractor to renovate and add on two rooms to the original eleven-hundred-square-foot space. One room she used for storage and the break area. The second room was her studio. She'd had windows installed across the entire upper section of the back wall. The windows were high enough that she wasn't distracted by whatever activity was going on outside and still allowed a substantial amount of north light to enter. Of the entire gallery, here was where she felt the most comfortable—among the clutter of her paints, brushes and canvases. She glanced around at the seven nearly completed paintings. They were lacking what she referred to as the "final pizzazz," which consisted of those last few highlights and details needed to take the painting beyond the ordinary. The pieces had to be finished in the next few days if she wanted to include them in the late-October show the gallery hosted as part of the annual holiday festivities. She rarely sold an original anymore without first having a hundred, high-quality Giclée prints made first.

She had never been able to work on just one painting at a time. Besides the seven nearly completed works, in the corner sat the one canvas that she ached to complete. The painting was of the clearing where her blind was located. The right side of the painting held a large blank area. The spot was reserved for the buck she had been trying to photograph. Gladys had asked her why she didn't just use one of the dozens of other deer photos she had, but Lee knew that only the buck would do. And not just any buck. She wanted to paint the majestic creature she had first seen in the clearing two weeks ago.

She sat in the overstuffed armchair in the corner. From there she could survey each of the seven works in progress. She set her coffee down, opened the yogurt and studied each canvas as she ate. Taped on the wall above each piece was an enlarged photograph, or in some cases a compilation of photos that she used as reference material. She knew that some purists considered it undesirable for artists to use photos. They insisted that the only way to achieve the true colors was to paint them while looking directly at them, but Lee had never liked plein-air painting. She had tried it several times but tiny bugs or trash blown about by the wind were forever getting stuck on the wet canvas. After she had switched from the horrible-smelling oil paints to acrylics, she was even more inclined to stay indoors, as any breeze or sun dried the acrylics so much more quickly.

She used the visual aids as a proportional reference. As far as she was concerned, nothing ruined a painting faster than having the image of, say, a bluebird sitting on a rail and the small bird appeared to be the size of an owl. She didn't use the references for much else. The colors and essence of the site were in her memory and if they started to fade, all she had to do was walk back to the area in question, since she took the subjects of her paintings directly from the region she lived in. She was certain that if she lived another three hundred years, she would never be able to paint or photograph all the wonderful things she saw on a daily basis.

Photography had been the love of her youth, but over the years, it had given way to her true passion, painting.

Lee had grown up in Houston, Texas, where her parents, Richard and Helen Randle, owned a chain of fine jewelry stores. Her father was a strict but fair man. He had insisted that Lee and her older brother, John, work at the main store with him on weekends and summers, but he also paid them a fair wage. They were required to save half of their salary. The rest was to be used for clothing and pocket money. They had started working as soon as they could reach the counter. At first, they were responsible for keeping the glass cases sparkling. As they grew, so did their responsibilities. By the time they were in high school they were working as sales clerks. Most people might have found it odd to find a seventeen-year-old explaining the finer points of a six-thousand-dollar diamond ring, but not the regular customers of Randle's Jewelry.

When she had eloped, her parents were devastated at first, but once they learned that she still intended to go to college, they slowly came around. She and Brandon moved to her parents' guesthouse where Brandon began working on his novel. Lee continued to work for her father and started college where she majored in photography. She enrolled in an art course and rediscovered her childhood love of sketching and painting. She took more art classes to develop what proved to be a natural talent.

It didn't take long for her to discover that Brandon suffered from a chronic case of severe writer's block. If there was noise, he couldn't write. If it was too quiet, he couldn't write. If it was raining, he couldn't write. If it was sunny, he couldn't write. She realized almost immediately that the marriage had been a mistake, but she was committed to making it work.

Then, in her sophomore year, she discovered she was pregnant. The prospect of becoming a father completely derailed Brandon. He began drinking and the closer her delivery date got, the more he drank. The worst part for Lee was that everywhere she looked she was confronted with beautiful, desirable women.

Lee was four months shy of her twenty-first birthday when her daughter, Sara Leanne Dresher, was born. Despite Lee's resolve to hold the marriage together, she finally had to accept defeat. They were divorced when Sara was sixteen months old, and Brandon left for New York.

For several months, Lee struggled with a sense of failure and inadequacy. She would eventually grow to realize that she had loved Brandon in a schoolgirl sort of way. She had never been in love with him, but rather with his dreams of adventure. It was hard, but she finally understood that she had used him to avoid admitting she was a lesbian.

After the divorce, Lee's determination switched from holding her marriage together to raising her daughter and making it on her own. She took a job as a photography assistant for a large merchandising company. Then she moved out of the guesthouse and into a small apartment. There was only one bedroom so she fixed a small bed in the corner for Sara, while she slept on a painfully small rollaway cot. Her parents begged her to come back home or to at least let them help her, but she was determined to survive on her own. She even refused to touch the money her father had made her save when she was younger.

She began having an affair with a married female coworker and ended up being fired when the affair was discovered. Ashamed of what she had done, she moved back in with her parents and agreed to continue with her education. After obtaining her Master's in Fine Arts, she went to work for a company that photographed items for art auction house catalogs. Photography soon became nothing more than a job and a rather boring one at that. If it hadn't been for the paintings she occasionally photographed, the monotony would have been unbearable. Oftentimes, she would spend as much time studying the brushstrokes and composition of a painting as she did photographing it. She started painting for relaxation, but at the same time, she continued to hone her skills.

When she turned twenty-five her father gave her a two percent interest in his stores, just as he had John on his twenty-fifth birthday. Since Randle's Jewelry had grown to include highly successful stores in Houston, Dallas, San Antonio and Corpus Christi, the gift more or less guaranteed that she would be financially secure for life. She invested most of the quarterly earnings and tried not to become dependent on it.

Sara was five when Lee met Lucy and fell in love. Lucy loved Sara and helped Lee to accept her sexuality for what it was. They dated for six months before Lee came out to her parents. Then she and Sara moved in with Lucy. The relationship lasted nearly three years until Lucy met someone else.

Devastated, Lee focused her life on her daughter and her painting. A few months later, she had her first showing in a small little-known gallery and was hooked. She quit her job as a photo assistant and began to paint full-time. They lived off the money she had saved until her paintings began to sell on a regular basis.

For her thirtieth birthday, she and nine-year-old Sara took a road trip. It was then that she discovered the small town of Christmas, Arkansas, and fell in love with it. The town was an artist's haven, catering to both art lovers and Christmas lovers. Each year from October through December, the town transformed itself into a Victorian holiday wonderland and tourists descended upon the community in droves.

In the spring after her thirtieth birthday, Lee returned to Christmas, purchased a small building on Main Street and opened her gallery. It quickly became successful in the already established art town. She and Sara lived in a rented home until they found the eighty acres of timbered land that made Lee's heart sing. She had a beautiful log home built on the site.

That had been a little over ten years ago. Sara was now in her third year at Trinity University in San Antonio, and Lee had never been happier.

After finishing the yogurt, she picked up a painting of two black bear cubs frolicking in a wildflower-dotted clearing. The mother bear was in the process of scratching her hindquarter on the trunk of a pine tree. As she set about arranging her palette and selecting her brushes, the outside world began to fade. By the time she had tied on her apron, she could almost smell the spicy scent of the flowers and feel the warm spring sun on her face.

CHAPTER THREE

The following Saturday, Lee arrived at the VFW Hall at five thirty in the morning. The place was already buzzing with activity. As soon as she stepped out of her truck, she heard her name being called and turned to see Clarissa Jenkins, the chairperson for this year's event, darting between people toward her.

Lee waved and waited. After seeing Clarissa being stopped twice, Lee decided it would take the energetic little woman a while to reach her so she moved to the passenger side of the pickup and opened the door. Inside were two sturdy cardboard boxes. One box held the four loaves of bread she had baked the night before. The other box held a large Crock-Pot of chili. Bread and chili were among the few things she knew how to cook. She called out to a couple of high school boys who were leaning against a tree. "Richie, can you and Joe give me a hand?" Both boys came running over. "Watch the chili. It's still hot," she warned.

"Did you make any of that jalapeño bread this year?" Richie asked.

"Two loaves, just like you requested," Lee assured him.

He smiled brightly and grabbed the box with the bread. In addition to two days of hard work, Decoration Days also featured an enormous potluck. This was a time when the townspeople and those in the surrounding area came together. It occurred to Lee that this might have been similar to what a pagan holiday celebrating the fall harvest must have been like in ancient times.

"Make sure you plug the Crock-Pot in," she called after them and then made a mental note to check to make sure they did. There was nothing worse than a bowl of cold chili. She checked on Clarissa's progress and saw she still had time. Lee went to the rear of the truck and dropped the tailgate. Inside were several plastic grocery bags that contained sandpaper, rags, paintbrushes of several different sizes and a box of stencils she'd prepared last week. She began to gather the bags.

"Lee," Clarissa trilled out. "I'm so glad you got here early. Everything is already falling apart. It's a complete disaster." She waved her hands frantically. "Oh, and I called Gladys and Dewayne this morning and asked them to stop by Jenny Morrow's place to help her load those tables she promised. Larry's back went out. I know that's not exactly news." She waved her hands again. "But that's not what I wanted to tell you. Ollie Waters is painting everything battleship gray."

"Clarissa, calm down before you have a stroke. I'm sure that whatever the problem is, it's fixable. Now, why is Ollie painting everything gray?" By "everything," Lee assumed that Ollie was only painting the signs gray and not the entire town. She gave up all hope that today would go smoothly. She handed Clarissa some of the bags and waited for her explanation.

"He bought eight gallons of the putrid stuff at an auction over in Mena," Clarissa began. "He insists it's not gray but silver."

Lee frowned. They were going to be painting wooden cutouts of traditional Christmas shapes. After they were painted, some would have informational details stenciled on. She had created a full listing of which cutouts to use as informational signs. The messages ranged from the larger-sized directional signs that would be placed along the highway to hopefully grab the uninformed travelers' attention, all the way down to the smallest elf-shaped signs that pointed the way to restrooms, visitors' centers and the like. Sam and Ruth Weidner from Weidner's Hardware had donated all the paint they would need.

"I think I'm missing something here. Why did Ollie buy paint?" She gathered the remaining bags.

"Who knows why that grumpy old codger does anything." Without waiting for Lee to reply, she took off toward the hall.

Despite the fact that Lee was at least five inches taller, she had to trot to catch up with the bundle of energy. They hadn't gotten far when Allison Carroll, a local butcher, stopped them.

"Howdy, Lee. Clarissa, where do you want the barbecue pits set up?" he asked.

Clarissa swung her arm up to point and barely missed him with one of the bags. "Put them around back on the south side of the tables." Still muttering, she took off again. "The wind is supposed to be out of the north today."

Lee nodded at Allison and smiled as he shook his head before walking away. Once more Lee broke into a trot behind Clarissa, but before she could catch up, someone else had already stopped her. Rather than waiting again, Lee took the bags from her.

"You're the chairperson of the sign committee. You have to talk some sense into Ollie," Clarissa called after her.

Lee nodded and took a deep breath. Talking sense into Ollie Waters was a tall order. He was one of the most stubborn people she had ever met.

She cringed when she stepped into the hall. The noxious fumes of oil-based latex house paint filled the air. Ollie stood at one of the back tables. He was indeed slapping gray paint onto a wooden cutout of a bell and making such a mess it was hard to distinguish him from the bell. She couldn't believe that he had already painted at least a dozen or more of the cutouts and had them leaning against the back wall.

The toxic odor did nothing to diminish the frantic pace. If anything, it was even more chaotic in here than it had been outside. They were all probably high on the paint fumes, she decided as she waved her hand in front of her face. The fumes were too strong to fan away.

She opened the window next to her as she tried to decide where to start. Several dozen wooden cutouts lay on eight long tables. On top of the cutouts sat piles of boxes and bags. The hall was supposed to have been used exclusively for the sign painters, but it looked as though it was rapidly becoming a catchall for everything. She would have to get control over the mess quickly or they would never get finished in time. The signs had to be painted today in order for them to be put up tomorrow.

"Just jump in feet first," she said aloud as she set her bags down. Then she turned and closed the door. Before she could speak, someone pushed the door open and bumped into her.

"I have breakfast rolls," Lilly Anderson said, holding up a large pan of sweet-smelling rolls. Lilly owned a dress boutique on Main Street.

"They smell wonderful, but the food goes around back," Lee reminded her. "The tents should already be set up."

"Oh, that's right." Lilly scurried off.

Before Lee could close the door, someone else approached. She directed them to the back and promptly locked the door. She stepped over to the light switch and flashed the lights twice. A deafening silence filled the hall. "Good morning," she called out loudly. "I'm sorry, but I'm going to have to ask everyone who is not on the sign committee to leave now and please remove anything that's not needed for the signs. We need to get started painting. If there's any food in here, it needs to be taken to the tents out back."

A low rumble of complaints floated around the room, but most people began to gather their belongings. Lee motioned for Rami Chandler, another member of her committee. "Stand here by the door and don't let anyone in unless they're here to paint."

Rami nodded briskly. Her family had operated the only grocery store in Christmas for three generations.

Lee set two other members to opening the remaining windows. If she didn't get some fresh air in there soon, they would all be sick. Then she headed over to deal with Ollie, who was now painting a Santa Claus cutout. Even from a distance, she could see that the thick globby paint he was using was definitely gray. "Good morning, Ollie," she said as she approached the table. He looked as though he had lost weight and there were dark circles under his eyes. She hadn't heard of him being ill. Normally, word got around whenever someone was sick, especially one of the older residents who didn't have family around to keep an eye on them.

Without bothering to looking up, he grunted what she assumed was supposed to be a greeting.

"Ollie, I appreciate you buying more paint, but we already had all we needed."

He didn't respond.

"Ollie, I'm sorry, but the fumes are going to make everyone sick." She wondered if he had been using the paint at his house, maybe that was why he looked so ill. He ignored her so she continued, "That's why we decided to use the acrylic paint, remember?"

This was not going well. In fact, nothing had gone right with the signs this year. It had started in June when the warehouse that stored the signs, which were normally used year after year, along with most of the street decorations, had caught fire and nearly everything had been destroyed. They had commissioned a local woodworker to cut the new shapes, but he had finished less than a fourth of them when he suffered a heart attack. His son took over the task of filling the order, but after several wasted weeks, he informed them that he wasn't going to be able to do the work. Several local amateur woodworkers stepped in to complete the task, but their time was limited and the pieces had been slow in arriving. As a result of all these delays, the signs that should have been ready weeks ago were still waiting to be completed.

Lee hated to be discourteous to anyone, but sometimes there just wasn't an alternative and as far as she was concerned, this was one of those moments. "Ollie, you have to stop using that paint. It takes too long to dry and we simply don't have time."

"We got all day," he growled as he continued to slap on the paint.

She had cringed when she learned that Ollie had signed up for her committee, because he was such a stubborn old cuss. He had a habit of trying to bully people. She didn't intend to become one of his victims. She reached over and grabbed the brush from his hand and leaned in. "Please, stop. I apologize for being rude, but we have less than twelve hours to get all of these signs painted and stenciled. This paint is the wrong color and it takes it too long to dry. So either listen to me or perhaps you would be happier helping someone else."

Ollie swiped his hands across the front of his already paint-soaked shirt. "I should've known you'd be a ball-bustin'—"

Lee slapped the brush hard against the table. "If you say what I think you're about to, I'm going to forget you're an old man." For once, she was grateful for every fraction of her five-foot-ten-inch frame. She took full advantage of it as she stretched across the table and glared at him.

He managed to meet her gaze for a second but couldn't hold it. He glanced at the small circle that had formed around them. He apparently didn't like what he saw, because he snatched up the brush, grabbed the cans of gray paint and stormed out.

Rami came over to her. "I put a couple of my young 'uns out front to send people where they need to be." Rami and husband, Lester, had eight children, all tow headed and blue-eyed. Lee had trouble distinguishing one from the other. "What are we going to do about those?" Rami pointed to the pieces Ollie had already painted.

"Let's get them outside," Lee said as she started toward the mess. "Maybe they'll dry enough that we can sand that gunk off or paint over it." She turned to the rest of the group. Most of her committee were there. "Start clearing everything off the tables. There's a large stack of newspapers over there in the corner. Use them to cover the tables." She stared at the ruined table Ollie had been using. She was certain the VFW folks weren't going to be too happy about that. If she couldn't clean the paint off, she would replace the table the next time she made a trip into Little Rock.

CHAPTER FOUR

On the following Wednesday morning, Lee left her house early. It was the first day of October and the Christmas season had officially opened for her small community. From now through the remainder of the year, the town would revert to Victorian times. Between the hours of eight in the morning and nine at night, the only modern vehicles allowed on Main Street were emergency personnel, and even those took the back route to the highway whenever possible.

A large field at the end of town had been converted to a parking lot for visitors. From the parking lot, visitors could either walk the short distance into town or they could ride free on a variety of horse-drawn vehicles, which ranged from four-seater buggies to flatbed wagons with hay bales for seats.

The quaint shops along Main Street presented lavish visions of a long-ago era—a time when things and people moved slower and life seemed simpler. The shops' windows were filled with tempting treats that were as varied as their individual owners. Visitors could indulge themselves in decadent baked goods, a luscious variety of homemade candies, freshly roasted coffees or creamy chocolate drinks. They could purchase handmade boots, clothing, delicate lace doilies and curtains, furniture and creations twisted and hammered from wrought iron. There was a wide variety of crafts including scented candles and soaps, wooden bowls and metal whirligigs. Then there were fine art pieces that included everything from Lee's landscape paintings to bronze castings.

The townspeople didn't stop at just dressing up their streets. Shop owners and their employees were required by city ordinance to wear historically correct costumes. Even the stores' cash registers and computers were hidden as discreetly as possible in order to perpetuate the feeling of a quaint little Victorian village.

Rather than going directly to the gallery, Lee went to the bakery that was owned by Clint Devonshire and Alan Loomis. As she strolled along the wooden walkway, she felt a sense of pride. The small town had so much more than just the beautiful scenery. She loved the fact that her small town accepted its tiny gay and lesbian community, which was comprised of more gay men than lesbians. That was okay with her. Most of the lesbians who lived there were paired up, but it didn't matter because Lee had realized a long time back that dating anyone in such a small town could easily lead to bigger problems. Sometimes it seemed as though every lesbian she knew had been with one or another at some point in time, so she never dated anyone who lived in Christmas or the immediate surrounding area. The fact was that in the last ten years she had seldom dated anyone. She liked being single. There were the rare times when in the wee hours of a long, dark night she would wonder if there was something wrong with her. After all, wasn't the act of pairing off a matter of human nature? Thankfully, those doubts seldom surfaced.

When she approached the bakery, she smiled. Clint and Alan

always went all out on their shop. Even Lee could almost believe she had stepped back in time when she gazed into the slightly frosted windowpanes that left just enough clear space to display three glowing candles and a platter of delectable baked goods that made her mouth water.

Alan had grown up on a farm just north of town. Clint was the son of a baker from Michigan. He, like Lee, had happened through the area on vacation. Whereas she had fallen in love with the land, he had fallen in love with the blue-eyed clerk at the convenience store where he had stopped for gas.

When she opened the door, a bell jingled to announce her presence. A wave of warmth laced with the scent of cinnamon, cloves, freshly baked bread and coffee tickled her taste buds. She put a hand to her stomach when it gave an embarrassing growl.

"Good morning to you, fair maiden," Clint called out as he came from behind the counter. He stopped when he saw her costume. "Or should I say, kind sir?"

The one thing that Lee refused to do for the community event was to wear a dress. Each year she donned locally made replicas of the Victorian walking suit. She'd had several suits of the short double-breasted frock coats made from ribbed coating in various subdued shades of blue, gray and green. Each coat had a matching vest that sported a broad collar rolled to match the shape of the coat and pantaloons made from either a striped or a solid matching color. The pants fit snugly around the waist, hips and thighs but widened considerably at the ankle to allow the material to fall gracefully over boots. Lee preferred to wear a modern but decisively more comfortable pair of men's shoes. The use of mock-leather gaiters made the shoes look appropriate to the period. An antique silk hat purchased from a shop in Little Rock and a pair of dark gloves rounded out her attire.

"You can call me anything you wish," Lee teased, "as long as you call me in time to eat."

At that moment, Alan floated in from the back and Lee laughed so hard she feared she would bust a seam in her pantaloons.

"God," she said as she wiped her eyes. "Don't we make a pair?

What on earth is that you're wearing?"

Alan swirled in a tiny circle. "This is a brocade bustle gown, circa eighteen-eighty-four." He ran his hand down the front. "You'll take note of these luscious pearl buttons." He frowned at Clint. "Although I'm embarrassed to admit that due to someone's ability to squeeze a dollar until poor George faints, I'm forced to wear buttons made of fake pearls."

Lee wiped her eyes again. "Is purple the only color it came in?"

"Oh, no," Clint replied. "He had at least ten other colors of material to choose from. He intentionally chose that one."

"How did you come by the wig?" Lee asked.

Alan patted the dark tresses that swept up into a high crown-like coiffure with springy ringlets falling on either side of his face. "My cousin John loaned it to me. He has a club in Texarkana and does a lot of drag shows."

Clint came from behind the counter and put an arm around Alan's and Lee's shoulders. Clint was wearing a dove gray suit very similar to Lee's suit. "What a trio we make. Thank God the citizens of our tiny hamlet have a sense of humor."

The doorbell jingled again and they turned to find Gladys and Dewayne standing in the doorway.

Dewayne gave a low rumbling chuckle. "Where is the camera when you need it?" He looked out of place in his ranger's uniform. Since he didn't officially work in town, the dress code didn't apply to him.

"Alan, where did you find that beautiful dress?" Gladys asked as she swooped in dressed in a tan and yellow printed tea gown.

"We're doomed now," Clint muttered to Lee. "I'll get the coffee."

Soon they were seated around a large circular table. After they had spent several minutes listening to Gladys and Alan drone on about clothes, Clint turned to Dewayne. "How are things out in the forest, Smokey?" The nickname stemmed from Dewayne's bear-like stature.

"We've found a few dead animals that we can't explain,"

Dewayne replied.

"What's killing them?" Clint asked.

"Someone is shooting them."

Lee leaned forward. "You mean poachers?"

"No. That's the puzzling part. The animals are shot and left." Dewayne looked at her. "Don't suppose you've seen anything unusual out your way, have you?"

"No. Not really." Lee thought about the strange woman she had seen, but it didn't seem likely that she was the culprit. "Why hasn't this been reported in the newspaper?"

Dewayne's face hardened. "The higher-ups made the decision to keep everything as quiet as possible. They're afraid it might scare away some of the hikers or campers."

Lee sipped her coffee. It seemed logical to her that the park service would benefit from the extra eyes that hikers and campers could provide. Unfortunately this appeared to be another one of those times when logic didn't seem to apply in a governmental decision.

"Gladys told me you saw a stranger on your land not long ago." Dewayne tore a cinnamon roll open sending a fresh cloud of delicious smells into the air.

"Yes. I saw a woman I didn't know, but she was just walking around."

"Oh, a strange woman in the woods." Alan wiggled his eyebrows at her.

"Take it easy, hotshot," Lee said. "Nothing happened."

"Of course not." Gladys and Alan chimed in at the same time.

"Lee, you have to start getting out more," Alan said.

Lee held up a hand. "Stop right there. If this conversation is going to be about my dating habits, I'm leaving."

Clint gave Alan a warning look. "Relax. We're going to talk about something else." He turned back to Dewayne. "So how serious is the problem?"

Dewayne finished off the roll before replying. "There's been a half-dozen deer, lots of smaller things, rabbits, squirrels, a couple of raccoons. The most troubling thing is we found a black bear that had been shot the other day. Whoever shot it only wounded it."

A flare of anger swept through Lee. There had been massive efforts by lots of folks to help reestablish the black bear population. The animals had virtually disappeared until recently, when their numbers had slowly started to rise.

Dewayne's voice dropped to a menacing rumble. "By the time we found it, there was nothing we could do for it. We had to put it down." He shook his head slowly. "I sure would like to catch this joker."

The ominous tone of his voice made Lee hope she would never be on Dewayne's bad side. As if he had read her thoughts, he turned to her.

"You be careful when you're out there tramping through the woods alone," he said with no signs of harshness left in his voice. "A stray rifle bullet can travel a long way and you know how dangerous a wounded animal can be."

Lee nodded, even though in truth she had never been faced with a wounded animal. Suddenly she thought about the magnificent twelve-point buck and felt a small wave of concern for him.

Dewayne wiped his hands on a napkin and finished off the last of his coffee. "I need to get rolling before the real wild animals arrive."

Lee knew he was referring to the tourists.

Dewayne stood. "I'd rather take my chances with a wounded mountain lion than a busload of those little old ladies fighting over a bargain bin."

"You should have seen them the time we ran out of raspberry-filled bonbons," Clint said, giving a mock shudder as the group rose to start their day.

CHAPTER FIVE

Lee and Gladys strolled back to the gallery together. It wasn't quite eight yet. They still had a few minutes before the early-bird shoppers arrived. The gallery was ready. All they had to do was open the door and wait. They had worked late the previous night, decorating the small tree with handmade paper Victorian ornaments, strands of popcorn and small candles that were simply there for decoration. They wouldn't be lit.

"I hope Dewayne didn't frighten you with all that talk about dead animals," Gladys said.

"No. I'm not frightened for myself, but I am concerned about the damage this person is causing." She shook her head. "I don't understand the senseless killing. Why would anyone do that?"

Gladys fussed with the front of her skirt. "It's probably someone with a grudge against the government."

"Then why take it out on the animals? I can think of several politicians who are much more deserving than an innocent, harmless animal." Their heels echoed on the wooden walkway.

"Girl, don't go there." Gladys giggled. "You know Big Brother is always watching and listening."

Lee chuckled. "That's probably what all those UFO sightings are. The boys in Washington have finally discovered what a hotbed of insurrection our tiny hamlet is."

They were almost to the gallery when a low, rumbling roar drifted from down the road. They both looked up.

"Here they come," Lee said as she watched two lumbering tour buses roll into the parking lot. When the doors opened the flurry of activity reminded her of a disturbed anthill.

They quickened their pace and were inside the gallery and ready when the first onslaught of customers stepped through the door a few moments later.

Lee quickly lost count of the number of people she waited on. Even without checking the tally, she knew it was an excellent sales day. Shortly after lunch, they'd had to rearrange the paintings on one wall to eliminate a couple of bare spots. As great as the sales were, she was relieved when she was finally able to lock the door for the night.

"My feet are killing me," Gladys said as she collapsed into a chair behind the counter.

"I can't decide which hurts worse, my feet or my back. I swear I think every year gets a little harder." She glanced at Gladys, who looked completely worn out. "Why don't you go on home? I can close up." She sat down on a stool beside Gladys as she contemplated leaving everything until tomorrow. She could skip going to the photography blind and come in early.

"No." Gladys pulled herself from the chair and headed toward the storeroom. "You run the cash drawer while I straighten things up and then we'll restock. I hate starting my morning out behind schedule."

She knew Gladys was right, but the thought of even a few more steps caused her feet to throb. When she heard the vacuum kick on she reluctantly gave in. She ignored the low hum of the vacuum as she ran the cash register receipts and batched the credit card sales. The sales were better than she had thought. They had sold over a hundred and twenty postcards, thirty-two lower-end prints, six of her Giclée prints and four original paintings, one of which was hers.

"How did we do?"

Surprised, Lee looked up. She had been so busy she hadn't noticed that Gladys had already finished. She smiled and handed over the sales receipt. With the commissions from the other artists' sales, the gallery had brought in just under six thousand dollars.

"Yes! Not a bad way to start the season." Gladys did a little jig. "You'll have some happy artists tomorrow."

Lee almost grimaced. The artists always came around a lot during the holidays to check on their work and to restock as needed. That meant that Melinda Thayer would be around more. It wasn't that Lee didn't like her, but Melinda was so blatant and persistent in her feelings for Lee that it had gotten rather annoying. "I think I could do without one of them making an appearance for a while."

"You're going to have to get tougher with her."

"I've said no a dozen times. You'd think she'd get the message." Lee put the money and receipts in a zippered bag before taking them back to put in the small safe she kept. The safe wouldn't stop a determined burglar, but she felt more secure leaving the cash there than she did driving home with it, and she wasn't about to drop it off in the bank's night depository. For some reason, not physically handing the money to a teller bothered her.

Gladys followed her, shutting off most of the lights as she went. Only the lights in the display windows stayed on. "Some people need to be given a little extra thump on the head before they catch on. Melinda is one of them."

Exhaustion suddenly hit Lee. "I'm too tired to thump anything."

"Are you going out to your blind in the morning?" Gladys asked.

Lee glanced back at her and wondered about the sudden shift in conversation. "I had planned on it. I really want to get a photo of that buck. I hope I didn't miss him this morning." She opened the safe before continuing. "Why do you ask?"

Gladys shrugged. "No reason. I was just wondering."

"Gladys, I'm on my own property. I'll be fine." She smiled. "If it makes you feel any better, I always carry my cell phone and the county sheriff's number is on speed dial. If I have any problems, I'll call him. I'm certain he can handle anything that comes along."

"I'd still feel better if you weren't out there alone."

Lee suddenly remembered the woman in the red sweater. She still didn't know anything about her. Not that she had really been trying to find out. She had been so busy at the gallery that she had barely thought of her. "Don't worry. I'll be fine."

They gathered their things and left by the rear entrance. Shopkeepers were permitted to park in the alleys as long as their vehicles weren't visible to the pedestrian traffic along the main street. Unfortunately, the only access to the alley behind the gallery was from the main street, therefore they had to arrive before the curfew and remain there all day or else park in the designated lot at the edge of town.

"You make sure you lock your doors tonight," Gladys called as Lee climbed into her truck. "And be careful."

Lee waved and watched as Gladys backed her bright red Toyota out and pulled onto the street. She wondered why Gladys was suddenly so concerned. Had there been more going on than what Dewayne had told them that morning? She glanced around the dimly lit alleyway and then, for the first time in years, she reached across and locked her truck doors.

As she drove out of town, her curiosity got the better of her and she turned off the main road onto the side road that ran by the old Peterson place. She hadn't been by it in months. As she drew nearer, she saw a faint light glowing through a front window. From the weak glow, she guessed its source to be either candles or perhaps a lantern. She was certain that whoever the visitor was it wasn't one of the Peterson kids. She would have seen them around town looking up old friends. As she slowed to the point of nearly stopping and stared at the dimly lit house, it took on a menacing persona. She shivered and quickly drove away. Tomorrow she would start asking around and find out who was staying at the house.

Her cell phone rang before she got home. It was her daughter, Sara, calling to see how the first day of the holidays had gone. Lee quickly filled her in on all the triumphs and tribulations of the past few days. "How's school?"

Sara gave a long-suffering sigh. "Are you sure this is going to be worthwhile in the future?" Before Lee could speak, Sara rushed on. "Never mind, I already know what you're going to say, but why did I have to choose such a boring career—a business major? Aargh!"

Lee did a slow count to three before attempting to interject. "I take it you're having a bad week."

"I want to come home. I hate these classes."

"Sweetie, you know there's nothing I'd like better than for you to be here, but—"

"Yeah, I know. I need an education."

"Thanksgiving will be here before you know it. You can come home for a few days then."

"Mom...about Thanksgiving." There was a slight pause. "Would it be okay if Dad had Thanksgiving dinner with us?"

The question caught Lee completely off guard. Her divorce had been amicable enough. Through Sara, she had sort of kept in touch with him, but she'd certainly never planned to share another holiday dinner with him. "I don't know, Sara. This sort of caught me by surprise." She didn't want to share a holiday meal with Brandon, but Sara had never asked before so it must have been important to her. "Why do you want to invite him? You know, he and I have nothing in common anymore."

"Mom, it's not like I have any crazy idea of getting you two back together again. I mean, I totally understand and support your choice of lifestyle."

"Don't call it a choice," Lee said sharper than she intended.

"I'm sorry. I didn't mean to be offensive." Again, she hesitated. "Look, we've always been honest with each other and the truth is Dad asked me to see if you would mind."

"Why? I mean, after all these years?"

"I told you before that he finally had a book published and it seems to be doing well. I think it has something to do with that. I mean, I think he's finally getting his life on track. He's even talking about going into politics."

"Politics." The Brandon Dresher Lee had known had never shown any interest in politics.

"Yeah, I guess I never mentioned it to you before, but he worked on a couple of big campaigns. He says that's when he caught the political fever and decided to reestablish a residency in Texas. He even ran for city council once."

"I didn't know," Lee said, surprised. "Still, I don't know why he wants to have dinner here."

"Maybe he just wants to share the moment of success with someone who, you know, knew him when he was struggling."

Lee decided not to point out the fact that just about anyone who had known Brandon Dresher from high school on would have known him as a struggling writer. "How important is it to you?"

"If you don't mind, and if you're not planning on inviting anyone, I'd like to invite him."

"All right, he can come for dinner, but, Sara, this is a one-time deal. And, to be completely honest, I'm not comfortable with it."

"Mom, he's not going to move in or stay the weekend." There was a touch of irritation in her voice. "He's just coming for dinner."

Lee frowned as a new thought hit her. "Does your father still live in New York?"

"Yes and no." When Lee didn't respond, Sara continued, "He spends a lot of time in New York, but he lives in Houston."

Lee didn't particularly care where he lived. The point she

had been trying to make to Sara didn't seem to be sinking in. She decided the direct approach would be better. "Sara, my point is he's flying all that way just to have dinner. He's definitely not spending the night here."

"Mother, he's flying out there to see me, and since I'll be there with you for Thanksgiving dinner, that's where he'll have to be."

Sara's switch from calling her "Mom" to "Mother" revealed her growing frustration. Lee let it go. She could make it through one meal with him if it meant that much to Sara. If he wanted to see Sara bad enough to fly all that way just for dinner, then why should she care? They talked for a few minutes more before Sara received another call and had to go.

Lee's thoughts quickly turned to the paintings that were waiting for her at home where she kept a second studio. By the time she pulled into her garage she had stopped worrying about the strange light at the Peterson place and the weirdo who was running around shooting animals.

CHAPTER SIX

Lee turned the alarm off and leisurely worked her way from beneath the blanket that was tangled around her legs. As soon as she was free, she pulled the blanket back up around her shoulders. She was already tired and this was only the second day of the holiday season. After arriving home the previous evening, she had spent a couple of hours painting in her home studio. She hadn't intended to work so long, but as usual whenever she was painting the time slipped by unnoticed.

This year the gallery had seemed to demand far more of her time than usual. In fact, the more successful it became the more time it took from her real love, painting. The gallery's annual fall show was going to be held on the last Saturday in October, which was only a little over three weeks away. She hadn't yet finished the pieces she'd hoped to have available. In order to allow time for the prints to be made she would have to have them completed at least two weeks prior to the show date and she didn't see how she could possibly finish them by then. Now she rarely sold a painting without having both limited- and open-edition prints and Giclée prints made first. That was where the real and recurring income was generated. As the demand for her art had grown, the only works that she didn't have prints made of were those that individuals had commissioned her to do.

Until recently, she and Gladys had been able to cover the gallery. She took Monday and Tuesday off, and Gladys took off Wednesday and Thursday. Then they both worked the weekend. Whenever either of them needed more time or the holiday rush became too much, she would call Betty Whittington to help. Betty was a retired art teacher from the local high school and could easily talk to the customers about the art.

Lee thought about calling Betty to see if she'd be interested in working the entire holiday season. If not, maybe she could hire someone else. The gallery could absorb the salary of another employee. That would free up her time to paint. Plus, she'd have more time to spend with Sara when she came home for Thanksgiving and the Christmas break. Of course, Sara usually worked at the gallery when she was home.

Lee had adopted her father's pattern of childrearing. While Sara was growing up, Lee insisted that she work in the gallery on weekends and during most of the summer. They would usually take the entire month of July off to travel, first to visit with her parents and brother, John, and then go on to someplace else that they could both agree on. Lee hated the humidity of Houston, which was beyond horrible in July, so she usually tried to arrange family vacations where they would all meet somewhere else.

Lee kicked the blanket off and sat up. She had been on the verge of dozing. After washing her face and brushing her teeth, she quickly dressed in dark jeans, a dull sage green flannel shirt, a dark jacket and her tan photography vest. She gathered her camera gear and headed for the blind. As she went, she began thinking about the woman she had seen. Was she living at the Peterson place or was someone else staying there?

By the time the sun appeared over the horizon she was comfortably settled in the blind. As time slipped by, she found herself watching for the woman rather than the buck. She blamed her lack of concentration on the recent bout of tiredness. She wondered if she should start taking vitamins. A complete physical a couple of months ago had revealed nothing, so whatever was wrong couldn't be too serious.

She continued to watch until a few minutes before eight when she became so antsy she couldn't keep still and gave up. As she headed home, she couldn't decide whether she was more disappointed about the buck not showing up or the woman's failure to reappear. Not one to remain despondent for long she reminded herself that Sara would be coming home for Thanksgiving. Then she started wondering why Brandon was suddenly showing an interest in sharing a holiday dinner with them. He had always been, at best, passively active in Sara's life. When she was younger, he would call her on a more or less monthly basis. He had never paid the court-ordered child support, and Lee had never pressed him. Thanks to her father's insistence that she and her brother save a large portion of the salary he had paid them, and later on, his generosity with the profits of his stores, Lee had always had her own money, and she suspected Brandon was struggling.

Birdcalls filled the morning air. As she strolled quietly along the well-worn path, she vaguely processed the sounds. Maybe Sara was right and Brandon just wanted to share his happiness with someone he knew. After their divorce, he had never remarried. She knew through Sara that he'd had a few women in his life, but nothing permanent. His mother had died a couple of years ago and his father was now in a nursing home suffering from Alzheimer's. He was an only child, so Sara was really the only family he had.

A sharp crack of a snapping limb brought her to a sudden stop. Remembering what Dewayne had said about the crazy shooter, she froze. She didn't want some idiot to mistake her movement for that of an animal and start firing. She turned her head slowly and listened for any further sound. Rather than the usual forest sounds, all she heard was a deafening silence. Experience had taught her that the creatures of the forest were never completely silent unless a human or some other dangerous predator was nearby. She felt certain that it wasn't her presence that had hushed them. Over the years, she had learned how to move and dress for her trips into the woods to cause as little disturbance as possible.

The hairs along her neck began to rise as she was struck by the eerie feeling that she wasn't alone and for the first time she felt fear. Never before had she been afraid of being alone out here. She lost track of time as she stood rooted to the path, not moving except to turn her head. As she carefully scanned the woods, nothing unusual caught her gaze. She thought about calling out, but if there was some crazy person out there, it was probably best not to bring any more attention to herself than necessary. The cell phone in her vest pocket suddenly seemed very far away. She fought the urge to run as she eased her hand to the pocket and tugged the zipper slowly open. Even as she reached for the phone, she knew that if she were in immediate danger, it was useless to call anyone. There was no way of knowing where Dewayne was. He could be anywhere within the national forest range. If she called the county sheriff, it was a fifteen-minute drive from town. Besides, what could she tell them? All she had heard was a twig snap. The rest was just intuition. Regardless, she held onto the phone. Its cold, solid form provided her with a small sense of comfort.

Gradually, the woods began to come back to life and within a few minutes it was as though nothing had happened. Whatever had frightened the wildlife was gone. Lee stood frozen for another few seconds before she began to move. She tried to maintain her normal pace as she told herself there could have been a dozen things that had frightened the birds. It could have been a bobcat or a fox. There was even a slight chance it could have been a black bear. Their numbers were increasing. She stopped to listen once more but heard nothing out of the ordinary.

After another moment, she started back along the path

she had worn down over the years, but rather than letting her thoughts stray as they normally would, she remained vigilant.

She arrived home without further incident. Still she was careful to lock the door behind her. As she made her way to the bathroom to shower, she was shocked at how late it had gotten. She had long since missed the eight o'clock no cars curfew. She would have to park in the parking lot at the edge of town. She hoped there would be a decent spot left.

After a quick shower, she put on one of the blue Victorian-era suits and took time to make an egg sandwich before leaving. She had barely reached her truck when her cell phone rang.

"I'm sorry I'm running late," she said without waiting for Gladys's voice.

"That's odd. You were always such a prompt child."

Lee blinked in surprise. "Mom. I'm sorry. I was expecting Gladys."

"I won't keep you but a moment. I just called to let you know that your father and I were thinking about coming to visit you and Sara for Thanksgiving."

Lee stopped short. Her parents rarely came to visit and never during the holidays. Those were prime retail days and her father practically lived at the main store in Houston during that timeframe.

"Hello. Are you there?"

"Yes, I'm here."

"If you're busy we understand."

"No. Of course it would be fine." Lee shook her head to clear it. "I mean it would be great. You just took me by surprise." Suddenly she grew concerned. "Everything's okay, isn't it? With you and Dad, I mean. You aren't sick, are you?"

"Mercy, no. John and his family are going to his in-laws this year, so we simply thought we'd come out and visit. It seems like ages since we last saw you and Sara."

Lee frowned. She didn't think it was wise to mention that they had all spent a week together in August. "When can I expect you?"

43

"Oh you know your father. He'll wait until the last minute to tell me when we're leaving. I'll let you know in plenty of time, though." She hung up before Lee could say anything more.

Lee sat in her truck and munched on the egg sandwich. She was definitely going to have to hire someone to help in the gallery. After a moment, she cranked the truck and backed out of the garage. She wondered what her parents would think about Brandon being there for dinner as well. She was sure they wouldn't mind, but they would probably wonder about why he showed up. She gave a short laugh. Why shouldn't they? She was certainly wondering why.

CHAPTER SEVEN

"Move the painting of the bear cubs over beside the one with the woodpecker," Gladys instructed as Lee struggled with trying to slip the hanger wire of another canvas over a hook. When it was finally firmly in place, she stepped back and pulled a paper towel from her pocket to wipe the sweat from her face.

"Gladys, you've had me move that thing three times already." She shifted her weight to her right foot. "These blasted shoes are killing me today." Normally she didn't mind wearing the Victorian-style clothing so much, but for some reason today she felt out of sorts.

"Are you all right? You seem"— Gladys waggled her hand— "a little upset."

Lee wanted to suggest that maybe it was because it was already after ten and she was exhausted, but she knew Gladys was tired also. "Sorry I'm so whiny. I know you're as tired as I am." The tourists were still rolling in during the day, which was great for business, but after three weeks, it could be tiring. Already there had been tour buses from Louisiana, Texas, Missouri and Kansas. The gallery had been busy that day. In the past week, she had sold four of her own original paintings, along with five others that she was showing on commission. Under normal circumstances, she would have been ecstatic over such a sales volume, but with the show scheduled for the following night, she was starting to worry that the gallery walls would look too bare. She glanced around at the empty walls. "Maybe we should remove some of these temporary wall panels."

"Why?"

"What if we sell several pieces tomorrow? The walls will look bare."

Gladys tapped her foot. "Lee, worrying about the future is pointless. The world could end any moment. An enormous meteor could come crashing out of the sky. A giant sinkhole could open up and—"

Lee held up a hand. "I get your point. I know I'm being crazy." She shook her head as she searched for the reason for her anxiety.

"I know you're tried, but we still need to hang four more of your paintings, plus your photos," Gladys said, "and don't forget that Melinda is bringing over twelve more of her sketches." She took a deep breath. "The walls won't be bare. Come on. Grab that painting. It's not going to hang itself."

Lee ignored her and glanced at the clock. It was going to be a long night. "Maybe we should stop having a show during the holidays. We could just keep the one in the spring."

Lee had mailed one hundred invitations to the event to previous patrons and collectors. She had hired a caterer and a string trio. She had used the group before. They always performed a delightful array of light classical pieces, poignant Celtic airs and a rousing variety of American folk songs. She had actually used both businesses on previous occasions and they never failed to impress her guests. The fall show was traditionally the gallery's biggest gala and she wanted everything to be perfect. Because the event was so important and benefited many other businesses besides the gallery, the city council issued a special exception for the night of the event that lifted the no-cars ban on Main Street and Victorian clothing requirement. Despite the lackluster economy, the gallery was doing well, and it appeared that this year's event would have record turnouts. The local motels and bed and breakfasts were already booked solid for the weekend.

"I think I'm getting too old for all this stress, or maybe I'm going through early menopause."

"I think it's time you found a girlfriend," Gladys mumbled. She put her hands on her hips. "This isn't like you. What's going on?"

"I don't know. Maybe I'm just premenstrual, or pre-insane." She gave a wry laugh as she studied Gladys's Victorian dress. "Just look at us. We may already be insane."

Gladys tugged at the dress. "You'd think we would've had enough sense to bring some comfortable clothes to change in to." She rubbed her lower back.

Lee felt badly about all the whining she had been doing. "Why don't you go on home? I can finish this."

"No, no. I know what you'll do. The minute I'm out of sight, you'll haul-ass home."

Lee bowed deeply from the waist. "Guilty as accused."

"Come on." Gladys waved toward the painting. "We still have a lot of work to do, so don't wimp out on me now. Grab the bear cub painting and move it over there by the woodpecker. They'll complement each other."

"That's what you said the first three times you made me move it." Lee took down the large thirty-six-by-forty-eight-inch painting.

Gladys moved out of her way. "I know, but it's so adorable I want to make certain it's in the best spot." Between customer rushes, they had spent the afternoon and evening arranging paintings on the stand-alone walls that would more than double the gallery's display space.

Lee hung the painting and used a hand level to make sure its alignment was perfect. Only then did she step back beside Gladys. "You're right. It does look better there."

"I can't believe you doubted me. I think we should hang those small eight-by-ten floral portraits there on the back wall."

As Lee moved to pick up one of the paintings, the gallery door opened. She stepped around from behind the wall in time to see Melinda Thayer hauling in a good-sized box. She wore a black printed tea gown with a pleated flounce bustle and short jacket. Lee recognized the dress as one of the patterns suggested by the costume committee. Upon seeing Melinda, her initial reaction was to run to the back, but she squelched the childish impulse. It wasn't as if she didn't like Melinda. They could probably be friends if Melinda wasn't so pushy. Lee wondered why she couldn't find this woman attractive. She had seen how Melinda's long chestnut hair and green eyes made men and more than a few women do a double take whenever she walked into a room. Lee didn't have an answer. Even with the few women she had dated, nothing had ever lasted for more than a few months. She had finally accepted the fact that she would probably spend her life alone and that her sex life would forever be only a notch above that of a nun, but that was all right. A life alone was preferable to one lived with the wrong person. Those painful days with Brandon when she blamed herself for everything that went wrong still hovered in the fringes of her memory. At least now when she woke each morning the only person she had to please was herself. She nodded and said hello as Melinda joined them.

"We missed you guys at the monthly chatterbox." The chatterbox was a meeting that the local artisans held at Sophie's Café. It was rare that anything outside of conversation and a good meal was achieved, but it was a nice social event.

"We sort of got behind," Gladys said as she gave Lee a knowing look.

"You've been busy." Melinda set the box down and nodded toward the paintings they were hanging.

"Everything sort of came together in the past few days," Lee admitted, looking to Gladys for a way to escape.

Instead, Gladys tossed her to the wolves when she gave a short wave. "I need to make sure those photographs are ready to hang."

Before Lee could think of anything to stop Gladys, she was gone. Lee pretended to study the painting.

"You didn't return my call," Melinda said.

Which one? Lee wondered. "I've been busy." When Melinda stepped closer, Lee moved away and hung the painting. Before she realized what was happening Melinda's arms went around her from behind and warm lips were teasing her neck, but even that shock paled in comparison to the one that exploded through her body. Lee tried to pull away, but her feet seemed to have merged with the floor. She felt herself melting back into Melinda's arms and struggled to stop herself, but Melinda's hands were moving along her sides, brushing her breasts. The kisses along her neck were growing more intense as was the throbbing between her legs. Lee again tried to pull away, but it felt as though she were wading through waist-high water. Her body felt heavy. Her movements only encouraged Melinda to grow bolder.

Lee couldn't stop the small gasp of pleasure that escaped her when fingers closed over her breast and gently squeezed the nipple. A rapidly waning voice of caution was telling her to put a stop to this, but Melinda's mouth on her neck was driving her beyond the point of caring. Then the cold slap of reason hit her when Melinda's hand slipped between her legs, and Lee remembered where they were. She stumbled forward. Melinda seemed shaken and surprised by her unexpected pulling away.

Lee tried to catch her breath. Her face burned with embarrassment, or maybe it was something far too dangerous even to consider. "Melinda, I'm sorry. I've tried to make my feelings clear to you, but you don't seem to be getting the message."

"Oh, I was getting the message." Melinda tugged her jacket back into place and winked. "I just came by to drop off my sketches."

Lee managed a weak nod.

As Melinda turned to leave, she glanced back over her shoulder. "I love a challenge," she said, flashing a smug smile.

Infuriated, Lee looked around for something to pummel, but then realized that if she was going to pummel on anything it should be herself. That was who she was upset with. She turned her attention back to the paintings, but she couldn't shake the feelings Melinda had stirred in her. Her hands shook so she could barely hold onto the canvas. How could she have stood there so passively? She was in such a state she didn't bother to pay attention to how she was arranging the pieces. She hardly noticed when Gladys came back.

"I see Melinda left her sketches and—girl, what are you doing?"

"What does it look like I'm doing?"

"Well, if I didn't know you better, my first guess would be that you're tripping on some bad stuff. You've hung that painting upside down."

Lee ran a hand over her face. "You're so much better at this. I should go—" She couldn't remember what she had been about to say. She glanced around as though she might find her train of thought lying nearby. Why had she just stood there and let Melinda paw her? The memory of Melinda's hands caressing her made her shiver.

Gladys placed a hand on Lee's arm. "Are you all right?" As she stepped forward, her worried gaze rose to Lee's neck. "What's wrong with your neck?"

Lee watched as Gladys's eyes grew round and her hand flew to her mouth.

Gladys's thin body began to shake and within seconds, she could no longer contain the laughter. It gurgled from her like water over rocks. It took her a moment to regain control, but she finally cleared her throat and pointed to Lee's neck. "I think you'll probably want to go...um...there's lipstick on—" She stifled a giggle.

Lee's hand flew to her neck as she spun and raced to the restroom. There were lipstick smudges along her neck and collar.

Her face burned. What had she been thinking? She grabbed a paper towel and scrubbed her neck until it was so red it was hard to tell if the lipstick marks were gone or not. She dabbed at the stains on the collar but couldn't completely eradicate them. The towel began to shred, making a bigger mess. She threw it away and took a deep breath before going back to face Gladys.

"These sketches are ready to hang," Gladys said as if nothing had happened. "What do you think of this arrangement?" She had the sketches lying on the floor.

Relieved that she wasn't going to have to face any further teasing, she gratefully went back to work. Despite her embarrassment over what had just occurred, she stopped to admire Melinda's pen-and-ink sketches, which ranged from simple country scenes to intricate botanical studies.

"I can't imagine what it must feel like to have that kind of talent," Gladys said as they stared down at the drawings.

Lee nodded. "I've always wondered why she hasn't tried to reach a larger market. I've talked to her about prints, but she doesn't seem interested."

"I could ask you the same question about reaching a larger market."

"I love not having to answer to anyone." Lee's feet began to throb again. "This arrangement looks good to me. Let's get it hung."

CHAPTER EIGHT

Lee made her way through the crowded gallery. Light strains of classical music drifted across the room. The musical trio, on violin, cello and guitar, were off to one side of the room. Neatly clad waiters floated among the guests with trays of stuffed mushrooms, deviled lobster canapés and cheese and olive rounds. To rinse these morsels down there were trays of assorted wines and sparkling flutes of Champagne. She spied Gladys and Dewayne talking with an elderly couple. They seemed to be discussing the works of Jake Drummond. His beautifully rendered watercolors were the first outside pieces she had accepted for the gallery. Gladys looked beautiful in a chic rose-colored dress with a matching short jacket. Her enthusiasm seemed to radiate across the floor. Again, Lee was struck with the realization that the gallery meant as much to Gladys as it did to her. There were times when Lee was so absorbed in finishing a painting that Gladys would completely run the gallery for days at a time. Lately there seemed to be less and less time for painting and Lee often found herself putting her artistic side on hold in order to fulfill the responsibilities of the gallery owner. She glanced at Gladys again. It was time to stop procrastinating and do what was right toward Gladys. Lee turned and nearly bumped into Melinda Thayer.

"You've been avoiding me all night," Melinda murmured.

Lee started to protest but knew it was true. "Look—" She stopped. Now wasn't the time or place for the conversation they needed to have. "We need to talk but not here and not now."

"We could step into the storeroom." The touch of suggestion in the offer irritated Lee.

"No. We can't. What happened last night was a mistake, and I'd prefer that we forget about it and move on." Lee noticed Gladys leave the elderly couple and start toward them.

Melinda nodded and said, "Why not let yourself go and have some fun? I'm not asking for any sort of commitment."

Gladys was drawing nearer. "We'll talk later." Lee turned to leave but stopped sharply when she saw the woman standing by the door. She was wearing cream-colored pants with a matching jacket and a turquoise blouse. As if feeling Lee's gaze upon her the woman turned and smiled shyly. Even from across the room it was easy to see that those amazing sky-blue eyes were now free of tears.

"What's wrong with you?" Gladys asked as she approached. "You look like you just won the lottery."

It took Lee a moment to realize that she was grinning like a fool. She tried to pry her gaze away from the woman but found she couldn't.

"Who is that?" Gladys had apparently followed her gaze. "Nice clothes. My goodness, is that an Elie Tahari jacket?"

"That's the woman in the clearing," Lee mumbled as she started making her way across the floor.

She saw a moment of indecision flash in the stranger's eyes and for a moment, she was afraid the woman would leave. She reached out an arm as if to stop her, even though she was still several feet from her. To her amazement, the woman started toward her. For a brief awkward heartbeat, they stood facing each other. Then they were both speaking at once. They stopped and shared a laugh tinged with embarrassment.

"Welcome to the gallery. I'm Lee Dresher."

The woman held out her hand. "Rebecca James...Becka, actually."

Lee took the small hand in hers and tried to stop smiling but couldn't. She suddenly recalled a photo she had once taken of an opossum. She felt certain she had the same silly grinning expression on her face as it had. "You're new to the area, aren't you?" She realized she was still holding Becka's hand and reluctantly released it.

"Yes."

Lee struggled to think of something to say. "Well, welcome to Christmas." She cringed. What an asinine thing to say.

"Thank you. I have to admit the town's name is what drew me here. Christmas all year long sounded interesting."

A waiter appeared with a tray of drinks. Becka took a glass of Champagne, but Lee declined. She noticed that Becka seemed to be constantly scanning the room.

"If you'd like I can show you around and give you a quick history of the town as we go."

There was a slight hesitation, and then Becka nodded. Before they could proceed, Gladys and Melinda suddenly appeared at Lee's side. She swallowed her disappointment and made the introductions.

"Have we met before?" Melinda asked as she shook Becka's hand.

Becka paled. Her body flinched as if she had been struck. "People are always telling me that." She smiled slightly. "If you'll excuse me, I see someone I need to speak with."

Before Lee could say anything, Becka moved off through the crowd.

"That was odd," Melinda said as she stared after Becka. "I'm sure I know her," she mumbled.

Lee was on the verge of venting her frustration on Melinda when Gladys took her arm. "Melinda, you'll have to excuse us. I need for Lee to mix and mingle." She led Lee toward the back of the room. Lee tried to catch a glimpse of Becka, but she had disappeared into the crowd.

Gladys grabbed two glasses of Champagne off a passing tray and pushed one of them into Lee's hand. "Here, hold this. It makes you look less intimidating."

Lee frowned. "I'm not intimidating."

"Says you." She moved them closer to the musicians. "You looked as though you were about to throttle Melinda."

"Becka James was the woman in the clearing."

"You mean the crying woman."

Lee nodded as she continued to scan the room. Above the noise of the crowd, she heard the dim tinkling of a bell. She turned just in time to see Becka slip out the door. She thrust the glass into Gladys's hand. "I'll be back in a minute."

Lee made her way through the guests as quickly as she could politely do so. By the time she managed to make it outside, Becka had already reached the end of the block. Without thinking, Lee raced after her. She had almost reached her when Becka suddenly turned and looked back.

Lee slid to a stop a few feet from her. For the second time since meeting this woman, she was at a loss for words. "You left so quickly," she said as she tried to catch her breath. She made a mental note to start exercising again.

Becka kept glancing back toward the gallery. "I've never been very comfortable in large crowds." She rubbed one hand over the other. "I saw the announcement about the show in the newspaper. I never dreamed it would be so well attended." Her hand flew to her mouth. "I'm sorry. I didn't mean to imply your gallery couldn't draw a crowd."

Lee shook her head. "It's okay. I understand." She slipped her hands in her pockets but quickly yanked them out. "Ah…do you really have to leave? I mean, I never got a chance to show you around. Or even tell you my fantastic story about how the town got its name."

Becka hesitated.

Lee realized that if Becka had been around town long, she'd probably already heard that Lee was a lesbian and here she was chasing her down the street. She was probably scaring her. She backed off quickly. "Look, I'm sorry. I didn't mean to—" She stopped. It wasn't like her to pursue anyone so actively—not that she was, she told herself quickly. She took another step back. "Thanks for dropping by tonight. I hope you enjoy your stay here." She turned and started back toward the gallery. Behind her, she heard the sound of a car door close. A moment later, the car pulled away from the curb. Lee tried not to notice the sleek Mercedes as it drove by, but she couldn't stop herself from following the trail of its taillights as it disappeared down Main Street.

As she walked back to the gallery, she thought about Becka James. Lee had discovered many years earlier that she noticed things that most people didn't. Maybe it was from years of staring at the world through the lens of a camera or because she had to study things so intently to paint them, but whatever the reason, she had seen the brief flicker of fear in Becka's eyes when Melinda spoke to her. Becka James was running from something or someone. Lee gave one last look down the road where Becka's car had disappeared. She should stay away from Becka. As she made a resolution to do so, she wondered if she'd be able to stand by her decision.

CHAPTER NINE

It was nearly midnight before Lee finally saw the last of the caterer's staff out and locked up behind them. She leaned against the door and gave a long tired sigh.

"Is it really over?" Gladys called from across the room.

"All that's left is the laughing or crying."

"You take care of the register, and I'll finish closing up," Gladys said.

Half an hour later, after the register had been run and the night's receipts locked away in the safe, they both collapsed onto the couch in the storage room.

"Are we laughing or crying?" Gladys asked.

"We are definitely laughing." Lee leaned forward and filled two glasses from the bottle of Champagne she'd set aside. She handed a glass to Gladys. "Sixteen paintings, twenty-two prints, six photographs, eight sketches, and Jake Drummond told me he had received a commission for a watercolor."

"Here's to hard work and hungry collectors," Gladys said. They raised their glasses in a toast. Gladys sipped her drink. "I saw a sold sign on the bear cub painting. Who bought it?"

Lee stretched her legs. "No one bought it. I put the sign there."

Gladys smiled as she leaned her head against the back of the couch and closed her eyes. "You finally saw what I did and couldn't part with it, huh?"

Lee pulled a certificate of validation from her pocket. The paper was something she provided with each of her paintings. It simply stated that it was an original work by her and held her signature. "Actually, I'm going to use it as a source of bribery."

Gladys opened her eyes slightly.

"Who are you bribing?"

"You."

"You know I love that painting, but I'm not going to tell Melinda to leave you alone. You're on your own with that."

Lee felt herself blushing as she recalled the encounter with Melinda the previous night. "I was sort of hoping you would agree to become my partner."

Gladys chuckled. "You know I love you girl, but you don't have nearly enough equipment for me."

"Not that kind of partner," Lee said as she swatted Gladys's leg with the paper. "I meant a business partner."

Gladys rubbed her eyes. "What are you talking about? I can't afford to buy part of the business."

"Hear me out before you refuse." Lee placed the paper on the couch between them. "You've been a part of the gallery almost as long as I've been. You work as hard as I do and you deserve more than a salary and a yearly bonus. You know I don't much care for the business side of things, and I have serious doubts that Sara will ever be interested in moving back here to live. I want to become less involved in the daily operation of the gallery and focus more of my time on painting and my photography, but doing that would shift a big burden on you. I could give you a raise to compensate you for the additional duties, but that still doesn't seem to be enough. I'm offering you a full and equal partnership in the gallery. We'll hire a full-time employee, and I'll still spend a lot of time here, but I'll be painting most of the time. I think it's time we changed Dresher's Gallery of Fine Art from a sole proprietorship to a partnership."

"That's not fair to you," Gladys protested, clearly flustered. "You can't just turn over half your business."

Lee shrugged. "I think it's fair. As I said, you'll be doing the bulk of the operational work. We'll need to hire another employee to help you. I'll still help during the busiest times of the year. We're running ourselves ragged. I should have already hired someone."

"I do agree we need another person, but I can't accept a full partnership."

Lee picked up the certificate of validation and smiled. "I'll give you the bear cub painting."

"I swear I don't know how you've succeeded in business." Gladys shook her finger at Lee. "You can't go around giving half of what you own away. It's not fair to you. What about Sara? You need to think about her future."

Lee's shoulders drooped. She couldn't tell Gladys that the yearly income she received from her current meager share of her father's jewelry stores was enough for her to live on comfortably for the rest of her life. Unless something unforeseen occurred, Sara would be financially secure as well. "I need more time to paint. I don't care about money. I want the gallery to thrive not for the sake of money but for the opportunity it gives me and the other artists whose work we represent. Haven't you realized yet that we artists are egomaniacs when it comes to showing off our work?"

"What if Dewayne gets transferred and we have to move somewhere else? Plus, we'll have to make some sort of agreement on your own art and the building and—"

Lee held up a hand. "All that stuff gives me a headache. Besides, that's why God made lawyers. We'll go over to Max

Bollard's office on Monday. Between the three of us, I'm sure we can work out the details. Do we have a deal?"

Gladys gazed at her for a long moment. A smile slowly brightened her face as she picked up the certificate. "I do love those bear cubs." She waved the paper. "I think we might be able to work this out, partner." She gave Lee a tight hug. "I should feel guilty about taking advantage of your senility," she said as she pulled away.

"You just wait until sales slow down after the holidays. You may not think it's such a great idea then." They sipped their drinks in silence for a moment before Lee said, "Why did Dewayne leave so early?"

Gladys set her nearly empty glass on a packing box at the end of the couch. "He got a call from Jefferson Depew over at the ranger's station. A guy from Little Rock came down to check on his hunting cabin this afternoon and found the place ransacked. He said it looked as though someone had been living there for a few days."

"Why did they pull Dewayne in on the call? Shouldn't that be handled by the county sheriff's office?"

"Yeah, but they found empty shell casings all over the place. Jefferson said it looked as though whoever broke in had been taking potshots at the hunting trophies mounted on the walls. The shell casings are the same caliber as those used in the shootings that have been happening on national forest property."

Lee thought about the last time she'd gone to the blind and the eerie feeling she'd had that someone was out there with her. She knew better than to mention it to Gladys. She'd have a cow. Lee suddenly realized that it had been over three weeks since she had gone to the blind. She had used the increased business at the gallery as an excuse, but now she wondered if maybe the experience had frightened her more than she had thought. After a moment, she decided she would go the following morning. She wasn't going to let one little scare in the woods keep her away. She turned her attention back to Gladys. "Where is the cabin located?"

"I don't know. Dewayne never said." Gladys stifled a yawn.

"I'll be glad when they finally catch this guy."

Gladys leaned forward and stretched her back. "It may not be a guy."

"What do you mean?"

"Well, I wasn't supposed to say anything, so don't repeat this. Jefferson told Dewayne that the county guys told him that they found a backpack filled with women's clothing in the cabin."

"It's not a woman. Women don't do things like that."

"Take off your rose-colored glasses, honey. Women can be just as mean as men."

Lee didn't agree, but she didn't want to argue. "Was there anything else that would identify who the backpack belonged to?"

"I guess not."

"Do you think they're making a mistake in not reporting these shootings to the press? I mean, maybe someone saw something that would help identify this person."

Gladys shook her head. "I don't know. I'd like to hope they know what they're doing, and not just keeping silent to keep from losing the business of a few hikers and campers." She stood. "Can you drop me off? Dewayne told me to call him when I was ready to leave, but I'm too tired to wait on him. I know it's a little out of your way."

"Oh, please. It's nothing." Lee stood. "Of course, it'll mean you have to ride in my 'old clunker.'"

Gladys folded her hands as if in prayer. "I retract every disparaging remark I've ever made about your fine ride."

Lee pounded a stray wine cork back into the Champagne bottle and placed it in one of the boxes of leftover food. "Here, take this. You can get Dewayne buzzed and take advantage of him."

Gladys made a snorting sound. "I'm so tired Denzel Washington doesn't even sound appealing."

"What about Will Smith?" Lee teased. Gladys was always swooning over the two men.

"Oh, honey, I said I was tired, not dead."

They packed the boxes with the leftover food into the back of Lee's truck. The painting of the cubs was too large to fit in the interior of the truck and Gladys refused to let Lee put it in the back. "I'll have Dewayne come by tomorrow. It'll fit in his SUV."

Soon they were driving out of town.

"So what's the deal with this Becka James woman?" Gladys asked. "You looked a little taken by her."

"No, I'm not. I'm just curious. She took off so fast I didn't really have time to talk to her. All I know is that she is the woman I saw crying in the clearing."

Gladys made a small sound.

"You have something else to say," Lee said. "What is it?"

"She sure left in a hurry after Melinda mentioned she looked familiar."

"Now, there you go. Melinda never said she looked familiar. She asked if they had met before."

"Same difference."

"No, it's not."

Gladys sat staring out the window.

"I know you're dying to say something, so out with it," Lee said.

"I don't have anything to say." Gladys hummed for a couple of seconds. "It does seem strange, though, that no one knows who she is. Where's she living? She wasn't wearing a wedding ring. She's not working for anyone we know in town. That jacket and the pants were definitely Elie Tahari originals, and those heels were by Christian Louboutin." She made another clucking sound with her tongue. "Did you see that sterling silver chain bracelet with the pavé diamond details? That was at least eighteen-karat gold woven through it."

Lee knew from her days of working in her father's jewelry store that the bracelet Gladys had just described would have been expensive. She had been so busy staring at Becka she hadn't paid much attention to what she was wearing. Still, she felt compelled to defend Becka or at least turn Gladys's attention away from her. "How do you do that?"

"What?"

"How can you look at clothes and tell who made them? How do you know she didn't buy them at Wal-Mart?" She knew it was useless for her to argue with Gladys about anything dealing with women's wardrobes or accessories. Gladys had forgotten more about fashion than she would ever know.

"Now you're being silly. Do you honestly believe she could have purchased those clothes at Wal-Mart?"

Lee relented. "No. Still, how can you be so sure this Elie person made them? Couldn't they be cheap design rip-offs like those fake Gucci purses they sell at flea markets?"

"You know paint. I know clothes. That jacket was Italian suede, and I'll bet you anything it cost at least a thousand dollars."

"No way!" Lee nearly ran off the road.

"Yes way!"

Lee thought for a moment. "She could be rich and decided to retire here."

"Maybe, but she doesn't strike me as the Hooterville type."

They were approaching Gladys's house, a sturdy frame home that was over two hundred years old. When she and Dewayne had bought the house it was on the verge of being demolished, but with a lot of hard work and determination they had slowly brought it back to life.

Lee waited until Gladys was inside before she drove off. As she made her way home, she found herself thinking about Becka James and her sky-blue eyes.

CHAPTER TEN

On Monday morning, Lee telephoned Betty Whittington, the retired art teacher who helped as needed at the gallery. Betty was out of breath when she answered.

"I almost missed the call. I was out back turning over the flowerbeds for the winter," Betty said.

Lee shifted the phone to her shoulder as she poured herself a cup of coffee. "I have to admit that every time I drive by your place I turn green with envy over your flowers. No matter what I do, my flowers never look as nice as yours do." She took her coffee and headed to her studio. As she walked through the gallery, she saw Gladys at the computer posting the previous day's sales.

Betty chuckled. "God gave us all a talent. Your flowers thrive on a canvas, mine in a flowerbed."

"I suppose so. Miss Betty, I'm calling to see if you'd be interested in working at the gallery full time."

There was a slight pause before the older woman responded. "No, I don't think I'd want to take on a full-time job. I like being able to take off to visit one of the grandkids whenever the fancy strikes me."

"Yes, ma'am, I understand completely. We need to hire another person, and you've always done such a wonderful job for us that I wanted to offer the position to you first."

"Thank you for thinking of me."

Lee was about to thank her and hang up when Betty said. "If you need help until you find someone, I can work until the week before Thanksgiving. I'm going to Baltimore to spend the holidays with my son, Ron, and his family."

"That would be wonderful. Hopefully, we can hire someone right away." With Betty working, she and Gladys would be able to have a day off occasionally—something they rarely got during the holidays. "When could you start?"

"I have to finish my flowerbeds. Would tomorrow be soon enough?"

Lee smiled before replying, "Tomorrow would be perfect."

After hanging up Lee called the local newspaper and arranged for them to run a help wanted ad in the weekly edition that would come out on Thursday. Then she called Max Bollard's office and made an appointment to see the lawyer the following afternoon.

She picked up her coffee cup and took a sip as she crossed off another item on her list of things to do. One of the many things she loved about living in a small town was that she didn't have to wait two weeks to get an appointment. Her gaze fell on the half-finished painting in the corner. She had been hopeful that the buck would be at the clearing this morning. It had rained the previous night and a lot of animals and birds were out moving around when she had hiked out to the blind. The cheerful birdcalls and chattering of the squirrels had erased the uncomfortable memories of her last trip. She hadn't been able to stay as long as she would have liked, but now, with Betty helping out, she could start spending more time at the blind each morning. Maybe she would soon get another chance to photograph him. For a brief moment, her fingers itched to paint him from memory, but she fought the urge. She wanted to capture everything about him as realistically as her skills would allow. Lee spied a stack of fresh canvases and a spark of excitement buzzed through her. It was time to start some new pieces. She needed to spend more time in the woods where she found her inspiration. She hoped it wouldn't take long to hire a full-time employee. Soon she would have much more free time to paint. A deep sense of contentment made her sigh as she pushed her chair back from the small table she used as a desk and stretched her legs out in front of her. A sudden piercing whine shattered her peace as a police car sped down Main Street. From the direction it came from, she knew it had to be the county police. She glanced at her watch. It was after nine. The no-car ordinance was well underway. Normally the two county patrol cars left out before eight and didn't return until it was time for a shift change and then they came in through a back street. This was a law-abiding county. When the sheriff was called out it usually involved an automobile accident. Lee stepped out to the gallery floor just as Clint Devonshire burst through the front door. From the open doorway, a far more frightening sound could be heard in the distance. An ambulance screamed toward the highway. In such a close community there was high possibility that the ambulance was going for someone they all knew. Lee watched as Clint's frantic gaze tore through the room, searching. He passed over her with hardly any notice. Then the look of concern deepened when it finally settled on Gladys. Lee saw Gladys stand and step away from the computer. Clint started toward Gladys with his hand out.

Lee moved closer to Gladys as if to protect her from what Clint had come to say.

"Sheriff Rogers was in the bakery when the call came in," Clint began. "A ranger has been shot." He grabbed Gladys as she started running toward the door. "Listen to me. They don't know who it is yet. Apparently a hiker found him and called it in."

Gladys pulled away from him, turned back to the counter and grabbed the phone. She hysterically punched in numbers.

After her second misdialing, Lee took the phone from her and motioned for Clint. He came forward and put an arm around Gladys's shoulders while Lee dialed the number Gladys called out.

Lee pressed the speakerphone button and the three of them stood staring at the receiver as Dewayne's cell number rang several times before finally going to voice mail. His deep rumbling baritone seemed to reverberate around the room. Lee left a short, tense message asking him to call the gallery.

"Why isn't he answering?" Gladys whispered as tears threatened to spill from her eyes. "He has to answer."

Lee hung up the phone and took Gladys's hands into her own. "Listen, it's probably crazy out there now and he may not have even heard the phone." She knew the excuse sounded lame. She pulled Gladys into her arms and hugged her. "Dewayne Downing is a tough guy. No matter what happened, I know he'll be all right," she said softly as she stared into Clint's concerned eyes and prayed she would be right.

"I have to go out there," Gladys said suddenly as she pulled away and turned to Clint. "Where did it happen?"

Clint shook his head. "I heard the dispatcher say it happened somewhere along the Black Fork Mountain Trail. I think the best thing for us to do now is go over to the hospital and wait for the ambulance to return." He looked at Lee as if to verify the suggestion.

Lee had hiked that particular trail dozens of times. The panoramic views up and down the Ouachita River and Big Creek valley continued to draw her back. The mountaintop trail was unsurfaced and rather steep at points. She didn't voice her opinion, but depending on where the shooting had taken place along the trail, it could be difficult to extract the victim.

Gladys was shaking her head. "I don't want to wait at the hospital. I want to go out there and see what's going on. I have—" The phone rang, startling them.

They stood staring at it. Gladys looked as though she had turned to stone. Lee answered on the next ring and nearly dropped the receiver when she heard Dewayne's voice. "It's Dewayne," she said as she handed the phone to Gladys.

"Are you all right?" Gladys asked as soon as she had the phone. "No. We tried to call you, but you didn't answer and I thought—" Her voice broke.

Clint and Lee stepped back enough to give Gladys some privacy.

"Oh, dear Lord," Gladys said as she swiped a hand across her tear-streaked face. "Is he going to be all right?" There was a pause as she listened. "How long will it take?" Another pause. "Is there anything we can do?"

The one-sided conversation soon had both Lee and Clint easing back toward the counter. Most of the rangers had lived in the area for a long while.

"It was Jefferson Depew," Gladys said after she hung up and dropped to the small stool behind the counter.

"How is he?" Clint asked.

"Dewayne said it didn't look good."

"What happened?" Lee asked.

"They aren't sure. All they know is a hiker found him about an hour ago. The hiker had a cell phone with him but couldn't get it to work. He finally had to leave Jefferson to get to an area where he could get a stronger signal. Dewayne was patrolling near the Black Fork Mountain Trail when the call from the dispatcher went out. He followed the directions the hiker had given." She looked up. "Jefferson was shot in the back. Dewayne didn't go into details, but apparently, all he could do was to try to stop the bleeding. He said he was afraid to try and move him so he just sent the hiker back down the trail to lead the ambulance team up when it arrives." She stopped and shook her head slowly, as if unable to believe what she had heard. "He knew I'd be worried when I heard and thank God, his phone was able to pick up a signal."

"It won't take the ambulance more than ten minutes to get there," Clint said.

The bell chimed and they all turned to find Betty Whittington, still dressed in her gardening clothes. She was a tall, thin woman. Her short slate-gray hair looked as though it might have been scrunched beneath a hat. "I came over as soon as I heard the news. Have you heard from Dewayne?" she asked.

"It was Jefferson Depew," Gladys said and quickly filled in the few details they knew.

"My goodness," Betty said. "I taught Jefferson and his brother, Grant." She crossed her arms across her waist as if hugging herself. "Joan Depew is six or seven months pregnant with their first child. Why would anyone want to hurt Jefferson?"

"This is going to be hard on his parents," Clint said. "I'd better get back to the bakery and start putting a basket together to take over. As soon as the news gets out, people will start showing up at their house to sit with them."

"I'll run over to the grocery store and grab some cold cuts and pick up a few other things they'll need," Lee offered.

Gladys pulled her purse from beneath the counter. "I'm going over to the hospital to sit with Joan."

"I'll be here. Call if you need anything," Betty said.

With that, the group dispersed to do what needed to be done. Members of their community were hurting. Each one of them knew that had the winds of fate blown disaster their way, the very people they were going to comfort would have been among the first to arrive to help them.

CHAPTER ELEVEN

By the time Lee arrived at the home of Jefferson's parents, Lincoln and Zelda Depew, several cars were already parked along the lane leading up to the house. Since the Depew homestead was located in the same general direction as her own place, she had taken time to go home and change into jeans and a sweater before driving out. Lee parked her pickup along the road, being careful to avoid the muddiest sections, then she placed a quick call on her cell to Gladys. As she waited for her to answer, she casually watched several men sitting on the Depews' front porch, which spanned the width of the white, two-story frame house.

"Any news?" she asked when Gladys answered.

"Not really. They had trouble getting him down the trail. You know how steep some areas of the trail are, and the mud from last night's rain didn't help. The ambulance finally made it back here about fifteen minutes ago. They took him directly to surgery." She lowered her voice slightly. "Dewayne is here. He followed the ambulance in." She took a deep breath as if to steady herself. "He said it'll be a miracle if Jefferson lives."

Lee squeezed her eyes shut and pinched the bridge of her nose. "I don't suppose they know anything about who did this?"

"One of the deputies found a shell casing several yards away from where Jefferson was found."

Lee opened her eyes and rested her head against the side window of the truck. "Let me guess. It appears to match all the other mysterious casings that have been showing up recently."

"Right."

"How's Dewayne doing?" Lee could only imagine how horrible it must have been for him to see Jefferson like that.

"He's pretty upset. The only positive thing about this horror is that everyone will be stepping up their efforts to find this person and put them away."

Lee noticed that Gladys hadn't given the suspect a gender. "Did they ever find out anything about that hunter's cabin that was broken into?"

"The casings matched the others that they've found and that backpack I told you about did have women's clothing in it. She wasn't alone. At least she wasn't all the time. Apparently the bedsheets held more than enough DNA samples for comparison if they ever arrest anyone."

Lee shuddered. She didn't want to pursue that line any further. She quickly changed the subject. "I'm out here at Jefferson's folks' place. Call me if you need anything." As she got out of the truck and started removing grocery bags from the back, three of the men on the porch came out to help her. As they drew nearer, she recognized one of them was Grant Depew, Jefferson's brother. The other two were Grant's teenaged sons, Hank and George.

"I'm really sorry to hear about Jefferson," Lee said as Grant approached.

He nodded slightly.

"How're your parents and Joan holding up?"

"Tolerable," he said as he began taking bags from her and

passing them over to his nearly grown sons. "Granny's having a rough time. She's not able to go over to the hospital and sit."

Lee recalled that she'd heard someone mention a few months ago that Ida Jane Depew had moved in with her oldest son, Lincoln. She vaguely remembered that the woman was blind. She handed him the last of the bags.

"It was right nice of you to bring this stuff by," he said as his gaze met hers. "If you have the time I'd appreciate it if you'd come up to the house and sit for a spell."

"Thank you. I'd love to meet your grandmother."

Grant gave a small smile. "You watch out for yourself. She may look old and frail, but she's a cagey old bird." He glanced away quickly. "And please don't be offended if she starts trying to get you married off, later on, I mean. It's just Granny's way."

"That would take a serious amount of work on her part," Lee replied as they started toward the house.

There had been a bit of culture shock for Lee when she first arrived in Christmas. It had taken her some time to adjust and catch on to some of the more subtle customs. She quickly discovered that business matters moved at a much slower pace than what she had grown to expect in the city. If you hired someone here to fix your furnace, the job could quickly fall into an as-needed basis. If someone else called after you did, and had a sick parent or child who would be affected by the lack of heat, your work order would be pushed back. You could just as easily find yourself on the receiving end of that help, as she had been a few years back when three weeks of almost constant rain had turned the dry creek behind her house into a raging river. Without her having to ask, dozens of people had shown up to help her pile sandbags along the creek bank. Afterward, when the creek had once more gone dry, Clayton Zelman had come out with his bulldozer, cleared the creek bed of brush and raised the height of the bank nearest to her house. He had gruffly refused payment when she offered. A few days later, she heard that the house he and three generations of his family had grown up in had been washed away by a flood when he was a teenager. She went

72

to the local historical society and dug through their records until she found a photo of the old homestead. After talking to a few of the town's older citizens to check certain details, she painted a landscape of the homestead and gave it to him. She could still remember the look in his eyes as he gazed at the painting. His wife informed her that Clayton had brought the painting home and hung it over the fireplace where his favorite print of Frederic Remington's *Night Herder* had been displayed for decades. Over the years, several people had mentioned to her how much that painting meant to him.

As they approached the porch, several of the men nodded or tipped their hats at her. She spied Ollie Waters and was shocked to see that his eyes were more sunken and the skin on his face sagging. She noticed that his clothes hung on his frail frame. He looked much worse than he had on Decorating Day at the VFW Hall.

"Hello, Ollie," she said as she idly kicked a large chunk of mud off the porch. He grunted an acknowledgment. She politely inquired about his health, but he fixed her with a glare that suggested he'd prefer not to speak to her, so she turned and followed Grant and his sons into the house. She tried to think of someone she knew who was friends with Ollie, but no one came to mind. He was so cantankerous it was hard to imagine anyone talking to him. She made a mental note to talk to Gladys tomorrow. Someone needed to get him over to see a doctor.

Lee had never been to the Depews' place before. Like many of the homesteads around Christmas, this one had been in the family for many years. Stepping into the living room was like taking a trip through history. The furniture was an eclectic collection that ranged from an antique bentwood rocker to a modern black leather sofa. Several generations of knickknacks filled two long shelves that ran on both sides of the massive fireplace which must have at one time been used for heating and cooking. A large section of another wall was covered with framed photos of what she assumed were the Depew family, past and present. There was a scattering of people sitting around the living room, but the heart of the house would be the kitchen. That was where she would find the female family members and their closest friends.

"Granny Depew," Grant called out as soon as they entered the kitchen. "Miss Lee Dresher is here to see you. She's brought enough food with her to feed an army."

Lee felt a sense of calm settle over her when she stepped into the enormous kitchen. She could almost feel the heartbeat of the generations of women who had ruled this room. Like the living room, the kitchen was a hodgepodge of old and new, and again it seemed completely natural. The new stainless steel refrigerator looked completely at home with the copper pots that hung from wooden pegs on the wall and the massive wooden table that was now laden with food. She nodded and waved to the dozen or more women who nodded at her. She recognized most of them. There were only a couple of new faces. One of them was the tall, thin woman sitting at the kitchen table. She wore a pale blue blouse with long billowing sleeves. Lee saw a glimpse of her ankle-length navy blue skirt beneath the table. She wore small dark-tinted glasses.

"Grant," Granny Depew replied calmly, "when are you going to remember that I'm blind, not deaf?"

"Sorry, Granny."

"Sorry is for sinners, boy. Now, bring that woman over here so I can see her."

Grant turned to Lee. "She can't really see, but she wants to touch your face," he said in a near whisper.

"I still haven't gone deaf, boy." Granny Depew held out a hand. "Ignore him and come on over here. I'm not nearly as fearful as I look."

The guys handed over the bags of groceries and made a hasty exit. Lee wondered if she should help with the things she had brought in, but the women were already disbursing the items onto platters.

Lee focused her attention back to the older woman sitting at the kitchen table. When Granny Depew placed a hand on

74

Lee's cheek, a sense of strength seemed to radiate from beneath the paper-thin skin. This was a hand that wouldn't hesitate to swat an unruly child's butt, and would be just as fast in offering a needed hug or wiping away tears. "Hello, Mrs. Depew. I'm so sorry about what happened to Jefferson." She leaned down at the older woman's urging. She closed her eyes and waited as her face was gently explored.

The soft hands dropped from her face before the older woman replied, "I love that boy, but Jefferson is bullheaded just like his daddy and his brother are. I worried about him being out there in those woods. It's not like it was in the old days. Now, there are dope dealers and poachers out there." She shook her head. "I heard they found one of those meth labs in those caves over south of the old railroad lines. I told Jefferson a thousand times to find himself a safer job. He said he liked being outside." She blinked fiercely. "Now, look at what's happened to the little nitwit."

Her harshness caught Lee off guard.

"I guess it's my fault," Granny Depew said. "I never should have named them after politicians." She patted a spot at the table to her left. "Sit down."

Lee admired the hand-hewn table as she complied. The marks from the carpenter's plane could still be seen in places. Years of use had worn several areas of the surface to a smooth, shiny finish.

"You're the painter lady." She took Lee's hand and held it.

"Yes, ma'am. I own a gallery in Christmas."

"I never understood that." Granny Depew began to rock slightly. "It never seemed like it was something to make a living from. No disrespect intended."

"None taken, Mrs. Depew."

"Call me Granny. Mrs. Depew sounds so old." She chuckled and continued on, "I reckon it's a gift from God. Jefferson had a gift for drawing. Did you know that?"

"No, actually I didn't." Lee recalled that Betty Whittington had mentioned having both of the Depew brothers in her art class. "Could Grant draw as well?" A soft round of laughter floated around the room.

"Grant never had time for nothing but chasing girls," Judy Depew, Grant's wife, replied.

"That stopped soon enough when he met you," Granny said.

"Thanks to you, Granny," Judy said.

"No need to be airing our dirty laundry," Granny replied.

Lee looked away when she saw Judy drop her head and turn away. She kept quiet. The silence that followed made Lee long to scurry outside. She knew it was an impossible wish, even if Granny Depew hadn't still been holding on to her hand. Just when it seemed that no one would ever speak, there was a sound of rustling plastic. She looked up to find Grant coming back in and behind him stood Becka James. Grant handed over the bags and left.

Lee felt her heartbeat accelerate slightly as Becka spotted her and smiled. The forest-green jacket with matching slacks and a black turtleneck looked sharp on her.

"Is that Becka?" Granny asked.

Lee looked at her, surprised.

"Yes, Granny, it's me," Becka replied as she came forward and kissed the woman's cheek.

As Becka leaned down, the glitter of a gold chain caught Lee's attention. Her gaze was drawn to the pendant that hung from the chain. At first glance, Lee thought the blue stone in the pendant was a sapphire. Then the light caught it and cast seductive twinkles of red and green. Lee could only stare. In all the years of working in her father's store, she had never seen such a magnificent gem. "That's a faceted benitoite," she said, unable to keep the awe from her voice.

Becka glanced at her.

"What's benitoite?" Granny asked.

Becka was still leaning toward Granny and Lee couldn't stop her hand from reaching out and taking the pendant. "Benitoite is a gemstone," she replied as one of father's favorite lectures came back to her. "It was discovered in the early nineteen hundreds along the headwaters of the San Benito River. That's where it gets its name. It's only been found in that one mine in San Benito County, California." She slowly manipulated the pendant and marveled at how the stone captured the light. The dispersion of a benitoite was equal to a diamond. In fact, it was sometimes referred to as the blue diamond. It was her father's favorite stone. He bought them for her mother and even wore one himself in a ring, but Lee had never seen one as large and magnificent as this stone. She estimated it to be over four carats. When her brain did the math, she let go of the pendant and tried not to gasp in shock. The gemstone must be worth at least fifteen thousand dollars.

She realized Becka was watching her closely. "You seem to know a lot about jewelry," Becka said as she stepped back.

"My father owns a jewelry store. My brother and I worked there during the summers and on weekends."

Becka's hand went to the pendant. "I doubt this is anything so special. I bought it in a pawnshop for less than a hundred dollars."

Lee held her tongue, but Becka was either lying or the pawnshop owner was the biggest fool this side of the moon. She thought about what Gladys had said about the cost of Becka's clothes. Her wardrobe today looked nice. The material looked to be of a high quality and the pieces were obviously well made, but that was about as far as her fashion sense went.

"It's nice to see you again," Becka said.

"You two know each other?" Granny asked as she motioned for Becka to sit.

"Sort of." Becka took a seat across from Lee. "I met Lee at her gallery the other night."

"We were just talking about her gallery," Granny said. "Did you like it?"

Becka glanced at Lee and actually blushed. "I'm afraid I wasn't able to stay long enough to really see much."

"You're welcome to come back any time," Lee said. Becka's slight nod left Lee with the impression she wasn't much interested in returning to the gallery. She was taken aback by the sense of sadness the thought brought with it.

Becka turned to Granny. "Grant said there hasn't been any further news from the hospital."

"Zelda said she'd call as soon as they let them know something. I suppose that won't be until after the surgery."

Becka patted the older woman's hand. "Jefferson has a lot of grit. He won't give up easy."

Lee had the feeling she was missing an important connection here. "Do you two know each other?"

Granny Depew nodded. "Little Becka is family."

"Family?" Lee asked, even more confused.

"My father was Thomas Peterson. He and Becka's great-grandfather, William, were brothers. They grew up in Tennessee, but my father moved to Arkansas after he and my mom were married. William stayed in Tennessee where he raised five children. One of his sons, Walter, moved out here and bought a place."

"The old Peterson place," Lee said as some of the pieces started to come together.

"Right," Granny said as Becka nodded in agreement. "William's oldest son, Richard, stayed in Tennessee. His daughter Jenny married Michael James and that's where our little Becka sprouted from."

"So it is you staying at the old Peterson place," Lee said. "I'd heard someone was living over there."

Becka seemed to hesitate a moment before replying, "Yes."

"We're trying to talk her into buying the old place and fixing it up," Judy Depew said as she came over with a large tray loaded with the fully cooked, sliced ham Lee had brought.

A young woman who appeared to be in her mid-twenties placed a plate of food in front of Granny. "Try to eat something, Granny."

Granny reached out and waited for the young woman to take her hand. "Lee, this is my great-niece Annabelle. She's the daughter of my little brother Howard's youngest son. Her family lives over in Mena."

The short, heavy set woman flashed Lee a quick smile before staring down at the floor.

"It's nice to meet you, Annabelle," Lee said as someone set an empty plate on the table in front of her.

"Annabelle likes to paint, too," Granny said.

Lee couldn't help but smile as Annabelle's face blossomed into a brilliant shade of red.

"Go get that picture you painted for me when you were little and bring it in here and let Lee see it."

Annabelle looked as though she would like to disappear. "Aunt Ida, I was ten years old when I did that. Ms. Dresher doesn't want to see that."

"Nonsense," Granny replied. "I can still see it in my mind just as clear as the day you gave it to me." She pushed at Annabelle. "Go on now and get it."

Annabelle stayed rooted to the floor.

"I don't hear no footsteps," Granny said as she folded her hands in front of her.

Annabelle glanced at Lee as if pleading her to put a stop to it.

Lee didn't know what to do. She decided it might help if Annabelle knew she wasn't the only person who had ever had to endure such humiliation. "When I was eight I tried to paint a self-portrait to give to my parents. It looked more like an ostrich." She stopped and shrugged. "Or maybe that's how I really looked then. Anyway, my parents still have the painting and they love to drag it out to show people." She looked at Annabelle. "I'm sure your painting can't possibly be any worse than my first one was."

"See," Granny said. "Now hurry up and go get it."

After Annabelle had reluctantly left, Becka leaned forward. "Granny, you embarrassed her."

"Horsefeathers. All that girl ever talks about is painting. How is she ever going to get anywhere with it if all she does is paint pictures that she ends up hiding in her closet? You didn't get where you are today by being a shrinking violet."

Lee's head came up. "What do you do?" she asked Becka.

"I'm a freelance writer," Becka said quickly.

For the briefest instant, Lee thought she felt the room go still, but it had happened so quickly she nearly missed it. Even Granny Depew seemed to grow quieter.

"What sort of things do you write?"

"Here is it," Annabelle said as she reluctantly handed the painting to Lee.

"That's not bad," Lee replied as she looked at the small scene of a cat lying on a rug in front of an armchair. Off to the side was a blazing fireplace.

"See," Granny said triumphantly. "What did I tell you?"

Annabelle's smile nearly doubled. "Do you really think it's okay?"

"If you were only ten when you did this, it's better than okay," Lee assured her as she studied the piece closer.

In relation to the rest of the room, the dimensions of the cat were off slightly and the flames of the fire appeared to be more on the outside of the firebox rather than inside, but there was a tremendous amount of detail in the rug, and overall it was a nice piece. With her use of bright cheerful colors, combined with the touch of innocence it portrayed, the painting would appeal to folk art collectors.

"If you're still painting, I'd love to see some of your other work," Lee said as she handed the piece back to Annabelle. "Maybe the next time you come over this way to visit you could bring some of your work by the gallery."

Annabelle nodded slightly. "I could do that. I mean, if you really wouldn't mind looking at them."

"No, I don't mind. You understand that I can't make any promises, but I do like this. I'd love to see some of your other work."

"Thank you. I could do that."

"Let's eat so we can get out of the way before the men come in," Granny said. "Do you girls have a plate?"

"Yes, Granny, we're all taken care of," Becka assured her.

"Good. Then eat."

Lee took a bowl of potato salad that someone passed to her. As she helped herself, she realized that Becka had never answered her question about her writing.

CHAPTER TWELVE

Another two hours passed before Zelda Depew called to let them know that Jefferson was out of surgery. The doctor told them that if he survived the next twelve hours his odds of recovery were fair, but the bullet had been so close to the spine they had been unable to remove it. As soon as he was stable enough to be moved, he would be transferred to a larger hospital where the bullet could be removed. Zelda told them that the surgeon didn't appear to be very optimistic about Jefferson's odds of recovery.

Lee's cell phone rang while the Depew family was listening to Zelda's news. She stepped onto the back porch when she saw the caller was Gladys. After a quick update that recapped the news Zelda had given, Gladys surprised her with some additional news.

"Dewayne talked to the sheriff and they found a lot of tracks in the mud," Gladys said.

"You mean whoever it was deliberately shot Jefferson?"

"They think it might have been an accident. According to the sheriff it looked like whoever did the shooting had been trailing a bear." Gladys gave a loud sigh. "It's all conjecture at this point, but they think the shooter might have mistaken Jefferson for the bear. He had spilled a cup of coffee on his uniform this morning as he was leaving the house. Joan said he changed his uniform but he didn't have another uniform jacket so he wore his regular jacket."

A queasy feeling gripped Lee's stomach. Could Jefferson have been mistaken for a bear and shot by the same person who had been shooting the animals? "Let me guess, the jacket was black."

"That's right." She stopped and Lee could hear Dewayne's voice in the background. "Lee, I have to go. Dewayne is about to leave to go back to work. I'm going to sit with Joan and Mr. and Mrs. Depew a while longer before I go back to the gallery."

"Forget about the gallery. I'll call Betty and ask her to stay on until closing time. She can call me if things get too hectic." There had been no tour buses through that morning so things had been slow.

"I still have to get a couple of things done," Gladys said. "Besides, it's best if I stay busy."

"All right. Call me if you need anything." Lee went back into the kitchen. She would stay a few minutes longer before going home. Before she could sit down, Granny Depew grabbed her hand. "I'd like to go for a short walk. Would you mind walking with me?"

"Not at all. It would be nice to stretch my legs." Lee helped her up.

"I can go with you," Becka offered as she stood.

"No," Granny Depew said. "I want to talk to her about painting, and I'm sure you would be bored."

Becka looked as though she was about to say something more but apparently thought better of it.

"We'll go out the back," Granny suggested. She placed a

hand on Lee's shoulder. "You're a tall one. You lead the way until we get outside." The back porch also extended the width of the house, but it had been screened in. When they made it to the screen door, Granny stopped and patted along the wall until she found what looked like a sawed-off broom handle that was leaning against the wall. "Let's go out by the pond. There's a path somewhere ahead that will take us directly there."

"I see a path that leads off into the woods."

"That's the one. It's not far," Granny assured her as she looped her arm through Lee's.

A thin line of timber ran along both sides of the path. In most places, Lee could see the fallow fields that lay beyond.

They walked in silence for a few minutes before Granny spoke. "So you like our Becka."

Lee glanced at the older woman. She wasn't sure what she meant exactly. "It'll be nice to have a neighbor," she replied cautiously. "As you know the place has been empty since Mr. Peterson died."

"I thought maybe you were interested in more than a neighbor."

Lee glanced at her again. Where was she headed with this?

Granny Depew shook Lee's arm. "Don't go getting all tensed up. I'm not judging. I've got more important things to worry about than what other people do."

Lee tried to relax, but she still wasn't sure what was going on.

"As you've probably guessed," Granny said, "Becka isn't a very happy young woman. She's got herself all twisted up and can't seem to find a way to get herself straightened out."

"She does seem to be a little jumpy."

Granny chuckled. "Jumpy, huh? In the last ten years, that girl has bounced around more than a mattress in a cathouse." She went on without waiting for Lee to respond. "She needs a good friend, someone like you who is stable. I think she could work through all this stuff if she would just talk it out. I've tried to talk to her and so has Annabelle, but"— she shrugged— "I guess us being family and all keeps her from saying all the things she wants to say."

"I'm surprised she doesn't talk to you about whatever is bothering her," Lee said. "You two seem very close."

"I think she's afraid of disappointing me. Not that she ever could," Granny Depew added quickly. "Besides, I ain't likely to be around much longer, so she can't always depend on me."

"Now, don't say that. You look to be pretty healthy to me."

"Then you'd better get your eyes checked. I'm eighty-seven. My old ticker is wearing out."

The thought of Ida Depew dying saddened Lee. She had only known the woman for a few hours, but she already liked her. "Maybe you should see a doctor," she said.

Granny waved her hand as if shooing a fly. "Doctors nowadays don't know their butt from a hole in the ground. All they want to do is write prescriptions that nobody can read and tell you what not to eat. My doctor told me not to eat eggs or nothing fried. I'd starve to death for sure if I listened to him. Then he tells me to stop drinking coffee and to start drinking eight glasses of water a day. I told him if I went around drinking eight glasses of water every day, I'd pee myself silly."

Lee tried to hide her amusement. "I guess he's worried about you."

The older woman made a hissing sound. "He's worried about paying off that fancy foreign car he zips around in and the mortgage on that big old house of his. That's what he's worried about." She suddenly changed the subject. "I've heard you have a daughter."

"Yes. Her name is Sara. She's away at college now."

"Does she know you like girls?"

Lee tripped over a tree root and nearly fell.

"Careful, you're supposed to be helping me," Granny said as she steadied Lee.

"I'm sorry. I didn't see that root sticking out."

"Why are you so nervous?"

Lee swallowed. She started to make some lame excuse but

instinctively knew that Granny wouldn't buy it. "It's not every day that someone asks me that question pointblank."

"Are you ashamed of what you are?"

Lee turned to face her. "No, ma'am, I'm not ashamed, but it's still not something people ask me about."

"Well, now I am. Does your daughter know you like girls?"

Lee took Granny's arm and started walking again. "Yes. She has known for years and no, it doesn't bother her."

"Becka likes girls too, you know."

Lee's step faltered, but this time she managed to keep going.

"See," Granny said as she patted Lee's arm. "The more you talk about it, the easier it gets."

Lee had to laugh. "I suppose you're right. So why don't you just tell me why we're out here?"

Granny patted her arm again. "I knew I was going to like you. There should be a bench coming up soon. Why don't we sit down and rest for a while?"

Lee looked around and sure enough about a hundred feet down the path was a wooden bench. "I see it. Come on."

As soon as they were seated, Granny stretched her legs out slowly. "I don't know when my body got so old. One day I was seventeen and dancing with all the young bucks in the county. The next thing I know my ankles are swelling over the tops of my shoe and the only bucks I'm interested in are the green ones that I need to pay off medical bills."

Lee nodded. "I can understand a little of that."

"Are you going to ask Becka out? I guess you do that, huh?"

Lee gave up being shocked. "Yes. Lesbians ask each other out on dates."

"So are you going to ask Becka?"

"Are you saying she wants me to?" Lee parried.

"That girl doesn't know what she wants, but I think she's interested in you."

Lee didn't say anything, but she thought that Granny's instincts had missed the point this time.

"All she does is hide away up there in that big, old, empty

house," Granny said. "She needs to get out and have some fun."

"Why is she hiding?"

This time Granny hesitated. "I think maybe that's something she should tell you herself."

"Is she in some kind of trouble?" Lee didn't want to get tangled up in someone else's mess.

"Her biggest troubles are in her head and heart. She needs to find some kind of peace."

Lee rubbed her forehead. "If you don't mind my saying so, I think maybe she needs to do that by herself. I can't fix whatever is wrong with her."

Granny began the slow rocking motion she had been doing earlier at the table. "Maybe you're right. I just thought that talking with you might help her."

Lee recalled times in her own life when all she really needed was a friend she could pour her soul out to without having to worry about being judged. If she had been able to talk about her feelings for Jean Braddock in high school, she might never have married Brandon. She chose not to wander down the path, without him there would be no Sara. She loved her daughter and would have married Brandon a dozen times over for that reason alone. So what harm was there in at least talking to Becka? "I suppose I could invite her to dinner."

"I think that would be perfect." Granny rubbed her arms. "Let's head back to the house. This breeze is a little cooler than I thought it'd be."

When they stood, Lee removed her jacket and wrapped it around the older woman's shoulder.

"Keep your jacket," Granny protested. "I don't want you getting cold."

Lee took her arm. "Trust me. I'm having enough hot flashes to power half the electrical appliances in Christmas."

Granny gave a resounding laugh and then said, "You just wait a few more years. You'll be longing for one of those heat waves."

As they walked, Lee asked, "Did you really want to talk to me about painting or was that just an excuse to get out of the house?"

Granny patted her arm. "Lord, I can't believe I forgot all about that. What did you really think about Annabelle's painting?"

Lee shrugged. "It was a little crude, but she was young when she painted it."

"Do you think she has any talent?"

"Based on what I saw, I'd say she does, but I'd have to see what she's done recently."

"They tell me she's much better," Granny said. "I think she needs to go to school somewhere to get help."

Lee nodded without thinking. "She could take some college courses."

Granny took a deep breath and slowly released it. "No. That wouldn't work with Annabelle. Money would be a problem. I hear college is real expensive now, and besides, the poor thing never took to school." She patted Lee's arm again. "What about you? Do you offer classes?"

"No. I'm sorry. I can't." It wasn't the first time Lee had been approached by someone interested in lessons, but she always refused. She didn't want to teach.

Granny made a slight clucking noise with her tongue. "It's too bad we don't have a little place around here where the kids could learn these things. Have you ever heard of the Hudson River school, those artists who all got together?"

Lee smiled. "Yes, ma'am, I've heard about it."

"Well, why can't we start something like that right here? But with classes."

"It would be expensive and there would be a lot of work involved," Lee said.

"It's a good idea, isn't it?"

"I suppose so. Christmas already has a thriving art community, so it's reasonable to assume an art school would do well."

"So you'll do it?"

"No!" Lee stopped so fast that the older woman was brought up short. "I didn't say I would do it. I don't have the time or the money to start something like that."

"Jefferson was good at drawing. Truth is, that's all he really ever wanted to do. I have a box full of pictures he drew for me. Course, Lincoln never gave him any encouragement." She shook her head. "Now, don't get me wrong. I love my son, but there have been times when I've found myself wondering who he is and where he got some of his notions. Overall, Lincoln is a good man and was a good father, but I always thought he was too strict on those boys."

They had reached the steps to the back porch. "Here we are back at the house," Lee said and felt ashamed that she was relieved. She liked the older woman, but she certainly did not intend to give art lessons, especially not now that she was so close to finally getting a chance to more or less paint full time.

When they reached the kitchen, Lee was both pleased and disappointed to find that Becka had left while they were out walking. It was getting late and Lee wanted to get home before dark. She said her good-byes and departed, but not before she promised Granny Depew that she would call Becka and invite her to dinner soon.

CHAPTER THIRTEEN

It started raining soon after Lee got home. She dialed her parents' home number and kicked off her shoes before going to the kitchen and opening a bottle of Merlot. She poured the wine into a jelly glass and headed back into the living room. She got ready to hang up. She didn't want to leave a message. If she made this sound like a big deal, her mother would be all over it. She was relieved when her father answered.

"Hello, sweetie. What's up?"

"Why does something have to be up just because I called?" She took a sip of her wine.

He chuckled slightly before replying, "It's after eight on a weeknight and you're drinking wine."

"How do you know I'm drinking wine?"

"I heard you sipping it, and I'll wager you're drinking it from a jelly glass, which would drive your mother insane."

She laughed. "I'm way too predictable."

"No. You're just too much like your old man. Now, what's up?"

"Dad, I was wondering what the current retail value of a four-plus-carat faceted benitoite would be."

He gave a soft whistle. "Are you sure it's a benitoite? One that large would be rare."

"I'm positive."

His voice changed and she knew he had slipped back into his jeweler mode. "Describe the color and clarity."

"Eye clarity," she replied, using the term he had taught her that indicated that the stone had been studied without the aid of any magnification. "It was an oval stone, medium blue with slight purple highlights."

He was silent and she could almost see him as he stood there tugging at his small goatee. "Without examining it, all I can offer is a ballpark figure, but I'd say its value is in the range of between twenty and twenty-four thousand."

Lee nearly choked on her wine. "It's really gone up."

"The mine has pretty much played out. I heard the owners were actually opening it up for tourists to go in and dig around. If that's true, then there's no known supply for new stones." He waited a heartbeat before he asked the question she knew was coming. "Where did you see such a stone?"

Lee didn't want to lie to her father, but she didn't want to have to explain everything that was going on. He would worry if he knew about the shooting and her mom would be on the next flight out. "A customer was wearing it. I was just curious." To divert any further questions she quickly changed the subject. "Mom called and said you guys were coming out for Thanksgiving. I'm surprised you would leave the store during the holidays."

"Normally I wouldn't, but it seemed to be so important to Sara that we all be together for the holidays that I decided the store could spare me for a few days."

Lee frowned. "Sara called you?"

"Yes. She seemed anxious to have a family holiday. Didn't she mention it to you?"

"She called to ask if she could invite Brandon."

"Brandon? Her father?"

"The one and only." Lee set the glass on a coaster before stretching out on the sofa. "I thought it sort of odd too, but she said he wanted to be around people who knew him when he was a struggling writer. Apparently, he's had a book published."

"It took him long enough," her father replied. "Maybe he'll get around to paying you all that child support he owes you."

"Dad, him being published is a miracle. We probably shouldn't expect two miracles in a row. Besides, we did fine. Thanks to you, I always had plenty of money I could fall back on."

"I hear your mom calling me. I'll see you at Thanksgiving." Her father quickly hung up.

She smiled as she set the phone down. Her father had never liked discussing money.

The rain continued throughout the night. Before turning in, Lee had set her alarm with the intention of going to the blind. When it went off the next morning, she discovered it was still raining. She turned over and tried to go back to sleep, but instead she started thinking about Granny Depew's suggestion. She found herself wondering why with so many artisans in the surrounding area no one had ever bothered to offer classes. People had asked about them often. It probably wouldn't be too difficult to start something simple. It certainly wouldn't be anything as prestigious as an art institute, but something along the lines of—she kicked the blankets off and sat up quickly. The last thing she needed was to get involved in anything that was going to take time away from her painting.

She went to the kitchen and put on a pot of coffee. After looking up the number in the phone book, she called the county hospital to check on Jefferson. The woman at the switchboard patched her through to the waiting area where one of Jefferson's cousins picked up and told her that there had been little change from the previous night. She took a quick shower and then dressed in the rose-colored Victorian-era walking suit. After pouring a cup of coffee, she went to her studio. This was her favorite room of the house. It was a corner room. Massive picture windows filled a large area of both outer walls and flooded the space with northern and eastern light. The back wall also had a French door that led to a balcony that ran the length of the back wall. Beneath the balcony was an equally wide back porch. As soon as she stepped into the room, her gaze settled on the partially completed portrait of a doe with twin fawns that rested on an easel. She reached for a brush but stopped. She really didn't have time. If she started painting, she'd quickly get lost in her work and would be even later in getting to the gallery. She ran a finger gently over the bristles of the brush as she eyed the three other paintings in various stages of completion that leaned against the wall. She could hardly wait until she would have more hours to paint. The local weekly paper wouldn't be out until Thursday. Impatient for results, she decided she would post a help wanted notice on the bulletin boards at both the grocery store and the hardware store. After one last glance at the unfinished canvases, she moved over to the window that overlooked the balcony. She started to go out and sit where she could see the birdfeeders she kept filled year round, but the chairs were wet, and she didn't feel like taking time to dry them. This window looked out over a vast area where she had planted a variety of flowers and vines that attracted both birds and butterflies. Deer, rabbits, ground squirrels and a number of other mammals enjoyed the area as well. She loved to sit by the window in the winter when the weather didn't allow her out on the balcony and watch them.

Her spirits suddenly lifted when she remembered she had the appointment with the lawyer that afternoon. She felt good about making Gladys a partner. It was absolutely the right thing to do. Her only regret was that she had taken so long in making the decision. She should have done it much sooner. She gazed longingly at the dabs of color that dotted the high slope to the east. The fall foliage was already beautiful this year and it hadn't reached its peak yet. It was a welcome change from the previous two years when the lack of rainfall had prevented the leaves from reaching their full potential.

As she studied the slope, she thought about Becka. The old Peterson place was located at the base of that slope. Her thoughts turned back to the previous day and her conversation with Granny Depew. She regretted telling her that she would invite Becka to dinner. She liked her life as it was now. She didn't want to get involved with anyone. "As if she was interested in getting involved with me," she mumbled aloud. Besides, it wasn't as if an invitation to dinner automatically meant an orgy. She scolded herself for being so standoffish and unneighborly. Becka was obviously going through a difficult time. What would it hurt to invite her to dinner? There was a good chance that Becka wouldn't even want to come over. It wasn't as though she had shown any burning interest in getting to know Lee. "That wasn't very neighborly of her," she muttered.

She grimaced as she sipped her coffee and found it had grown cold. A glance at the clock told her time had rushed past while she had stood there daydreaming. If she didn't leave now she would have to park in the tourist lot. As she turned to go, she caught a peripheral glimpse of movement. Her first thought was that it might be the buck she had been trying to photograph. She set her coffee down and picked up the binoculars that she kept handy for bird- and nature-watching. The first time she swept the area where she thought she had seen the movement she found nothing. It wasn't until the second, slower pass that her heart stuttered as she brought the image into focus. A man dressed in camouflaged coveralls, like those that hunters wore, was leaning against a massive pine tree near the edge of the woods. She might have missed him completely had the rifle he cradled in his arms not been projected in a straight line. She had worked with landscapes enough to know that there were rarely any straight lines in nature. The man seemed to be staring directly at her. She started to step back but stopped. The windows of her studio were treated with a special tint that allowed the light in but blocked ultraviolet rays. This special treatment made it nearly impossible for anyone outside to see in unless it was at night and she had a light on. She knew that it worked, because when she sat on the balcony she couldn't see inside the room.

She continued to watch the man for several more minutes until he slowly turned and slipped into the woods. When he disappeared from her sight, she sat on the small stool and started to wonder why Ollie Waters would be standing in the woods behind her house with a rifle. He could have been hunting, but she owned the land where he had been and all of her property was clearly posted. She had never kept it a secret that she strongly disapproved of anyone hunting for sport.

After a careful check of the woods, she finally put the binoculars down and took her cup back to the kitchen. As she rinsed it, she thought about the last time she had seen Ollie. He had been sitting on the Depews' front porch yesterday. The events of the day replayed in her mind. She saw herself climbing the porch steps, walking a few paces and kicking the clump of mud off the porch. It had rained the night before Jefferson was shot. Gladys had even mentioned that the mud had made it difficult for the rescue workers to bring Jefferson down the trail. Had there been mud on Ollie's shoes? She shook her head. She was being ridiculous. Even if Ollie had stepped in mud out on Black Fork Mountain Trail, it wouldn't have still been on his shoes by the time he reached the Depew home. "That's why you run a gallery and not the police department," she told herself as she placed the cup in the dishwasher and dried her hands.

She had never liked Ollie, but she didn't think he was capable of harming anyone. A new thought struck her. Maybe that was why he had looked so ill? Perhaps he had been tracking the bear and shot Jefferson by mistake. She could see Ollie defying the hunting laws. He had probably hunted this entire area long before hunting restrictions and laws were enforced. She shook her head to drive the thoughts away. Gladys had told her a woman was involved and she had never seen Ollie with a woman. As far as she knew, he had never even been married.

After grabbing her keys, she went into the garage. Normally

she hit the garage door button by the kitchen door as soon as she stepped out, but today she got into her truck and locked the doors before opening the garage with the remote. The back of her neck began to tingle as the door slid up. A part of her half expected to find Ollie standing out there waiting for her. When no one appeared in the driveway, she slowly backed out, watching for any movement that might indicate someone's presence. As soon as the truck was clear of the door, she hit the close button and for once waited until it was securely in place. As she backed out of the driveway, her fear began to be replaced with anger. This was her home, and she had never before been afraid. There were more nights than she cared to remember when she had forgotten to lock her doors. Now, thanks to one ornery old man, that had all changed.

"I'll be damned if I let that old fool scare me," she spat as she threw the truck into gear and headed down the graveled lane that led to the main highway. She didn't know exactly where Ollie lived but she intended to find out, and he'd better have a danged good reason for skulking around her property.

She had only driven about a half a mile when she saw someone walking along the roadside. She wondered why anyone would be out here since this road only led back to her property. In fact, her property bordered both sides of the road. For the briefest instant, she thought it might be Ollie but realized that this person was wearing a dark green jacket. The hiker stopped and turned to look back toward her. It was Becka James. Lee eased the truck to a stop.

"Do you need a ride?" Lee asked after rolling down her window.

"No, thanks. I was just out for my morning walk."

Lee wondered if she should mention that she was walking on private property, but she decided against it since Becka wasn't hurting anything. Then she thought about Ollie wandering around out there with a rifle. She didn't want to frighten Becka, but she certainly didn't want Ollie taking potshots at her either. "Do you think it's safe to be out walking like this? I mean, after what happened to Jefferson?" Lee regretted opening her mouth as soon as she saw the frightened look in Becka's eyes.

"I thought it would be safe enough here," Becka replied as she glanced around. "I'm not on national forest land." She turned to Lee. "Am I?"

"No. This isn't national forest land, but still you might want to be careful." Lee didn't want to leave her alone out here. "Why don't you let me give you a ride back to your place? I'm headed in that direction anyway."

Becka tilted her head slightly and smiled. "No, you aren't. You know my place is at least a mile out of your way."

Lee shrugged. "How can you be so sure? Maybe I was on my way to see you."

"I doubt that, but I'll take you up on the offer anyway." She moved around to the other side of the truck.

Lee reached across and unlocked the door. As she waited for Becka to get in, she scanned the edge of the woods and back as far as she could see into the interior. It wasn't until Becka had gotten into the truck that Lee noticed she was wearing camouflaged pants.

CHAPTER FOURTEEN

Lee turned away when Becka noticed her staring at her pants.

"Are they a bit over the top for around here?" Becka asked shyly.

"No, but they might be dangerous later on during hunting season." Lee put the truck in gear and took off. "Of course, no one is supposed to be hunting out here anyway. You might even be safer wearing them with that crazy shooter running around loose." She stopped chattering. "Sorry, I guess this whole thing has me a little shook up." She was dying to ask Becka how well she knew Ollie Waters. Could they be in this together? Then she recalled what Gladys had said about the bedsheets in the hunter's cabin. The mere thought of Ollie touching Becka made her sick to her stomach.

"I have to believe it was an accident," Becka replied,

interrupting Lee's deliberations. "Jefferson is such a gentle soul. I can't imagine anyone wanting to hurt him."

"How well do you know Ollie Waters?" The question even surprised Lee. She hadn't thought before it popped out her mouth.

Becka frowned slightly. "Who?"

"Ollie Waters. He was at the house yesterday." Lee tried to talk her way out of the question. "I didn't realize he was a friend of Jefferson's."

"Oh, you're talking about the older man. He's sort of…um…grumpy."

Lee chuckled. "That's putting it mildly."

"I don't know him. Someone said he was a friend of Granny's."

Lee latched onto the explanation. She wanted to believe Becka. "I keep forgetting that Granny Depew lived around here."

"Until Grandpap died." She stopped a moment. "I guess that was about fifteen years ago."

"I've only been here a little over ten years, so I never knew him."

"This is where my parents and I would spend our vacations. We'd either stay here with Uncle Walter and his family or we'd stay with Granny and Grandpap for a couple of weeks every summer. I was an only child, but here there were always scads of kids around to play with and I loved it."

"I have an older brother, but he wasn't much fun to play with." Lee looked at her and smiled. "He was horrible at baseball, too short for basketball and couldn't ride a skateboard."

"Let me guess. You were great at all those things."

"Well, I don't like to brag, but"— she laughed—"I was good."

"Granny told you I'm a lesbian, didn't she?"

Lee sobered and nodded. "She mentioned it while we were walking."

"What else did she tell you?"

99

"Just that you were going through a rough time and she thought you might need a friend to talk to."

"Is that all she said?"

"No. She said that if you wanted me to know anything more you'd tell me." Lee concentrated on negotiating the turn onto the road that led to Becka's place. "Oh, she also said I should invite you to dinner."

Becka looked at her for a long moment before turning to gaze out the window. They remained silent until Lee pulled into the driveway.

"I guess you were on your way to the gallery," Becka said.

"Yes."

"I suppose you've had breakfast, too."

"No. Actually all I've had is a half cup of coffee."

"I have plenty of fresh coffee and a box of doughnuts that I picked up yesterday, if you'd like to come in."

Lee looked at the house. "I'll stay if you promise to have dinner with me at my place on Friday night."

"Can you cook?"

"Not really, but I've never poisoned anyone, although now that I think about it, I'm not sure I've ever fed the same person twice."

"That doesn't say much for either your culinary skills or your relationship skills."

Lee shrugged. "I've never claimed to be good at either one."

"Then I don't feel so bad about feeding you a slightly stale doughnut."

They got out of the truck and made their way inside. Lee was shocked to find that the living room contained nothing but a foldable lawn chair, a small plastic table with a Coleman lantern and a cardboard box filled with books. "Whoa, you give a whole new meaning to a monastic lifestyle."

Becka glanced around the room. "It is sort of pathetic, isn't it?" She went to the center of the room and slowly turned. "I don't know how long I'm going to stay. I didn't want to buy stuff and then have to leave it or get rid of it."

Lee looked at the empty socket where the ceiling light should have been. "I have a couple of lightbulbs I could spare, if you'd like one."

Becka's laughter echoed through the nearly empty room. "Thanks for the offer, but I'm afraid they wouldn't do me much good." She waved a hand. "I never had the electricity turned on."

"Please tell me you have running water."

"Sort of."

The room was surprisingly warm. Lee pulled off the Victorian jacket and draped it over the chair. "What does 'sort of' mean exactly?"

"Come on. I'll show you." Becka led the way into another room where there was a large fireplace. The ample mound of ashes testified that the fireplace had received a lot of use. In fact, embers still glowed in it. An old-fashioned coffeepot hung from the pot crane. The only furniture in the room was a card table and a chair. "The fireplace produces all the heat I need, as well as providing me with a continuous source of hot water." She pointed to the coffeepot before moving to a table Lee hadn't noticed earlier. It was against the wall. "Here I have all the conveniences of a modern coffee bar." There was a small metal coffeepot of the type that Lee had seen among the camping supplies at the hardware store, a pump pot for coffee that was very similar to the ones Alan and Clint used at the bakery, a small box of artificial sweetener and another of powdered creamer. Before Lee could think of anything to say Becka motioned for her to follow her. "This is the kitchen and you'll notice that I have a well-stocked pantry." She waved to the shelves fastened along one wall where a decent variety of canned vegetables were stacked. "And over here is the running water you were so concerned about."

"That's a hand pump," Lee said, completely appalled.

Becka grabbed the handle and pumped it until water poured from the mouth and down into the antique sink. "Now it's running."

Lee covered her mouth with her hand to keep from blurting

out her shock.

"Ah, I can see you're concerned about my living arrangement. I have a fire to heat my food and water for bathing. There is a full bath down the hall and while I do have to fill the tub manually, it drains on its own. I've worked out a very simple procedure to make the commode work. I just fill the tank with water. I have the same conveniences most people have. Mine simply require a bit more work to make them operational." Becka leaned back against the sink and crossed her arms.

When it became obvious that she was waiting for Lee to respond, Lee dropped her hand. "All right, I have to admit that I find this a little shocking."

"Why is it so shocking? This is how the people who originally built this house would have lived. In fact, they had it worse. They had to use an outhouse."

"That's true, but they didn't have a choice."

"Does my having the choice make it wrong?"

"I didn't say it was wrong." Lee was starting to regret ever coming inside.

"You have disrespected my ancestors."

Lee could tell by Becka's smile and her tone that she was teasing her. "I apologize. I never intended to besmirch your family, but I still think you've taken this back-to-nature thing a bit far." She glanced around. "Don't you get tired of eating food from a can?"

"When are you free for dinner?" Becka asked without answering her question.

Lee shrugged. "Provided there are no tour buses rolling through town, I can pretty much set my own hours at the gallery."

"Great." She put a finger to her chin as if thinking. "What sort of wine do you like?"

"I normally drink red wine."

"Do you have a favorite label?"

"Whatever is on sale at the grocery store," Lee admitted.

Becka frowned. "Never mind. I'll take care of the wine

selection. You come by tonight, and I'll show you how the pioneers really ate."

"I don't know," Lee said, a little dubious at the prospect. "What are you planning to cook— possum on a stick or raccoon ravioli?"

Becka folded her arms again and tilted her head. "I think I'll just wait and surprise you." She paused before adding, "If you think you can handle it." Her voice held a challenge that suggested more than cooking.

Lee struggled not to gulp. "What time?"

"You're the working woman. You tell me."

"Is eight too late? That way I won't have to worry about a crowd hitting the gallery."

"Eight is fine and feel free to stop by earlier if you like."

"What can I bring?"

"Just bring an appetite. I'll take care of the rest."

Lee nodded and started toward the door.

"Didn't you forget something?"

She turned back to find Becka holding up a doughnut.

"You're feeding me breakfast and dinner. We'll have to be careful. People will start to talk." She took the pastry.

"You don't strike me as the type who worries about what people have to say."

"I guess it depends on what they're saying." Lee gazed at Becka and knew she was treading on dangerous ground. Becka had problems and she didn't want to be pulled into them. "What about you? Do you worry about what people say?"

The animation in Becka's face disappeared. "Sometimes it seems that all I do is worry."

Lee regretted being the cause of the anguish that filled those beautiful blue eyes. She longed to remove it and that scared her. Instead, she held up the doughnut. "Thanks for breakfast. I'd better get going." She rushed out to her truck. When she looked back, Becka was standing in the doorway waving. Something about the simple act left Lee feeling sad.

CHAPTER FIFTEEN

The rain had started again during the night. Lee had to park in the tourist lot where there were only a handful of cars. Most of them she recognized as belonging to local residents. She tried not to grumble as she picked her way through the mud puddles to where one of the wagons sat waiting to drive her into town. The wagon had a canvas covering, but she was soaked long before she even reached it.

"Nasty weather today," Allison Carroll called down as he offered his hand to hoist her up. "I wish I could offer you a dry seat, but everything is soaked." He pointed his thumb over his shoulder. "At least out here you don't have to smell wet canvas."

"How are you doing, Allison? Here I was feeling all sorry for myself about having to be out on a day like this. Do you have to stay out here in this mess all day?"

"Just until this afternoon, then someone else comes to relieve me. I don't mind it so much. If it starts getting too bad I just have a little pick-me-up."

She looked at him and laughed when he pulled a flask from his coat pocket.

He shook the reins slightly and the two mules started forward. "You're welcome to a nip if you'd like."

"Thanks, it's a bit early for me but check back with me later. I may need it if this mess keeps up."

"After a few nips of this, I won't even care if it snows."

"Oh, man, don't even mention snow. I'm nowhere ready for that."

"Have you heard anything more about Jefferson Depew?" he asked.

The local tendency toward sudden changes in conversation had bothered her when she first arrived, but over the years she had grown accustomed to it and sometimes even found herself doing it. "I called the hospital this morning and talked to his cousin Reid. He seems to be about the same."

"Clarissa Jenkins said she'd heard he might not be able to walk anymore." A cold gust of wind hit them and prompted Allison to urge the mules to a little faster pace.

"I suppose it's a possibility."

"Bad business," he muttered. "Can't see why anyone would want to hurt him."

Lee started to ask him what he knew about Ollie Waters but decided against it. She didn't want Ollie to find out that she had been asking about him. She was positive he hadn't been able to see her through the window that morning. He couldn't know that she had seen him and for now, she wanted to keep it that way.

He stopped the mules in front of the gallery.

"Enjoy your day," Lee said as she hopped down.

He smiled brightly and patted his jacket. "Ol' Jim and I plan on having a right cheerful day." He nodded. "Let me know if you need a little something extra to perk up your coffee."

She laughed and waved before rushing into the gallery.

Business was slow, as it tended to be during bad weather. Despite the fact that the paper containing her want ad hadn't been released yet, two women came in to apply for the job. They had both heard about it through a friend. Lee took both applications, but she already knew she wouldn't hire either of them. One was a major gossip and the other one never held a job for more than three months. As she placed the applications into a file folder, she realized that she had discovered another advantage to living in a small town. She wouldn't have to bother with checking references. She would probably know everyone who applied.

Later that afternoon she and Gladys went over to Max Bollard's office and started the process of making Gladys a legal partner in the gallery. Lee was somewhat surprised when Gladys handed him a paper that listed a couple of stipulations. The first one was that Lee's artwork would be handled on a commission basis the same as the other artists were. The gallery would still get its usual thirty-percent commission, but the bulk of the money would go to Lee. The second was that Lee would maintain full ownership of the building and the partnership would lease it from her at a fair market value. Lee agreed to everything except the rental. She reasoned that during slow times the gallery couldn't bear the burden of the lease expense and a full-time employee. Gladys argued that it was the only fair thing to do. In the end, Max settled the argument by suggesting that the gallery pay for any minor repairs that could reasonably be expected to occur in connection with the normal operation of the business and it would pay the property taxes and insurance on the building. In turn, Lee would charge a rental fee of one dollar per year. When Lee questioned the token sum, he explained it was just a symbol to show Uncle Sam that her intention wasn't to make a profit from a rental property but rather maintain a profitable gallery.

When they left his office, Lee stopped. The rain had slowed considerably, but the streets were still empty of shoppers. "Betty can handle things for a while longer. Let's go over to the bakery and celebrate our new partnership with one of their decadent desserts."

Gladys's hand skimmed along her hip. "I really shouldn't. I swear I gain ten pounds every year during the holidays and then spend the next six months trying to get rid of them." She looked at Lee a moment before adding, "I only had a bowl of oatmeal for breakfast and an apple for lunch." She grabbed Lee's arm. "Let's go. I hope they have the croissants with the cream cheese and raspberry filling that Alan makes, or the blueberry scones with that topping of thick, sweet cream."

"I want one of the chocolate rolls with the pastry that melts in your mouth," Lee said, already savoring the rich buttery treat.

By the time they reached the bakery, they were practically running. They burst through the door in a wave of laughter and anticipation.

"Prepare for a female chocolate emergency," Alan called when he looked up and saw them.

From the back of the bakery, Clint began to mimic a wailing siren.

"Stop it," Gladys scolded as she scanned the display of goodies. "Oh, no. They have both, so now what am I going to do?" she lamented.

"Have one of each," Alan said.

"Isn't that just like a man," Gladys said without taking her eyes from the display. "Dewayne can eat half a dozen doughnuts and never gain an ounce. All I have to do is sniff one and I gain a pound."

"Honey," Alan said, "don't you know that this place is like Vegas? What happens here, stays here." He waved his hands. "No calories leave this building."

"Yeah, they all stay right here," Clint said as he came out patting his stomach.

When Gladys couldn't make up her mind which dessert to choose, Lee ordered them both. "We'll split them," she said.

Since there were no other customers in the shop, Clint and Alan joined them at a table. The conversation quickly turned to

Jefferson and the shooting. After a few minutes of discussion, Lee decided to share that morning's experience with them. They would know what to do.

"What do you guys know about Ollie Waters?" she asked.

"He's a cantankerous old coot," Gladys said, picking up the last of the crumbs from her plate.

"I'll second that and add homophobic to the mix," Clint said.

Lee looked up in surprise. Had Alan made the comment she might have blown it off as him exaggerating, but not Clint. "Do you really think so?"

"I think he tries to pretend he's not, but I've seen the way he looks at us sometimes when he thinks no one is watching." He got up to refill their coffee cups. "Why? What has he done now?"

Lee thought about it for a moment, then decided to tell them about what had happened. "I saw him standing behind my house this morning. He was at the edge of the woods, and he seemed to be watching the house." She fiddled with her cup. "I guess it made me a little nervous because he had a rifle."

They all gaped at her.

"Ollie Waters was standing behind your house with a gun and this is the first I've heard about it," Gladys said, clearly miffed.

"I was going to talk to him—"

"Oh, no, you're not," the other three chorused at once.

"Look, I don't want to make a federal case about this until I know what he was doing. You know how he is. He was probably back there hunting."

Gladys was digging in her purse. "Lee, I can't believe you sometimes. There's a crazy man running around shooting animals just for the sake of killing. Jefferson Depew is lying in the hospital on the verge of death, and you don't think seeing that crazy old coot standing behind your house with a rifle is a big deal. Sometimes I wonder about your sanity." She finally found her cell phone and started punching in numbers.

"Who are you calling?" Lee asked, although she already

knew the answer.

"I'm calling Dewayne."

"Why? There's nothing he can do. Ollie was on private property, not national forest land. Besides, I don't want this to get blown all out of proportion until I know what he was doing back there."

Gladys gave her a look of disbelief. Dewayne must have answered then because she waved Lee off. "Dewayne, you need to go pick up Ollie Waters and find out why he was standing behind Lee's house this morning with a rifle. Yes, that's what I said. He had a rifle. No, he wasn't shooting at her or else I would have said so. Now, stop wasting time and go get him." She closed the phone with a decisive snap. "There." She turned to Lee. "You see, that wasn't hard at all."

They all sat staring at her.

"What's wrong?" Gladys asked.

When no one answered, Alan suddenly fanned himself with his hand. "That was so butch. I think I'm in love with you." He stopped and gave her a dubious look. "At least I would be if I weren't so scared of you."

They all began to laugh as Gladys smiled. "That did feel very empowering," she said, and joined in on the laughter. "I think I'll have another half a pastry."

"Another round coming up," Alan said as he jumped up to refill their plates.

CHAPTER SIXTEEN

Lee left the gallery a little after seven. It had been another hectic day after all. Grateful that the rain had finally stopped she went to the parking lot to her truck. She took her time, delaying the inevitable as long as possible. Why had she accepted the invitation to have dinner with Becka? She had been so busy with the gallery lately that she had let chores at the house slip. There were a dozen things waiting to be done and besides she needed to paint. Plus, that whole episode with Ollie had spiraled into the big melodrama that she had wanted to avoid. After Gladys called Dewayne that morning, he had called the sheriff. Richard Early, a deputy sheriff, came by the gallery and took her statement. Within twenty minutes of his departure, the phone began to ring as the local gossip mill kicked into full swing. In the end, it had all been for nothing because as of an hour ago, no one had been able to find Ollie Waters. Deputy Early had advised her not to go walking in the woods alone and to take extra precautions about locking her doors. Then Dewayne arrived with a pistol that he tried to give her. She didn't admit to him or Gladys that the thought of having a gun in the house frightened her more than finding Ollie skulking in the woods.

A new thought came to her. Maybe she could use the events of the day to beg off dinner. As she cranked the truck, she realized she didn't have a phone number for Becka. She probably pounded out messages on a tom-tom, she thought as she recalled Becka's strange living conditions. She told herself to get over it and stop whining. Tonight was going to be a onetime thing. She grimaced when she remembered that she had more or less invited Becka to dinner on Friday night. Perhaps tonight would go so badly that Becka wouldn't want to come Friday night.

She drove as slowly as she dared but still arrived nearly thirty minutes early. As she stepped out of the truck, she pounded the heel of her hand against her forehead. She hadn't thought to bring anything, but Becka had told her not to bring anything. Still it didn't seem right to show up empty-handed. Why hadn't she gone home and changed her clothes? These damn suits are getting too comfortable. She was on the verge of getting into the truck and rushing back to town for a bottle of wine. No, that wouldn't do. Becka had said she would take care of the wine. A bouquet of flowers would be better or would that suggest more of the night than she intended it to? She was still trying to decide when the door to the house opened.

Becka stood on the front porch in a soft orb of lantern light. "Can you see well enough to find the walkway?" she called. The slightly musical tone in her voice made Lee smile.

"Yes, I can see." She headed up the path and again wondered why she hadn't thought about going home to change. For someone who didn't want to do this, she had sure managed to forget several things. As she approached, she saw that Becka was wearing a dress of some flowing material that hung to mid-calf. Her shoes were sandal-like and seemed much too skimpy for the brisk night air.

"I wondered if you would come," Becka admitted as Lee stepped onto the porch.

"I almost didn't."

They stood staring at each other for a long second.

Becka broke the silence. "Let me guess. You couldn't stay away because you've heard all the rumors about my wonderful …what was it you called it…oh, yes, raccoon ravioli."

Lee tried to look disappointed. "Dang, I was hoping for possum on a stick. I've been thinking about it all day."

Becka suddenly broke into a brilliant smile. "Great, because that's exactly what I made."

Lee took a step back and realized a second too late that Becka was having fun at her expense. "Very funny," she replied and rolled her eyes. "I can see I'm in for a real treat tonight, a comedy show and dinner."

Becka looped her arm through Lee's. "Oh, come in and don't be a Grumpy Gus. I think you'll be both surprised and pleased with dinner."

"I'm sorry. I'm not usually this way, but–"

Becka shushed her. "No excuses tonight. Let's enjoy what I hope you will find to be a nice dinner. Come on in."

Lee stepped into the room and was greeted by a wonderful aroma. "Something smells delicious."

"That would be the roasted chicken," Becka said. "Please have a seat and I'll get us a glass of wine." She gestured to what looked like a card table that had been placed in front of the hearth. It was draped in a light-colored cloth. Two table settings awaited them.

The light from the fireplace along with the candles on the table cast a warm glow over the room. Lee no longer noticed the stark emptiness of the place. "You've been busy." Lee pulled out one of the metal chairs at the table.

She tried to relax as Becka went to the other side of the room. She noticed the two Dutch ovens and a small roasting pan sitting on the fireplace hearth. "Did you cook the chicken in that roasting pan?" Lee knew that Dutch ovens were used to cook over an open fire, but surely she hadn't tried to use the roasting pan. It would have been much too thin.

"A good chef never reveals her secrets." Becka was pouring the wine at another candlelit table. "You don't really buy wine just because it's on sale, do you?"

"I'm afraid so."

Lee rubbed her thumb nervously across the linen tablecloth. "I can't see paying forty dollars for a bottle of wine that tastes the same as a five-dollar one. I'm perfectly contented with my cheap Merlot and jelly glass."

"That is so not right." Becka shook her head. "And you thought I was living under appalling conditions." She handed Lee a tall, fluted glass and sat down across from her.

Lee sipped the white wine and wondered if she should say something about its body or bouquet, not that she really knew anything about either of those things. She was grateful that the glass gave her something to occupy her hands.

"I suppose I'm a bit of a wine snob." Becka stopped and grinned. "That's not true. I'm a huge wine snob."

Lee glanced around the room.

Becka apparently saw the look. "I know. After seeing the way I live, you probably think I'm some sort of weirdo."

"No." Lee tried to think of something positive to say about Becka's living arrangements. "Why do you live like this?" She knew she was being inexcusably rude, but her curiosity propelled her forward. "Judging from the clothes you wear and the car you drive, you certainly don't seem to be hurting financially, and—" She stopped sharply. She had gone far beyond simple rudeness. "I'm sorry. It's none of my business."

Becka stared into the fire.

Mortified by her ill-mannered outburst, Lee wondered if she should get up and leave.

"I'm not sure I can explain it," Becka said so quietly that Lee had to lean forward to hear. Becka turned to her. "Have you ever been in a situation that most people would die to attain?"

Lee blinked. "I'm not sure I know what you mean."

"You're already an artist of some renown," Becka began. "What if you woke up tomorrow morning and suddenly found yourself a national celebrity?" Her voice grew more urgent. "Overnight, your paintings start being compared to world-famous artists." She leaned forward, staring at Lee intently. "But with the fame comes all the other stuff. Everyone wants something from you—to use your name, your time. You can't leave your house without photographers or tabloid reporters hounding you. They go through your trash, follow you everywhere you go, and they don't care whether the stories they print are true or not." She stopped and fell back in her chair as if the rant had exhausted her.

Lee sipped her wine as she struggled for something to say. She had no idea what was going on, but it was obvious she had stomped on a raw nerve. "I don't think I would care to give that a try," she replied lamely. "I'm perfectly content in my little gallery."

Becka's entire persona shifted as she suddenly smiled and leaned forward. "Ignore me. I can be a bit over dramatic sometimes." She took a taste of her wine. "What do you think of the wine?"

Lee took a sip. "It's fine…good," she added quickly.

Becka shook her head and made a clucking sound. "Your introduction to good wine begins now. I want you to hold the glass up to the light and tell me what you see."

Eager to get the conversation back on a more comfortable level, Lee complied. "I see hundreds of little bubbles."

"Is that all?"

"Well, I see the glass, too."

Becka sighed. "You call yourself an artist." She held up her glass. "I see a pale rosé tinged with a slight coppery hue and a cascade of delicate bubbles."

Lee gave her a sarcastic look. "I didn't know you wanted me to go drag queen on you. Give me another chance. I'll do better next time."

"Close your eyes."

"Why?" Lee's need to reestablish a higher comfort level certainly didn't extend that far.

"I believe that Victorian garb is starting to affect you," Becka said as she gave Lee a knowing look. "Now close your eyes."

Lee did as she was asked.

"Relax. I'm not going to attack you—unless you want me too, of course."

Lee's eyes flew open.

Becka swatted her arm. "I'm messing with you. Close your eyes."

Once more Lee did as she asked.

"Now, this is a Lucien Albrecht Crémant D'Alsace Brut Rosé. I want you to take a small sip and let it slowly glide over your tongue. Then tell me what you taste."

Lee tasted the wine. "It tastes a little like Champagne."

"That's right. It's a sparkling wine made from Pinot Noir grapes. Now take another sip."

Lee raised the glass.

Becka's voice grew softer. "This time hold it in your mouth a moment."

Lee complied.

"Now, ever so gently move your tongue through it and savor the various flavors." Becka's voice seemed suddenly closer. Lee fought the urge to open her eyes to see where Becka was. An inkling of desire scampered through her lower body. She was so busy wondering where Becka was that it took her a moment to recognize the feelings for what they were. When she did, her eyes flew open and she swallowed the wine so quickly she choked.

Becka waited patiently until Lee stopped coughing. "That wasn't exactly the response I was looking for."

"I guess I'm a lost cause," Lee said as she wiped tears from her eyes. Now she remembered why she had stopped dating. She was no good at it. To her surprise, Becka didn't give up on her.

"Nonsense. Try again."

Lee reluctantly closed her eyes and took another sip. This time she focused on the taste and tried to ignore Becka's voice.

It took a moment, but suddenly a hint of floral crept across her tongue. It was followed by a teasing suggestion of fruit. She swallowed and opened her eyes. "Strawberries and something floral," she replied proudly.

Becka beamed. "I knew you would be good." Her eyes widened as if in surprise. "At wine tasting, I mean. You have a great mouth…ah…palate." She jumped up and moved over to the fireplace. "I made a vegetable medley. I hope you like it." She was rattling off the vegetables.

Lee didn't pay much attention to her spiel. The light from the fire shined through the thin material of Becka's dress and provided a breathtaking silhouette of her body. Mesmerized by the vision, Lee's eyes devoured the slightly rounded hips. She brazenly allowed her gaze to drift up the inside of Becka's legs. Only a strong rein on her emotions kept her from reaching out and allowing her hand to trace the path her eyes were taking. She continued her voyeuristic journey as Becka used an iron hook to remove the lid from one of the Dutch ovens. The aroma of basil and squash teased Lee's nostrils, but it wasn't enough to stop her from staring at Becka's body. The view was too tempting. She gave a small cry of disappointment when Becka broke the moment by stepping back from the fire.

"Would you mind bringing the plates over?" Becka asked. "This pot is too heavy to carry."

The spell was broken. Lee eagerly grabbed onto the distraction, grateful for anything that would take her attention away from the lusty thoughts that were beginning to germinate. She held the plates as Becka spooned the vegetables onto them. Next, Becka removed the lid from the roasting pan. She took a knife and meat fork that rested on a small stool that Lee hadn't noticed earlier and sliced the chicken.

"That smells heavenly." Lee inhaled deeply as Becka placed the meat onto the plates. "How on earth did you manage to cook that in a roaster?"

"That's the secret," Becka said. "I didn't. Have you ever heard of a process called string roasting?"

Lee shook her head as she set the plates on the table. She was trying to keep her stomach from growling. Suddenly she felt ravenous. "No, I can't say that I have."

"Good, then it'll be my secret." Becka walked back to the side table. "Would you prefer a nice California Cabernet Sauvignon, or I have an excellent Pinot Noir from Oregon's Willamette Valley?"

Not wanting to admit she didn't really know what the difference between the two was, Lee took the easy way out. "I'll have whatever you're having."

"Then we'll start with the Pinot Noir."

Becka handed her a glass.

"It's cold," Lee said, surprised. She normally left her wine on the kitchen counter.

Becka looked at her, appalled. "Oh, please tell me you aren't one of those people who drink red wine at room temperature."

Lee looked up. "Guilty as charged. I thought you were supposed to."

Becka sat in the other chair. "That's a horrible misunderstanding of the original meaning of the term. Red wines are meant to be served at the room temperature of a cellar, which should be around fifty-five degrees. The cooler temperature serves to reduce that unpleasant alcohol taste on the palate."

The wonderful aromas of basil and the roasted chicken filled the room. "If I promise to be a good wine student later, can we delay the lecture long enough to eat? I swear I don't think I've ever smelled food as wonderful as this and suddenly I'm starving."

Becka slid into her chair and winked. "I should have known that once you found something you wanted, you would be the impatient, passionate sort."

CHAPTER SEVENTEEN

Lee placed her silverware across her plate. "I have to admit, that was one of the best meals I've had in ages."

"I'm glad you enjoyed it." Becka began gathering the empty plates. Lee stood to help, but Becka stopped her. "I'm just going to put them in water."

"I can help," Lee insisted, but Becka was already rushing off.

Lee stood and moved over to the window to look out. From her previous trips around this area, she knew there was a meadow that separated the house from the nearby forest, but with only the vague illumination of a crescent moon, none of it was visible now. As she stood staring out into the darkness, she again thought about Ollie Waters and wondered if anyone had located him yet.

"Do you think it's too cold to take a walk?" Becka asked as she returned to stand by Lee.

"I guess that depends on what you consider is too cold. I would imagine the mud from this morning's rain would be a bigger issue."

"Oh, right, I forgot about that." Becka turned to the window. "It's too dark for you to see, but the tree line starts a few yards out there. It seemed as though the woods were much farther away when I was a child visiting here."

"They probably were. No one has been keeping the land clear. If someone doesn't move in here and start maintaining the place, the forest will eventually reclaim everything."

"Do you see that as a bad thing?" Becka asked as she again slipped her hand under Lee's arm.

At first, the gesture had made Lee nervous, but she was getting used to it. Apparently, it was just something Becka did. There were no hidden meanings or intentions behind the move.

"Not necessarily, but then I love the environment in its natural state. My only objection would be to lose this lovely old home." She ran a hand along the window casing. "Look how smooth this is. Someone took a lot of patience and care to handrub this."

Becka stared up at her. "I can't imagine you being married and having a child."

"Why not?" Lee glanced down at her before turning her attention back to the darkened window. When Becka didn't answer right away, she continued. "I was really young." She hesitated a moment. "I had an experience in high school that terrified me."

Becka made a small murmuring sound. "Let me guess. It involved another girl."

Lee chuckled. "Yes. I wasn't ready to accept the reality that I was a lesbian." She shook her head. "I wouldn't be ready for several more years."

"So who was this woman who captured your heart?"

Lee ran a thumb over the smooth wood. "It wasn't exactly my heart that was throbbing for her."

Becka giggled. "I can't believe you said that."

"It's true." She gazed at their dim reflection in the window as she told Becka about her lust for Jean Braddock. When she finished, she shook her head. "I've never told anyone about Jean."

"I'm honored you trusted me enough to tell me." Becka squeezed her arm slightly.

Lee tried to ignore the soft pressure of Becka's breast against her arm. There was something strangely comforting about the touch. She stepped back quickly. "It's getting late. I should head home. Are you sure I can't help you with the dishes or something?"

"You can't leave yet." Becka pointed to the second Dutch oven that still sat on the hearth. "I made a peach cobbler for dessert."

"Peach cobbler, you say." Lee rubbed her hands together gleefully. "I suppose it would be impolite of me to leave before dessert."

"It most certainly would be, especially after I worked so hard on it." Becka gave her a small push toward the table. "Have a seat while I grab us a couple of plates."

Lee sat down. "I'm going to be spoiled the next time I'm asked out to dinner. Gladys always makes me wash the dishes."

"Oh, don't worry. I'm only being polite because this is your first time over. From now on, I'll not only expect you to help do the dishes, but I've heard a rumor that you're an excellent woodcutter."

"Who has been telling you those horrible lies?" Lee pretended to be shocked. She had surprised the locals when she bypassed the services of local woodcutters and cut her own fireplace wood. She never told anyone that she'd been so terrified of the chainsaw when she first bought it that it had sat in her garage for two solid weeks before she even removed it from the carton. Even after all these years of using it, she still maintained a healthy respect for the machine's vicious chain.

"I guess you do go through a lot of firewood, since you're using it for heating and cooking."

"I'm getting much better about learning how to plan my

meals ahead of time," Becka called from the kitchen.

Lee squirmed slightly. She shouldn't have drunk the wine, because now she needed a restroom and she had no desire to go running out to some darkened outhouse. She tried to think of something else. It was useless. There was no way she could sit through dessert and then make it all the way home without going. Reluctantly she stood and started toward the kitchen. "Becka, do you have a flashlight I can use?"

"Sure, there's one on the mantle. Do you need something from your truck?"

"No. I have to go to the outhouse." The firelight revealed Becka's face as she peered around the doorway. "I don't have an outhouse, but there's a bathroom down the hall if you don't mind using it." She smiled brightly.

"How can you have an indoor bath if you don't have running water?"

"Did you hear anything I said to you this morning? I told you I just pour a bucket of water in the back and flush it. The septic tank is fine." She stepped back into the room and handed Lee a flashlight. "Straight down the hallway, second door on the right. There's already a bucket of water in there, just bring the empty bucket back with you." Becka's voice broke slightly with laughter. "I normally just wash my hands with some of the water from the bucket."

Lee took the flashlight and hurried off. She was surprised to find a very modern bathroom. It was even nicely lit, thanks to a couple of candles. The lid on the tank had been removed. That and the bucket of water sitting by the vanity were the only indication that something was amiss. After finishing her business, Lee was a little hesitant on how to handle the flushing matter, but with the aid of the flashlight saw that it wasn't an issue at all. There was already water in the tank. She pushed the handle and chuckled as it flushed like every other commode. While she waited for the flapper to fall back into place she poured some of the water from bucket into the sink to wash her hands. A small stack of hand towels sat on the vanity. Lee couldn't help but smile as she carefully refilled the tank with the rest of the water in the bucket. She took the bucket to the kitchen, refilled it at the pump and carried it back to the bathroom.

"Thank you," Becka said when Lee returned.

Even before Lee reached the table, she smelled the spicy aroma of cinnamon and cooked peaches. As she sat down at the table where a large serving of peach cobbler was waiting for her, she noticed that a fresh log had been added to the fire.

"That's quite an operation," she nodded back toward the hallway. "It would certainly discourage me from drinking anything after three in the afternoon."

"I know you must find all this inconvenient and ridiculous."

Lee shook her head. "No. That little trip to the john actually made me think about all the water I waste on a regular basis. We should all try to cut back some." She grinned. "Although I wouldn't advocate cutting back quite as drastically as you have." She tasted the cobbler. "This is delicious."

"Thank you. It's my mom's recipe. I wasn't sure what you'd like, but then I remembered her peach cobbler and how everyone loved it."

A new thought struck Lee. "What do you use for refrigeration?"

"I'm glad you finally asked, because it's something I worked out all on my own. First of all, I try to keep perishable items to a bare minimum. But, to protect those items that are unavoidable, like leftover food, I bought a five-gallon plastic container with a tight lid and a pail handle to which I tied a rope. I put all my perishable items in plastic bowls and then store them inside the five-gallon container, which I lower into the ice-cold water of the old well on the back porch."

Lee nodded. "I'm impressed."

"It'll work for now. Granny told me the well dries up during the summer, but hopefully I will have made up my mind long before then."

"You're really into this pioneer thing, aren't you?"

Becka ate a small bite of dessert before replying. "If I were completely honest I would have to admit that there are times when I miss some of the modern conveniences, but for the most part, I do love the simplicity of my life now. If I decide to stay here, I'll certainly start making the necessary arrangements to have the electricity turned on." She tilted her head. "Heck, I might even go hog-wild and buy a television and have it connected to a dish. Until then, I'm happy with things as they are." She took a deep breath before slowly releasing it. "I can't describe it exactly, but it's sort of like kicking off a pair of tight-fitting shoes after a long day of being on your feet."

Lee nodded thoughtfully. "I sort of know what you mean." They finished their cobbler in silence.

"Would you like some coffee?" Becka asked. "I should have asked earlier."

"No, thanks." Lee placed her fork on her empty plate. "I don't think I'll need anything else to drink."

"You're so spoiled." Becka gathered the dessert plates and headed off with them. "What would you have done if I'd really had an outhouse?" she asked when she returned.

"I don't know. I'm grateful I didn't have to find out."

Becka sat back down at the table.

"How do your parents feel about your moving back here?" Lee asked.

Becka glanced at the fire. "They aren't very happy with me right now. They think I'm making a horrible mistake." She turned back to Lee. "Let's not talk about our pasts tonight. We'll have plenty of time to face that later."

Lee stared into the beautiful blue eyes that seemed to glisten in the firelight. It wasn't until much later that night as she tossed and turned in her bed that she wondered if it could have been tears that made Becka's eyes shimmer so.

CHAPTER EIGHTEEN

The following morning, Lee had come back from another fruitless visit to the blind when her phone rang. When she heard Dewayne's voice, she thought he was calling about Ollie Waters, but his news was much more distressing. He called to let her know Gladys had slipped on some mud and fallen in the driveway.

Lee kicked off the boots she had been wearing and reached for her work clothes. "How badly hurt is she?"

"Nothing is broken, but she twisted her back. The doc says she can go home in a few minutes, but she'll have to be off her feet for a few days, and no lifting for a couple of weeks." His voice was muffled for a moment before he came back on. "She wants to talk to you." He lowered his voice. "Don't let her talk you into anything."

Before Lee could respond, Gladys was on the phone. "Don't listen to him. I'm fine. I can sit at the counter and work," she insisted.

"I don't think so," Lee replied. "You're not going to be any good to the gallery at all if you hurt yourself worse and have to be out for months."

"What difference will it make if I sit there or at home?" Gladys demanded.

"No, ma'am, I'm not buying your bill of goods today. You go home and get into bed like the doctor told you." Lee tried to make her voice as assertive as Dewayne's rumbling tone, but somehow it just didn't sound the same. "Is there anything I can do to help you?"

"No." Gladys gave a sad sigh that made Lee feel bad. She knew how hard it must be for her to be stuck in bed knowing there was work that needed to be done at the gallery. Gladys added, "Dewayne is taking today off and he has already made arrangements for our neighbor, Ms. Harper, to come over to sit with me while he's gone."

"I'll drop by to see you later, but you have him call me if there's anything you need."

After hanging up she flopped back on the bed and struggled not to give in to the frustration that was threatening to spill over. She absolutely had to find someone now. Without Gladys there to help her, she would be working day and night and still never catch up.

As she lay staring at the ceiling, her thoughts turned back to the previous evening and she found herself growing calmer. The evening with Becka had been very pleasant, despite the lack of modern plumbing. She smiled as she recalled how amazingly simple things had been at Becka's place. Maybe going back to a simpler life wouldn't be so horrible.

"As long as I can keep my running water," she said as she hopped up and started dressing for work.

After she had finished dressing, she made her way to her studio. She left the lights off and slowly approached the window where she had seen Ollie the day before. Because it was overcast, the interior of the woods was too dark to see whether anything was there or not. She wanted to wait and see if it got lighter, but she didn't have time.

She went downstairs to the kitchen and grabbed an apple and a chunk of cheese before she pulled her car keys from the hook by the door. When she opened the door to the garage, she stopped sharply. She had forgotten that she had backed her truck in the previous night. The act had been an impulse. She decided it provided her a faster getaway if needed. "Never mind how long it took me to get it backed in," she mumbled.

She was relieved to find no madman with a gun or even a wild marauding animal charge in when the heavy door opened. Still, after she pulled out of the garage, she waited until the door was completely closed before she drove off.

As she traveled down the lane to the highway, she found herself looking for Becka. She was torn between hoping to see her again and hoping she wouldn't. Last night had been pleasant—too pleasant, in fact. It would be very easy to get accustomed to spending time with Becka, but she didn't intend to let that happen. The woman had too many personal problems. She was very happy with her life as it was, she told herself. She kept telling herself that long after she had pulled out onto the highway and headed toward town.

When she reached the gallery, she decided to park in the visitors' lot even though she had beaten the early no-traffic curfew. She wanted access to her vehicle in case Gladys got worse or called her.

The drivers were still hitching up their teams to the various wagons. Lee waved to a few of them as she walked to the gallery.

She managed to wait until ten before she went to her studio and dialed the cell phone number Becka had given her the previous night. When she heard Becka's voice, she couldn't keep from smiling. "I wanted to call and thank you again for the delicious meal."

"I'm glad you enjoyed it."

They had already agreed that Lee would cook for Becka on Friday night. "I'm embarrassed to say that even with modern conveniences my own cooking skills don't come close to your level."

"I'm sure it'll be fine." Lee realized the gallery doorbell had chimed several times. "I'm sorry, but I need to go back into the gallery. Gladys hurt her back this morning, so we're a little shorthanded around here."

"Weren't you already trying to hire someone?"

"Yes, so now I'm really understaffed."

After hanging up, Lee rushed out to the gallery. There were seven or eight people browsing around the floor. She straightened a bin of prints before joining Betty at the counter.

"Have you had any bites on the job?" Betty asked.

Lee knew Betty had already worked more days than she really wanted to. "A few," she replied, "but nothing suitable." She waited until one of the customers was out of earshot. "I really appreciate your staying on as long as you have. I know you hadn't planned on working this long."

Betty shook her head. "I don't mind so much when I'm not busy, but I've already made arrangements for Thanksgiving. I feel terrible about leaving you alone."

"You shouldn't. I'm sure I'll find someone before then." Lee wished she felt as confident as she sounded. Thanksgiving was a month away. Betty was leaving the week before to see her grandchildren, which only gave Lee three weeks to find someone and get them up to speed. She tried not to sigh. It didn't look as though she would have any free time to spend with her parents and Sara. The doorbell chimed again. Lee greeted the young man and woman who entered. Something about them caused her to take a second glance. The man wore a large coat that was much too heavy for the current temperature. The woman had a long loose shawl around her shoulders. Lee turned around until her back was to them. She had intended to alert Betty to watch them, but Betty was already on the move with her feather duster.

When Lee first opened the gallery, she had been dumbfounded

when she discovered that someone had stolen a sixteen-by-twenty framed painting. Since then she had lost one other small etching and averaged losing a couple of unframed prints and a dozen or so postcards every year to shoplifters. Now anytime anyone walked in with extremely loose clothing, a baby stroller or large packages, the staff went on high alert.

Her suspicion of the young couple grew when they split up. For her to follow one she would have to leave the register. She moved as far away from it as she dared and cursed the freestanding walls that they erected during the holidays. They were both a blessing and a nuisance. The extra space they provided allowed her to show stock, but they also blocked her view.

The door opened again. Despite her best intentions, Lee's attention was momentarily diverted as a dozen or more people poured in. They all wore teal T-shirts that indicated they were members of the Poplar Bluff, Missouri, Garden Club. She looked around, hunting for the young couple. She couldn't see either of them. The door opened again and this time she smiled. It was Becka. Lee grabbed her. "Stand at the register. I'll explain later." With Becka covering the front, Lee took off to find the young couple. She quickly spotted Betty, who had the woman covered. Lee continued her search for the man. When she finally spotted him, he was headed toward the door. She moved toward him and noticed that his left arm was rigid at his side. No one walked like that. He moved at a steady pace but would still reach the door before she could. Once he was outside, he could easily outrun her. "Sir," she called.

He didn't acknowledge.

"You in the long coat, please stop." She increased her pace in an attempt to close the distance between them. Other customers were beginning to stare.

The man started moving faster. A few members of the garden club were still standing near the door, but she couldn't ask them to help. She'd rather lose the painting than have a customer or employee hurt.

Suddenly all of the frustration of the past few days seemed

to shoot to her feet and she sped after him. Everything seemed to shift into slow motion as she saw him reach the door. She watched his hand glide through the air and close around the doorknob. The act had slowed him down enough for her to tighten the gap between them. Then the door was open and the nearly empty sidewalk lay before him. He was going to get away, and she knew by the time she returned the woman would be gone as well. Not this time, she told herself as she reached deep inside and summoned a reservoir of strength she didn't know existed. She used it to launch herself at him. It felt as though she floated through the air forever before gravity won over and stopped her upward projection. It would only be a moment before she hit the floor. She made one last desperate grab at his arm, but he looked back over his shoulder in time to see her and twisted away. He stepped out the door. He was going to get away and all she would have to show for her trouble was the nasty fall she was about to take. Then her hand connected not with the floor but the tail of his flapping coat. She managed to wrap her hand into the material more securely as she threw herself sideways. The sudden shift was enough to send him tumbling. She heard the wooden frame crack as it crashed to the sidewalk. Her body slammed against the floor. Thankfully, most of her body was still inside the doorway and the carpet absorbed a lot of the impact. The man was down and struggling to stand. On hands and knees, she scrambled after him. She was so intent on grabbing him that she was caught completely by surprise when a heavy boot suddenly appeared in her peripheral vision. She threw her right arm out to protect herself. The toe of the boot caught her wrist. She thought she heard a snap just before the blinding pain radiated up her arm. The pain knocked the last of the fight out of her. There was another brief flurry of activity as the guy ran off. At that point, Lee no longer cared. They could have been looting the entire shop and she would have been helpless to stop them. There was a moment when everything was again frozen, and then people surrounded her. She tried to move her wrist and was rewarded with pain so intense she nearly fainted. Then

Becka was by her side.

"They got away," Lee whispered as Becka leaned over her.

"Let the law worry about them," Becka said. "How badly is your wrist hurt?"

"It's okay." She didn't want to admit that she thought the wrist was broken.

"Can you stand if we help you?" Becka asked. Several members of the garden club were trying to help. They tried but it was too awkward.

"I think I'd better do it alone," Lee replied through gritted teeth. She cradled her injured wrist against her breast and slowly made her way to her feet.

One of the women from the club stepped forward with the painting. "I'm afraid the frame is cracked, but the painting doesn't look damaged," she replied as she handed it to Becka.

Lee saw that the painting was one of Jake Drummond's. Other than the frame, it didn't appear to be damaged. She turned when she heard running footsteps and saw William Rogers, the city marshal, and one of his deputies hurrying down the sidewalk. Within minutes, half the town would be arriving either to check on her or to be on the front line of the latest gossip. She stepped back inside and despite the pain nearly smiled when she found Betty steadfastly guarding the cash register. Betty rushed toward her.

"She got away from me," Betty said, nearly in tears. "Are you okay?"

"I'm fine. Please don't blame yourself. It's all my fault. I don't know what possessed me to tackle him."

"He could have hurt you," Becka said so sharply that Lee glanced up at her. She was surprised to see how pale she was.

"You're the one who looks ready to keel over," Lee said. "Maybe you should sit down."

The marshal stepped inside. "What's going on?" he demanded.

All of the customers started speaking at once. He finally held up a hand and pulled out his radio.

Lee listened as he called the deputy down by the visitor parking and told him to hold any cars attempting to leave. "I'll need someplace where we can interview all these folks," he said as he clicked the radio back onto his belt.

"You can use the studio if you like," Lee offered.

The marshal nodded to his deputy and pointed toward the studio. "Take 'em back there and get their statements. Make sure you get a number where we can reach them if need be." He moved closer to Lee. "Are you all right?" he asked when he saw her hand.

She looked at it and saw that it was already starting to swell. It was obvious that she was going to have to go to the hospital to have it checked, but first she wanted to get things settled with him. A large crowd was starting to gather at the door. She turned to Betty. "Why don't you go ahead and start closing up? I probably won't be coming back today, and I'd rather you not be here alone." Now that everything was over, she realized how stupid it had been of her to go after the guy. He could have had a gun. If that boot had caught her alongside the head rather than the wrist she could have been in much worse shape now.

Betty nodded. She grabbed Becka and together they began to usher the gawkers gently away from the door. While they were closing, Lee quickly gave William Rogers a detailed report of what had occurred. She also gave him a detailed description of the two shoplifters.

After she finished he pointed to her wrist. "You'd better get on over to the emergency room and have that looked after." He slipped the pad he had used to take notes on into his pocket. "I'll call you if we get anything on these two."

Becka, off to one side, came over as soon as the marshal put away his pad. "Come on. I'll drive you over to the hospital."

"Go on down and get your car," the marshal said. "If anyone says anything to you about it just tell them I said you could. There's no need for her to walk all the way over to the parking lot."

Becka thanked him and rushed off.

"Betty, you may as well go on home," Lee said. "I'll give you a call later on."

"Are you sure you want to close?" Betty asked. "I could call a couple of ladies from my sewing club to come over and sit with me."

"No. That's fine. One day won't kill me."

Betty gathered her things. "You call if you need anything," she said before leaving.

Lee and the marshal were left in the gallery. "I could have walked to the parking lot," she protested.

"Yeah, and you could have passed out in the middle of the street." He peered at her over his wire-rimmed glasses and grinned. "That's not good for business, you know."

"Do you think you'll catch them?"

He shrugged. "Probably not. I haven't heard from the parking area, so no one has tried to leave yet. They could have parked anywhere along any of the side roads and walked over. If you didn't recognize them, I'm guessing they aren't from around here. It was probably just a couple of kids looking for a thrill." He rubbed his chin. "I'll put a notice out over the radio, but without knowing what they're driving, the chance of anyone recognizing them is pretty slim. It never ceases to amaze me what people will try to get away with." He leaned against the counter and crossed his arms. "Last week I got a call from the feed store. Someone had broken in the back door during the night and stolen six bags of deer corn."

Lee tried to ignore the throbbing in her wrist. "I guess it's getting close to deer season."

"Crossbow and muzzleloaders have already started," he replied. "Modern gun will kick off in a few more days. Do you hunt?"

"The only shots I take are with a camera," she said.

Before he could respond, Becka returned.

"Thanks for coming over, Will," Lee said as she fumbled to lock the gallery door with her left hand.

The marshal took the keys from her and locked the door.

Then he saw them out to the car. He nodded as he closed the car door for her. "You keep your eyes open and let me know if you see those two around again." As he stepped away, he turned back to her. "But if you see them again, use your cell phone to call me rather than trying to tackle the guy, okay?"

CHAPTER NINETEEN

When they reached the hospital, Lee refused to let Becka drive her up to the emergency room entrance. Instead, they parked in the back lot and walked in.

Lucy Ralston, Clarissa Jenkins' sister, met them at the door with a wheelchair. "Marshal Rogers called and said you were on your way over." She motioned to the chair. "Have a seat. You're in luck, because Dr. Lyman is on duty today and she has already ordered x-rays for you."

Dr. Lyman had been Lee's personal physician ever since Lee first moved to Christmas.

"Such service," Becka said as Lee sat down. "I'll wait for you somewhere around here." She patted Lee's shoulder.

"There's a waiting area just around that corner," Lucy said as she started wheeling the chair down the hall.

Dr. Lyman was waiting for them at the door to an examining

room. "If you're going to play football, I suggest you suit up first," she admonished as she carefully probed Lee's wrist. At the age of sixty-four, Dr. Lyman was practically a legend in the area. Until about fifteen years ago when the hospital had finally been built, she had been the only doctor in the area, and as such she had delivered a good number of the local population. She would be the first to tell anyone who was interested that her biggest sin was vanity. She had a standing weekly appointment with a local beautician and went to Hot Springs once a month for a leisurely spa weekend. Her clothes were tailor-made, and she never stepped out of the house without her makeup being perfect. Her soft-spoken voice and mannerisms made her popular with old and young alike. "How is Sara?"

"Good," Lee replied. "She's bored with school, but then that's really nothing new for her." She gritted her teeth when Dr. Lyman tried to bend the injured wrist. "Is it broken?" If it was, she didn't want to think about how long it would be before she could paint again.

Dr. Lyman continued her examination. "Let's wait until we see what the x-rays show. Do you need something for the pain?"

"No. I'd rather not."

The doctor clucked her tongue. "Everyone's so brave. Personally, I yell for a pill at the first inkling of pain." She nodded to Lucy. "Take her to room four when you're finished in Radiology." She placed a hand on Lee's shoulder. "I'll be in to see you in a little while. Don't you worry. We'll get you fixed up as good as new."

A few minutes later, Lee tried not to be anxious as the technician carefully manipulated her hand and wrist to take the necessary x-rays. As soon as he was finished, Lucy arrived, wheeled her to an examining room and placed a cold pack on the wrist.

"Lie down and rest," Lucy instructed as she finished applying the cold pack. "Don't let that pack stay on more than twenty minutes." She pushed the wheelchair toward the door. "I'll try to come by and check on you, but we're shorthanded today, so if I'm delayed, remove the cold pack after twenty minutes."

Lee knew exactly what Lucy meant about being shorthanded but didn't bother to comment. The pain was getting worse and she was beginning to regret her decision to decline the pain medication. After Lucy left, Lee tried to find a comfortable place to rest her injured wrist but nothing seemed to help.

She would have to make some sort of arrangements for the gallery. She would probably be able to go back to work tomorrow, but she doubted she'd be able to lift anything. It wasn't fair to expect Betty to do it all. To date, there had only been two applications for the job. Her ad in the weekly paper would come out tomorrow. Hopefully it would generate some response. It seemed like forever before Dr. Lyman finally came into the room.

"Sorry to keep you waiting. Master Leopold Weingarten finally decided to make his appearance—all eight pounds and six ounces of him. We've been awaiting his arrival for the past sixteen hours." Dr. Lyman popped two x-rays onto the reader and peered at them.

"Lisa Weingarten?" Lee asked, hurting too much to form a complete sentence to inquire about her. Lisa's baby made her think about Joan Depew. "How's Jefferson Depew doing?"

Dr. Lyman shook her head. "He's being treated by Dr. Akers, so all I know is secondhand information. It sounds as though that poor boy is in for a long haul. From the cafeteria gossip I've heard, he's being transferred to Little Rock to have the bullet removed." She took down the x-rays she had been studying and put up two more. "Well, little lady," she began, "the good news is that you don't have any broken bones." She turned to Lee. "The bad news is that you have a nasty sprain. If I thought you would listen to me, I'd send you home with a sling and tell you to take it easy and not to be lifting anything, but I know you better than that." She gave Lee a knowing look. The previous winter Lee had gone in to see Dr. Lyman for a cold that she hadn't been able to shake. The doctor told her to go home and stay in bed for a few days until she felt better. Lee didn't listen and instead went back to work. The cold developed into bronchitis. It got so serious that she had been on the verge of having to be hospitalized.

"I'll be good," Lee promised, even though she had no idea how she could possibly get through a single day without using her arm. "How long before I can start painting again?"

"If there are no further complications, I'd say three maybe four weeks." She shook her finger. "It could be a lot longer if you don't give your wrist time to heal properly. You don't want to end up damaging a ligament."

"I'll be careful." Lee wouldn't do anything that might prevent her from painting.

Dr. Lyman smiled brightly as she scribbled. "I know you will, because I'm going to call Lucy back in here, and she's going to take you over to have a nice cast put on." Dr. Lyman handed her a prescription. "These will help with the pain. Take a whole one with a glass of milk or some food when you get home. Since you don't even take aspirin, be careful. These might be a little stronger than you like." She peered over her glasses. "Is there someone who can drive you home?"

Lee knew Lucy had probably already told Dr. Lyman about her coming in with Becka. She was sure that by now speculation was running high about the nature of their relationship. She merely nodded.

"The medication will help you sleep through the night," Dr. Lyman said. "If you don't like the fuzzy feeling it causes, then you can cut it in half after that. I know how stubborn you are so it's up to you whether you get it filled or not. But I recommend you do, and the pharmacy on the first floor can fill it for you." She started toward the door. "So you be thinking about what color cast you want. They have so many pretty colors now. As an artist I'm sure you'll appreciate that." She picked up Lee's chart. "I want to see you in my office in two weeks. Call and make an appointment tomorrow." She was out the door before Lee could protest.

It was over an hour later before Lee finished with the cast and took care of the bill. As she came out of the billing office, she noticed the pharmacy down the hallway. She preferred not to take any medication, but all the movement during the x-rays and application of the cast had caused her wrist to start throbbing again. In order to be able to function she needed something to alleviate the pain. She stopped and had the prescription filled and then went back over to the waiting room.

Becka's eyes widened when she saw the cast on Lee's arm.

"It's not broken," Lee said. "Dr. Lyman is punishing me because I didn't mind her the last time I was in to see her."

"How long does that have to stay on?"

Lee glanced at the black cast. She had chosen the darkest color, since the brighter colors would have been more obvious when she traveled to the blind. She was certain she could set the camera up with one hand. "I don't know. I have to see her in two weeks. Hopefully she'll take it off then."

"Are you finished here?"

Lee nodded.

"Then I'll drive you home."

"No. Just drop me off at my truck. I can drive—" She stopped short. Her truck had a standard transmission. She couldn't shift with her injured wrist and she certainly couldn't reach across and shift with her left hand. "Damn," she muttered.

"What's wrong?"

"My truck isn't an automatic. I won't be able to shift gears."

Becka tilted her head. "I'll drive you home today. Then tomorrow or whenever you're ready to go back into town I'll come over and pick you up. You can use my car until you're able to drive, and I'll use your truck."

"Can you drive a stick?"

"Please, I'm a country girl. I was driving a standard before my legs were even long enough to reach the pedals."

"If you couldn't reach the clutch how could you shift?" Lee asked as they started toward the exit.

"My daddy duct-taped blocks of wood to the pedals."

Lee peered at her to see if she was joking, but she seemed serious. "Are you sure you don't mind?" Her wrist throbbed and nothing she tried offered any relief.

"I wouldn't have made the offer if I hadn't meant it."

Lee spotted a water dispenser by the door. "Thanks. I appreciate the help." She reached into her pocket for the bottle of pain relievers. Dr. Lyman had told her to take the pill with milk, but surely it wouldn't hurt to take it with water just this once. "I was going to wait until I got home to take this, but since you're driving I think I'll take it now." She fumbled with the childproof cap.

"Here, let me help." Becka took the bottle and removed one of the small blue pills. She handed the pills to Lee and then got her a cup of water.

"Thanks." Lee swallowed the pill and tossed the cup. "My truck isn't nearly as nice as your fancy car." Her wrist throbbed in unison with her heartbeat. She wondered how long it would take the medication to start working. Hopefully, not long.

"Yeah, well, wait until we get a big rain and that so called fancy car bogs down in the mud on that lane leading up to your place." Becka moved to Lee's left side and slipped her hand around Lee's arm. "You'll be calling me up to bring your truck over to pull you out."

As they walked out of the hospital arm-in-arm, Lee experienced a slight sense of exhilaration. Maybe the pill was already starting to work. She had never been an overly touchy-feely sort. She didn't hug everyone she met the way some women tended to do, but having Becka holding her arm felt right. Almost as if she had read her thoughts, Becka moved a little closer to her. As they walked across the parking lot, Lee noticed that her wrist didn't seem to be hurting so badly anymore.

CHAPTER TWENTY

Becka held the car door for Lee. "Let me help you with the seat belt."

As Becka leaned across her, Lee could smell the slight perfumed scent of her hair. She closed her eyes and inhaled. What would Becka's bare skin smell like? Shocked by the thought, she shook her head sharply.

"Are you all right?" Becka pulled back and peered at her.

"Um...yes...I'm fine."

"How strong are those pills?"

"I guess I'm just tired." She tried to remember when she had last eaten, but she was finding it difficult to think of anything other than how close Becka was standing to her.

Becka's face softened. "Of course you are. Let's get you home and tucked into bed."

A jolt hit Lee's core when she experienced a vision of Becka in her bed. She shook her head again.

Becka hurriedly closed the car door and ran to the other side.

"Hang on. We'll be there in a few minutes." She cranked the car and slipped it into gear before squeezing Lee's left hand. "Try to stay awake until we get there. I don't think I could carry you in."

Lee sat up and tried to look alert. "I'm fine."

Becka was silent as she maneuvered the car out of the parking lot and through the edge of town to the main highway.

Lee tried to focus on the scenery that she had seen a thousand times, but the cotton balls in her head kept multiplying. The steady hum of the tires on the pavement became a counterpoint melody to her nodding.

"Are you and Melinda Thayer involved?"

Lee snapped awake. She hadn't realized she had been dozing. "No." The word sounded as though her head was in a barrel. She blinked her eyes and willed them to stay open. "Melinda is too aggressive." She tried to turn her head to look at Becka. The wobbly movement reminded her of the action of having a super-zoom lens mounted on a too small tripod. She tried to hold onto the armrest on the door so she wouldn't tip over, but it hurt too much.

"Does that mean you don't like overly aggressive women?" Becka glanced at her.

"The right woman can be aggressive."

"Is there a woman in your life now who could be that aggressive?"

Lee nodded heavily.

"Who?"

The voice was far away, but Lee ignored it. The sound of the tires on the pavement was so much nicer to hum along with. She tried to concentrate. She wasn't humming. Someone else was.

"Who is the woman?" Becka asked.

Suddenly, a hand shook her good arm.

"Lee, stay awake and talk to me."

She opened her eyes. The sound of the tires had stopped. She heard someone talking and turned to gaze at the woman beside her. There was something familiar about her, but Lee couldn't clear the fog in her head enough to see the woman clearly. The woman's mouth was moving. Lee focused all her attention on the mouth. It was a nice mouth, she decided as she reached out and touched it with her fingertips. It was soft and warm. She tried to lean over to kiss it, but something kept tugging her back. Her hand dropped to the seat. It was too heavy to hold up any longer.

She leaned her head back.

"Lee. Lee, wake up."

Lee struggled to open her eyes, but there just wasn't enough energy in the world to do so. Instead, she focused on opening one eye. "You're very beautiful," she whispered to the face that floated before her. "I'd like to kiss you, but they won't let me."

"Who won't let you?" the face asked.

Lee plucked at the restraint holding her back. She knew the name of the object but couldn't call it to mind. Finally, she gave up and tried to shrug, but like the rest of her body, her shoulders had turned to gelatin. Something was wiggling in her pocket. It tickled and she began to laugh.

"I need your keys. You stay in the car until I get the door open."

Lee gave a long sigh and closed her eyes. This was a comfortable place to sleep. She didn't know if she had spoken or merely thought the words, but it didn't matter because they were true. She let herself freefall back into the cottony world of oblivion. The peace didn't last long, though.

"Can you walk?"

Lee protested as someone tugged at her waist. She seemed to be sitting sideways in the seat.

"Wake up. You never told me you lived in a log house. Tell me about it. Did you build it yourself? Lee wake up and talk to me."

She ignored the voice and allowed herself to drift. He head nestled onto a soft shoulder.

"Lee, talk to me. Come on woman. I'm not just talking to hear my jaws rattle. You have to help me. I can't carry you."

There was a loud grunting noise as arms wrapped around her

waist. Lee felt herself being eased from the nice warm car. The cold air revived her slightly. "Where am I?"

"Home," Becka wheezed. "Can you please walk?"

Irritated that her peaceful slumber had been disturbed, Lee grumbled, "Yeah, I can walk. It's you who keeps stumbling all over me."

"You're a real comedian, aren't you?"

The voice seemed familiar. Lee took a deep breath and blinked her eyes hard until she could focus on the face. "You're Becka."

"Yes, and you're heavy."

"It's not nice to tell a lady she's heavy," Lee said and stumbled. They landed in a heap against the car. Her eyes started to close again, but suddenly someone was slapping her face. "Hey, hey," she said as she attempted to get away from the annoying hand. "That's not nice."

"Lee Dresher, you need to wake up and do it now!"

The authority in the voice made Lee pull herself upright. "I'm awake, Mom."

"Well, stay that way until I get you into the house. Now come on and walk."

Lee did as she was told, but she looked around, confused. Had her mother been there a moment ago, and if so where was she now? It took her a moment to realize that they were walking up the front steps to her house. Realization that her bed was only a few feet away made her move faster.

"That's it," the voice prompted.

Lee kept blinking and putting one foot in front of the other until she saw an oasis drawing closer—her sofa. She had slept on it many times. She tried heading toward it, but the stranger was determined to take her elsewhere. Lee looked longingly at the sofa and made up her mind. That was where she was going. She shook off the helping hand and made it to the end of the sofa before she collapsed, more or less on it. The last thing she remembered was hearing someone mumbling about something being heavier than a bag of rocks.

CHAPTER TWENTY-ONE

Lee heard the crackling of twigs breaking, as when someone stepped on them. She squeezed herself into as small a shape as possible and froze, just as she had seen the animals she photographed do whenever she was careless in approaching them.

The sound seemed to be drawing nearer. She tensed every muscle in her body in a desperate attempt to maintain her position, but her courage failed her. She began to run. Her feet tangled in the underbrush and pitched her forward. The only pain she felt was her throbbing wrist. She tried to stand, but something kept dragging her down. The sound of footsteps grew nearer. Even without seeing the face, she knew it was Ollie Waters. As she waited for the impact of the bullet to hit her, a series of thoughts flashed through her mind. She wouldn't be around to see Sara graduate. She wouldn't be there for her wedding day or for the birth of her children. Sara was young and strong and would be able to go on with her life, but the death of their only daughter would devastate her parents. The footsteps had grown so close she could feel their vibration seeping through the ground beneath her. Suddenly, she regretted not hugging Sara and her parents more or telling them she loved them. She tried to scream that she was too young to die, but no sound emerged. There were so many things left on her to-do list—visit the Grand Canyon, climb to the top of the Eiffel Tower. She'd never even seen the Alamo. At the top of her list of regrets was the knowledge that she would never know the soul-binding love that her parents shared.

In the distance, she heard Becka calling her and a spark of hope flared. Maybe Ollie would be frightened off by Becka's approach. At the same instant, a far more horrifying thought bloomed. He might shoot Becka also. That she wouldn't allow. A primeval rage roared from her core as she launched herself upright.

"It's okay."

"Run. He has a gun." Gentle hands pushed her back onto the sofa.

"Lee, it's me, Becka. You're having a bad dream. It's the middle of the afternoon and you're safe in your living room. No one is going to hurt you."

Lee struggled to open her eyes. The room seemed to be slightly off-kilter and it took a moment for Becka's face to come into focus. She tried to speak, but her tongue refused to cooperate.

"Here, try some of these ice chips." Becka spooned a few through Lee's parched lips. "You scared me so badly, I called Dr. Lyman. She said you'll be fine, but that you're not to take any more of the pain pills without eating first."

Lee watched Becka's lips move. Why had she never noticed how full and sensuous they were before? She tried to tell Becka how beautiful she was. From the look on Becka's face, she knew she hadn't understood. Lee tried again. Becka leaned forward as if to hear better and all Lee had to do was turn her head slightly to kiss her. The lips were even softer and fuller than she had imagined they would be and for one long moment, she savored them. A rush of desire seized her when she felt Becka's lips respond, but the ecstasy was short-lived when Becka pulled away suddenly. Lee tried to protest, but Becka placed a hand against her cheek.

She gazed into Lee's eyes and said, "I want this too, but not now, not this way. You don't know what you're doing now. I don't want you to do anything you'll regret later." She kissed Lee's forehead. "Dr. Lyman said you should sleep. Close your eyes and rest. I'll be right here beside you."

Lee wanted to kiss Becka again and tried to reach out for her, but she could feel herself slipping back into the cottony haze. She tried to fight it by reaching for Becka again, but her muscles would no longer obey.

"I sure hope you're still this determined when you do wake up," Becka said as she moved back slightly. "I promise I won't—"

Sleep overtook Lee before she could hear the rest.

Lee slowly surfaced into consciousness. Her mouth felt as though someone had packed it with gauze, and she couldn't remember the last time she had been so thirsty. Even without opening her eyes, she recognized that she was lying on her sofa, but she couldn't remember why. She tried to move and a sharp stab of pain stung her wrist. Slowly everything fell into place— even the dream and kissing Becka. Her eyes flew open. Becka was asleep in the recliner across from her. A low-burning blaze in the fireplace gave off enough light for her to read the clock on the mantle. It was a little after midnight.

She studied Becka's face as she struggled to remember what had really occurred and what had been a dream. The nightmare about Ollie Waters had obviously been just that. What about the kiss? Had she kissed Becka? She gazed at Becka's lips and suddenly knew without a doubt that it had not been a dream. She closed her eyes in mortification. How could she have done such a thing? What must Becka think of her?

"I sure hope you're still this determined when you do wake up."

She opened her eyes again. Becka had said that. Or had she? Lee shook her head. No. Becka had definitely said that.

"How are you feeling?"

Lee flinched. She hadn't noticed that Becka had opened her eyes. "Better," she croaked.

Becka got out of the chair. "You seem alert enough now for some water. I'll get you some."

Lee nodded and listened to the sound of Becka's footfalls padding across the hardwood floor and then the tile in the kitchen. It was a strange yet nice sound. Except for Sara, it was rare that anyone ever came over. Why hadn't she invited Dewayne and Gladys out more? Or Alan and Clint? She remembered the dream she'd had and the list of regrets she'd felt. She didn't know where the Alamo aspect had come from, but she had always dreamed of going to Paris. Why hadn't she gone already? Money wasn't the issue. It was time to stop procrastinating. She and Sara should go in the summer. She experienced a minor bout of nerves when she heard Becka returning.

"Here you go." Becka seemed slightly hesitant when she approached the sofa. Rather than sitting on the side as she had before, she knelt down and helped Lee with the glass.

Lee sat up slightly and took a sip of the water. It tasted so good she ended up drinking the whole glass before handing it back.

"Do you want some more?" Becka asked.

"No. I'm fine."

Becka took the glass.

Lee studied the woman before her as Becka carefully placed the empty glass on a coaster on the heavy slab coffee table. She was searching for any sign that would give her a clue as to how Becka felt about what had happened between them.

Lying on the sofa suddenly seemed too intimate of a position. Lee tried to sit up. The room spun crazily around her.

Becka grabbed her. "Whoa. Take it easy."

Lee took a deep breath as she tried to move her joints. "I feel like my body is made of rubber."

"That pill knocked you for a loop." Becka sat on the sofa beside her. "I almost didn't get you inside. I was afraid I'd hurt your wrist, so I didn't even attempt to remove your jacket." She stopped for a moment. "I'm not sure how much you remember." There was a slight pause. "You were sleeping so hard and for such a long time that I got concerned and called Dr. Lyman. She told me that you're a…and these are her words, not mine… 'medication wuss.'"

"Remind me to thank her," Lee said as she continued to try to shake off the clinging spider webs of sleep.

An awkward silence followed. Within seconds, it began to rebound around the room like a Chinese gong. Lee tried to ignore it and think. Every time she had jumped into a situation, especially those dealing with personal relationships, it had proven disastrous. If nothing else, her impulsive marriage to Brandon should have taught her to approach anything dealing with the heart with caution. She liked Becka. Yet what did she really know about her? What were those issues that Granny Depew had hinted at? How objective was the older woman?

In truth, she didn't actually know the Depew family very well. Until the incident with Jefferson, her acquaintance with them had been limited to saying hello when they met on the street. She probably knew Jefferson the best, but now that she thought about it, most of that was through hearing Dewayne and Gladys talk about him. Perhaps Becka already had a lover. Had that been what Granny Depew hinted at? She tried to remember the exact conversation but couldn't. Something about Becka being in a bad place and needing a friend to talk with. That might explain her desire to hide away like a hermit. She recalled the first time she had seen Becka in the clearing. How she had sat down on the rock and cried as if her heart were broken. Had she been crying for a lost love? She flinched slightly when Becka placed a hand on her good arm.

"I didn't mean to startle you," Becka said as she eased closer to Lee. "I called you twice, but you were a million miles away."

Lee blinked. The flickering firelight illuminated Becka's face. Becka's hand still rested comfortably on her arm. It felt nice—too nice, in fact. She knew she should probably stop this before it went too far. She found herself staring at Becka's mouth again. What if these feelings were nothing more than lust? It had been a long while since she'd made love to anyone. "I'm no good at relationships," she said.

"I'm not in a position to even offer one," Becka replied. Neither of them moved.

"Is there someone waiting for you somewhere?"

"No. I'm not with anyone, but there are things going on with me that prevent me from—"

Lee leaned over and kissed her softly. Sitting on the sofa made it awkward.

"Wait," Becka said as she moved over to kneel between Lee's legs. "I've waited too long for this to mess it up now," she whispered, slipping both arms around Lee's neck. "Now, kiss me like you mean it."

For once, Lee did her best to follow orders. The kiss deepened as Becka pressed her body farther between Lee's legs.

The heat from Becka's body competed with the heat that was rapidly building in Lee. She placed her good hand on Becka's back as she pushed herself closer to Becka's straining body. Her breath caught as curious fingers made their way inside her collar and teased her neck and throat.

Their kisses grew more urgent. Lee's left hand slipped around and caressed the side of Becka's breast before growing bolder. She caught a hardened nipple between her thumb and finger and gently teased it. She was already dreaming of how it would feel in her mouth.

Becka's arms clasped Lee's waist, pulling her still closer.

Lee couldn't stop the rocking motion her hips were starting to make. She reached to open the buttons on Becka's blouse.

A loud boom broke not only the moment, but the east window as well. The window was only a few feet from where they sat. Lee threw herself to the floor, and tried to ignore the pain that stabbed her wrist as she dragged Becka down with her. She had lived in the country long enough to recognize the sound of a high-powered rifle when she heard one, and this time she was terrifyingly positive that she wasn't dreaming.

CHAPTER TWENTY-TWO

Lee ignored the pain in her wrist as she swept an arm out and grasped the opposite side of the heavy slab coffee table. By using both hands, she managed to turn it over onto its side. She pulled it closer so that they were cocooned in a V-shaped foxhole fashioned from the sofa and table. She was eternally grateful that she had purchased all of her wooden furniture from a local artisan who built his creations from dense chunks of hardwoods. She hoped the thick logs of the walls and the table would be enough of an obstruction to stop a bullet.

Becka started wiggling away, but Lee grabbed her. "Where are you going?" she hissed.

"My purse is by the chair."

Lee stared at her in amazement. "Now is not the time to worry about your purse!"

"My cell phone is in it."

Lee cringed. She hadn't even thought about calling for help. "Mine's in my jacket pocket." She tried to get it, but her arm was blocked by the weight of the table pressing against it. "I can't reach it. Can you? It's on the right-hand side."

Becka leaned across her and patted around until she finally found it. She reached into the jacket and removed it, then handed it to Lee.

It only took Lee a moment to hit the speed dial button to the county sheriff's office. Marge Littleton, the night dispatcher, picked up almost immediately.

"Marge, this is Lee Dresher. Someone just shot out my front window."

"At the gallery?"

"No. I'm at home."

"You live in that log house on the old Crane homestead, don't you?"

"Yes. Can you get someone out here?" Another loud boom ripped the night air and the sound of shattering glass from the general direction of the kitchen followed.

"Marge, I have to hang up. I think the shooter is Ollie Waters. He just shot out another window. Please get someone out here now!"

"Sit tight. There's a car on the way." There was a slight hesitation. "Lee, it can't be Ollie Waters. He's in intensive care. He stumbled into Kelsey's diner out on the highway this afternoon. Someone had shot him."

Lee froze. It had been scary enough to think of Ollie being out there shooting at her, but somehow not knowing who it was frightened her more. She shook off the ridiculous reasoning.

Becka leaned closer. "Tell her to warn whoever's coming to be careful. The shooter is using a deer rifle. He could easily kill them before they ever reach the house."

Lee relayed the message.

"I'll let them know. You sit tight. Whatever you do, don't go outside. We don't want the responding officer to mistake you for the shooter."

152

Lee disconnected and grabbed Becka's arm. "Come on. We can't stay here. There's too many ways for him to get into the house." She struggled to her knees and tried to keep as much weight off her injured wrist as possible. "Stay low and follow me." For the first time in her life, Lee regretted not having a gun in the house to use for defense. Even as she wished for it, she knew she still would never own a weapon. I'd probably shoot myself, she reasoned as she made her way toward the stairs. Her ultimate goal was to reach her studio.

There was a stretch of about six feet where they would have to pass through the light from the fireplace. If anyone was on the ridge out front, she and Becka would be sitting ducks. She hoped there was only one shooter and that he was still out back.

"We're going upstairs," she whispered to Becka. "Once you take off don't stop no matter what happens. When you reach the top of the stairs, turn right and go all the way to the end of the hall. That's my studio. There's a balcony, so if whoever is out there manages to get inside, we'll still be able to get out of the house."

Becka nodded.

Lee squeezed her hand. "You ready?"

"Yes."

Lee took a deep breath. "Go."

Becka sprinted away like a deer. She had reached the bottom of the stairs before Lee had even left the floor. When Lee took off, she expected to feel a bullet ripping through her at any moment. Her feet hit the bottom step, and she took the stairs two at a time. She could hear Becka ahead of her and quickly closed the gap between them. They made it to the studio with no further incidents. Lee flipped the inadequate thumb lock on the doorknob. It wouldn't deter a four-year-old, but at least no one would surprise them. She reached down to the outlet beside the door and unplugged the night-light. She kept the light there because the one drawback to the tinted windows was that they also made the room much darker at night. Once the small light was extinguished, the room was pitch black. Maybe the medication was still clouding her judgment, or it could have been because she was so frightened, but for whatever reason it took Lee a moment to orient herself.

"Give me your hand," she whispered. She took Becka's hand and started moving toward the corner. She almost fell when her toe caught the edge of one of the easel's platform legs. Becka helped her maintain her balance. Lee carefully extended her hand until it encountered a metal file cabinet that sat against the interior wall. It wasn't much protection, but it was the best she could do. "Sit here." She squatted down beside Becka. "I'm going to see if I can spot anything moving around out there."

Becka grabbed her arm. "No."

"It's all right. As long as there's no light on in here, they can't see me."

"I think you should stay away from the windows. Whoever is shooting may just be taking potshots at the windows. He could hit you by accident."

Lee thought about Jefferson and decided to heed the advice. She stayed beside Becka. Now that she was in the studio, she was beginning to wonder if she had made the right decision. They could jump from the balcony if need be, but it was at least a nine-foot drop, maybe even a little more. She tried to plot the escape. How long would it take them to reach the balcony and get over the rail? She wondered if it would be better to wait on the balcony. It was wide enough that they could sit next to the wall without being visible below.

She mentally reviewed the objects in the room, looking for something that she could use as a weapon. The deadliest thing she could recall was a half-inch blade that she used to open boxes.

Her large wooden easel stood a few steps away, but it was much too heavy for her to pick up and swing. There were a few frames hanging on a peg on the far wall. Some were heavy enough to hurt if you were hit with one, but they certainly wouldn't be effective against a rifle.

"What's that noise?" Becka grabbed Lee's arm in a grip so tight her arm began to tingle.

The only thing Lee could hear was her own heart pounding. She was on the verge of dragging them out to the balcony when she heard the sound, too. It was a siren screaming down the road. Relieved that help had arrived she sat down on the floor just as Becka jumped up. Becka had only taken a couple of steps when the large picture window on the north wall exploded. Millions of shards of safety glass rained over the room.

Lee watched in horror as Becka's arms flew into the air. It seemed to take an eternity for Lee to get up. Even as she was standing, she saw Becka falling.

CHAPTER TWENTY-THREE

Lee screamed as she dropped and started crawling on her stomach toward Becka. Even with the missing window, the room was so dark it was hard to distinguish anything. The first thing Lee grabbed was Becka's leg. She followed it up, terrified of what she would find.

"It's okay," Becka whispered. "I'm all right."

Lee's heart nearly flew out of her chest when a hand closed over her arm.

"Lee, stop screaming. I'm all right. I tripped over something. I'm not hit."

Lee hadn't realized she was still screaming until Becka put an arm around her and started rocking slightly. She also hadn't realized how hard she was crying. She wrapped her arms around Becka and held her tightly. "My God, I thought he shot you." She was crying so hard she was starting to hiccup.

Becka tried to calm her. They both froze when they heard footsteps pounding up the stairs.

"Lee Dresher, this is Sheriff Rogers. Can you hear me?"

"In here," Lee yelled. Together they felt their way to the door. It took Lee a moment to get the door open. She had forgotten that she had locked it. By the time they stepped out into a brilliantly lit hallway, the sheriff was already headed down the hallway toward them.

There was a moment of confusion as Lee and Becka tried to both talk at once. He finally held up a hand to stop them. "How badly are you hurt?" His gaze was flying back and forth between them.

Lee turned to Becka and felt her knees weaken. The side of Becka's head was covered in blood. She gasped. "He did hit you."

Becka's hand flew to the side of her head. She flinched. "No. I think I hit a chair or something when I fell."

Lee took a closer look and saw that indeed there was a small gash at the edge of her hairline.

"Other than that, you're okay?" the sheriff asked.

Becka nodded.

"And you?" He turned to Lee.

"I'm fine. Did you see anyone when you came up?"

He shook his head. "No. I have a couple of deputies looking around outside, but I'm not going to send them out into the woods. Anyone sitting out there with a high-powered rifle could easily pick them off." He hooked a thumb over his belt. "I want you two to follow me back into town. I'll get your report there and then you need to find someplace to stay for the night." He must have been expecting them to argue, and when they didn't he seemed a little flustered and started moving them downstairs.

From the foot of the stairs Lee could see emergency lights flashing wildly around her front yard.

"Why don't you two follow me?" he suggested. "You don't have to worry about the place. I'll leave a couple of deputies out here for the night."

Lee didn't say anything, but she could have told him that the only thing that she cared about in the house would be going with her. She looked at Becka and nodded.

The next few hours were among the longest Lee could remember. After they went to the sheriff's office and gave their statements, Sheriff Rogers insisted that Becka go by the hospital to have the cut on her head checked. Becka tried to get out of it until Lee joined forces with him. When they reached the hospital, they discovered that the gossip mill and Dr. Lyman were already several steps ahead of them. After Dr. Lyman cleaned the cut on Becka's head and determined that it wasn't deep enough to require stitches, she wanted to x-ray Lee's wrist again, but Lee refused.

"I told you I'm fine," Lee insisted as Dr. Lyman closed the door to the examining room. She felt certain her wrist hadn't been damaged further during the event. Dr. Lyman was probably just in search of more gossip. She immediately regretted her unkind thoughts. It was three in the morning and the doctor had made a special trip in to the hospital. "Thanks for coming back down here."

Dr. Lyman shrugged. "I was already up. I don't sleep much. When I heard your name on my police scanner, I thought I'd come over to see what you had gotten yourself into now."

Lee wondered if she was the only person in the entire county who didn't own a police scanner. Most people said they merely used them for weather emergencies, but she suspected they were used more as a source of information on what was going on in the area.

Dr. Lyman patted Lee's shoulder. "Let me at least take your blood pressure. I'm an old woman. I've earned the right to be obstinate."

Lee tried to rein in her impatience as she sat down.

"Why did you think it was Ollie Waters shooting at you?" Dr. Lyman asked without preamble.

If Lee hadn't lived in Christmas for so long, the question

might have shocked her, but she knew how quickly these things spread. She gave in and told her about seeing Ollie standing in the woods with the rifle. "How is he doing?" she asked when she finished.

"He's still unconscious. He lost a lot of blood, but he's a stubborn old mule. It's going to take a lot more than that to stop him."

"What happened?" She tried to ignore the fact that she was being just as guilty of gossiping as Dr. Lyman.

Dr. Lyman wrapped a blood pressure cuff around Lee's arm. "No one knows for sure. He stumbled through the door at Kelsey's and collapsed. The ambulance brought him in. He'd been shot through the side. It appeared that he might have accidentally shot himself, but from the angle of the wound, it seems he had been shot from above. But where and by whom?" she shrugged. "I don't understand what's going on," she said as if to herself. "This sort of thing doesn't happen here."

Lee knew only too well how wrong that statement was. "Was it the same caliber of bullet as the one that hit Jefferson?"

"I don't know. I leave it up to the police to figure that out." She patted Lee's knee. "Since you won't let me take another x-ray, I can't tell if you've done any further damage. How do you feel?"

"Like a house fell on me—thanks to those pills you gave me."

She made a dismissive sound. "As usual, you didn't listen. I told you to take the pill with food." She waved a hand. "I can't believe how sensitive you are. I'm going to start giving you baby medicine. You're sensitive to everything I give you because you never take any medicine."

"I could start smoking pot again," Lee offered and smiled when Dr. Lyman scowled at her. "Don't worry. I'm just joking. It gives me a headache."

Dr. Lyman shook a finger at her. "Sheriff Rogers will give you a headache if he hears you talking like that." She stood and took a couple of steps toward the door.

Lee was about to stand up when the older woman turned back to her. "So, I'm your physician. You know you can tell me anything and I won't repeat it."

Lee nodded and wondered where this was headed.

"What's going on with you and that young woman who was with you?"

Lee chuckled. "I don't believe you. What's going on is that my doctor gave me a prescription that put me in orbit and Becka drove me home. I was so zonked she was afraid to leave me alone."

"So she doesn't normally stay with you?"

"No. I live alone and have for years. You know that. Becka is living over at the old Peterson place."

Dr. Lyman tapped her chin thoughtfully. "Do you think the shooter was shooting at you or her?"

Lee frowned. "What do you mean?"

"Nothing. I'm just thinking about all that's happened recently. She moved into the old Peterson place, and then Jefferson Depew was shot. You saw Ollie watching your house, and then he's shot. She drives you home and now someone is shooting at your house?"

"What does any of that have to do with Becka?"

The doctor shrugged. "Maybe nothing, but no one has ever shot at your house before, have they?" Before Lee could respond, the doctor opened the door and disappeared, leaving Lee with a lapful of unanswered questions.

CHAPTER TWENTY-FOUR

When Lee made it back to the waiting area, she was surprised to find an exhausted-looking Dewayne sitting with Becka, Clint and Alan. She glanced at her watch. It was after four in the morning. Dewayne stood when Lee approached. "You guys having a party or what?" she tried to joke.

"Are you okay?" he asked. There was a different sound to his voice. It was lower in volume and decisively more menacing than his normal tone.

"I'm fine." Remembering the dreams she had, she stepped forward and hugged him, then moved over to hug Clint and Alan. The shocked look on all their faces made her feel bad that such a simple gesture from her caused such a reaction.

"I'm sorry they woke you guys," she said.

"Gladys called to tell us," Alan said in a voice that shook slightly. "We were worried sick."

"What's going on?" Clint asked. "First there was the mess at the gallery and then at home. We were going to close the shop and come out to check on you—since you don't answer your phone," he said pointedly.

"Oh, that's my fault," Becka said. She turned to Lee. "Your cell phone kept ringing, but you were laying on it and I couldn't get to it."

Dewayne and Clint looked away suddenly, but Alan just smirked.

Lee rolled her eyes. "I had taken a sleeping pill that…" She saw the smirk on Alan's face spread and knew it was useless to try to explain. "Never mind."

"We finally called Betty and she told us your wrist was hurt but not broken," Clint said. "What happened?"

Lee wondered who had told Betty the final condition of her wrist. It could have been any number of people. She was too tired to stand so she motioned for them all to sit. "I don't know," she said after they were all seated. "It seems like everything has gone crazy these past few days." She looked at Dewayne. "I guess you heard about Ollie."

He nodded. She glanced at the other two, who were nodding also.

"Let's hope that when he regains consciousness he can explain what he was doing behind your house," Clint said.

"I feel awful about accusing him. I guess he really was hunting." Lee noticed that Dewayne was watching Becka. Did he believe, as Dr. Lyman obviously did, that all this mess was somehow directed toward Becka? Could they be right? After all, what did any of them know about her? When Granny Depew said Becka was in trouble, maybe she had meant exactly that. She rubbed her forehead. She was too tired to think about it now.

"Come on," Dewayne said, motioning to Becka and Lee. "You two can spend the night with us."

Becka shook her head. "Thanks, but I'm going home."

Lee felt a stab of disappointment. A part of her had hoped to continue what they had started hours ago. She tried not to show her feelings, but she caught Alan's look of astonishment before he busied himself with examining his thumbnail.

"I thought I'd crash on the sofa at the gallery," Lee added much too late to be believable.

Dewayne stood. "Gladys told me to bring you both back with me, so that's what I have to do."

Too exhausted to think, Lee suddenly began to laugh. There was just something hilariously wrong with this gentle giant being intimidated by such a tiny wife.

Soon they were all laughing except Dewayne. He waited patiently until they settled down before he turned first to Lee and then Becka. "Ready to go now?" He looked at Becka. "You can follow me."

Becka nodded as they both stood.

Lee found herself dozing as Becka followed Dewayne the short distance across town. When they stepped into the house, Gladys was lying on the sofa waiting for them.

"Shouldn't you be sleeping?" Lee asked.

Gladys pinned her with one of her deadly stares. "How can I sleep? Dewayne gets a call from Sheriff Rogers that some madman is shooting at your house, and I then find out that you nearly got yourself killed taking down a shoplifter at the gallery." Her hand went to her hip. Even when she was lying down it looked intimidating. "Now, can you tell me why I had to hear that from Marge Littleton?"

"That was my fault," Becka said. "I should have called you. Lee had that reaction to the medication—"

Lee nudged Becka with her elbow, but it was too late. She could almost see Gladys's hair rise.

Dewayne stepped forward. "These two are probably exhausted." He grabbed each of them by the arm and rushed them down the hallway. When he reached the end of the hallway where the lamps in two rooms burned softly, he stopped suddenly as if unsure of himself. He let go of them and cleared his throat. "Both guestrooms have been fixed up...and...um...yell if you need anything. Our room is on the other side of the house." He took off and left them standing in the hall.

They watched him disappear into the living room and pick Gladys up from the sofa as if she weighed no more than an armload of towels. A moment later the living room light went out.

Lee and Becka stood in the hallway for a moment before Becka sighed. "I guess the rest is up to us."

Lee nodded. This was not what she had planned.

Becka leaned forward and kissed her on the cheek. "Don't look so disappointed. We'll have plenty of time. Sweet dreams." She entered the bedroom closest to her and smiled before she closed the door.

Lee went into the other bedroom and stared at the big empty bed. Maybe she would buy a gun after all, because right now she felt like doing some serious damage to the jerk who was responsible for her having to sleep alone tonight.

Lee saw the oversized T-shirt that had been left folded on the bed. It was just like Gladys to think of little things like that. She looked at her watch. It was already after five. She debated whether she would feel worse if she slept for a couple of hours or if maybe it would be better to just stay awake. She would have to open the gallery in a few hours. The bed looked so comfortable she decided to stretch out for an hour or so. She stripped and pulled the T-shirt on. She doubted she would even be able to sleep, knowing that Becka was only a few feet away. As she crawled between the sheets, she wondered if Becka had a similar shirt. She told herself not to think about that or she'd never get any rest. She pulled the linens up beneath her chin.

The sun shining in her face woke Lee. She groaned as she peered at the clock beside the bed. It was after ten. The gallery wouldn't open on time today. She lay still for a moment to plan her day. She needed to call Betty and tell her to come on in, and then she would have to go back to the house to get clean clothes and wash up. But first, she would drop Becka off at the parking lot so Becka could take her truck. She did a mental erase when she remembered the broken windows at home. Betty couldn't handle the gallery alone. She would have to close the gallery for the day. Then, she needed to get someone out to the house to cover the broken windows. Plus, she'd have to deal with the insurance company and the repair guys... She practically growled as she kicked the covers off. The day was nearly half gone, and she hadn't even started.

She spotted a bathroom through a side door and headed toward it. She was surprised to find a small bundle of her own clothes lying on the vanity. There was even a plastic bag filled with her shampoo and other toiletries. Someone had obviously gone to her house and picked up the items. When she saw a pair of her favorite panties sticking out of the pile of clothes, she blushed. Surely Dewayne hadn't been the one to go out there. With Gladys's back hurting, the only other logical person would be Becka. The thought of Becka handling her underwear brought on an entirely different sort of blush. In deference to the cast, she took a quick bath rather than her usual shower. By the time she was dressed and made her way to the living room, her mood had taken a dramatic turn for the better and she was humming.

CHAPTER TWENTY-FIVE

When Lee stepped into the living room, she found Gladys and Becka chatting away.

"I'm glad to see that yesterday's excitement didn't keep you from getting your beauty sleep," Gladys said as Lee walked in.

"Don't pick on me. I've been traumatized and I haven't had a cup of coffee yet."

Becka hopped up. "Sit down. I'll get you some coffee." She headed toward the kitchen. "How do you like your coffee?"

"Black," Lee replied.

"I guess you two aren't too far along if she still doesn't know how you take your coffee," Gladys said as soon as Becka was out of earshot.

"Stop it." Lee took a seat across from Gladys. "There's nothing between us."

"That's not what your eyes said as they followed her out of

the room," Gladys said.

"How's your back?" Lee asked, changing the subject.

"It's much better, thank you." Gladys replied. "And how is your wrist? Do you need another pain pill? I heard that Becka practically had to carry you into the house last night."

"My wrist is well enough to smack you on the noggin if you don't stop picking on me," Lee replied. "I need to call Betty—"

Gladys suddenly became all business. "I've already called her, and she was going to contact a couple of her friends to go over and sit with her. The gallery is open and she's not alone. I told her to call me if it got busy and I'd send you over. You're less than ten minutes away."

Lee started to speak, but Gladys stopped her.

"Before you get all crazy the way you can when you have too many things to do, Dewayne and Clint went out to your house this morning and nailed plywood over the broken windows, so you don't have to worry about that."

Tears suddenly stung Lee's eyes. "I don't know what I'd do without you guys."

"You would do just fine," Gladys said, all traces of her usual teasing gone from her voice. "I can't tell you how frightened I was last night when they called." She sniffled.

"Gladys, I've never been so scared in my life. There was one point when I thought Becka had been hit." She looked up. "I don't think I could have taken that."

Gladys looked at her for a long moment and smiled slightly. "Could it be that you've officially been bitten this time?"

"Bitten by what?" Becka asked as she came in with a tray containing coffee and a plate of pastries.

"A love bug," Gladys said and grinned.

Lee wasn't sure whether her face or Becka's was the reddest.

Gladys let them off easy. "Becka drove out to get you both some clean clothes this morning. On the way back in she stopped by the bakery and picked up some goodies."

"Did you two wait for me?" Lee asked.

Becka and Gladys exchanged guilty-looking glances. "Of

course we did," Gladys replied. "You don't think we would eat without you, do you?" She plucked a cookie from the plate Becka held out to her.

"Yes, I do," Lee answered. "I'll bet this is your second round, in fact."

As they munched on the baked goods and drank coffee, Lee noticed a ceramic pumpkin sitting on a table by the window. She had forgotten that tomorrow was Halloween. Since she lived in the country she never got trick-or-treaters coming to her door there, but most of the townspeople and a few of the rural ones would bring their kids to the shops on Halloween night. She knew she should come in and keep the gallery open for the kids, but honestly, she was too tired. Traditionally, the days on either side of Halloween were slow days for tourists. They were all busy with their own lives. She considered whether she should talk to Gladys about closing the gallery for a few days. It would give Betty a break and this would be the ideal time to do so.

"Have you had anyone interested in the position at the gallery?" Gladys asked.

Lee shook her head. "No. I'm hoping the paper will generate some attention." She started to make her suggestion about closing the gallery for a few days when Becka spoke up.

"In all the excitement that happened yesterday," Becka said, "I completely forgot to tell you why I came in."

They turned their attention to her.

"Lee, you remember my cousin Annabelle?"

"Yes. She was visiting Granny Depew the day Jefferson was shot."

"Correct. I saw the notice you put in the grocery store and I called her to let her know. She's thinking about moving here and if she does she's interested in the job." Becka leaned forward slightly. "That's why I had stopped by the gallery. I was picking up an application for her."

Lee looked at Gladys who shrugged. Lee wasn't sure if hiring a member of Becka's family was a good idea. If things between them did develop—she stopped herself sharply. This wasn't the time to dwell on that.

"She has worked at Wal-Mart ever since she was in high school," Becka continued. "So, she has a lot of people experience." She paused. "I shouldn't be speaking for her. I was just supposed to pick up the application."

"I'll get one for you," Lee said. Annabelle might be a perfect choice. After all, she did want to be an artist.

"In the meantime, if you just need someone to stand around and watch the register while you tackle shoplifters, I could help out," Becka said.

"I won't be tackling any more shoplifters," Lee replied. "Thank goodness it's not a major problem for us. It seems to be more of an issue during this time of year."

"People taking advantage of the crowds, I suppose," Gladys replied.

The phone rang before Lee could agree. Gladys picked up the extension that was lying beside her. Lee stood to pour herself another cup of coffee when she heard Gladys say, "I'll tell her to come right over."

Lee waited for Gladys to explain.

"That was Dewayne. They need you to go over to the sheriff's office. They may have the two that tried to steal the painting yesterday."

Lee set her cup on the tray. "Wow. How did they catch them?"

"I think they want to talk to you about that. In fact, they want to see you both."

Lee nodded as Becka stood and pulled her car keys from her pocket.

"We can't drive," Lee reminded Becka. "We'll have to walk or catch one the wagons as they pass." It was times like these when the ordinance against cars on Main Street during the holiday season became a royal pain. "After I've finished there," Lee began, "I suppose I'll go by the gallery. I still need to call the insurance company and get them out to the house."

"Why don't you two stay here a few more nights?" Gladys

suggested.

"Thanks, but no. I need to get home," Becka replied.

"Me, too," Lee said, but in truth she was a little nervous about returning to the house. A part of her felt certain that the shooting hadn't been directed at her personally. She just happened to be the lone house in the woods that the creep stumbled across. Whoever it had been was probably long gone by now. As she and Becka said their good-byes and left, Lee tried not to dwell on the fact that she'd had the same thoughts after Jefferson had been shot.

She and Becka walked to the corner and caught a ride on one of the horse-drawn carriages. They rode across town in silence. It seemed as though neither of them knew what to say. When they arrived at the sheriff's office, Dewayne was waiting for them at the door. When she saw him, it suddenly struck her that something else was going on. Dewayne had no jurisdiction outside of the national park territory. Why would he be involved with the shoplifters? She stopped so sharply that Becka nearly plowed into her.

Dewayne came out to meet them.

"This isn't about the shoplifters, is it?" Lee asked him.

"I think you'd better come on in and talk to the sheriff," he said and motioned for them to follow him.

Becka and Lee looked at each other and followed him inside.

He led them through the building. To Lee's surprise, he asked Becka to wait in a small side room before he led Lee farther down the hallway. He stopped by another door and motioned her inside before he followed her in. The room was so small Dewayne seemed to fill it all by himself. With Sheriff Rogers and a woman who Lee didn't recognize already in the room, the cramped space was bordering on claustrophobic. Lee was amazed to discover that she was standing inside one of those viewing rooms she had seen in so many movies.

Sheriff Rogers introduced the woman merely as Angela Foster. He never bothered to explain who she was or why she was there. "We would like for you to see if you recognize any of the people we're about to show you," he said to Lee.

"All right." Lee sensed a wave of tension that seemed too intense for a couple of shoplifters.

Sheriff Rogers pressed a button on a small intercom. "Pete, send the first group in."

A light on the other side of the one-way mirror came on and a few seconds later a line of men filed in. Lee had no trouble picking the man out even before she was asked. "The third one from the left is the guy."

"Are you positive?" the woman asked.

"Yes. That's him."

"Have you ever seen him anywhere else?"

Lee shook her head. "No." She turned to look at them. "Why?"

"Bring in the women," Angela Foster said.

Sheriff Rogers again pressed the intercom. When the women strolled in, it took Lee a moment to find the one who had been with the man. "Can you ask them to turn sideways to the right?" Lee was certain she recognized the woman, but today her hair was a different color and Lee wanted to be certain she was correctly identifying the right person.

The sheriff spoke into the intercom and a moment later, all the women turned. "That's her," Lee pointed. "The last one."

Again, Angela Foster asked her if she was positive.

"Yes. I'm sure."

"Have you ever seen her before?" Angela asked.

Lee shook her head. "No."

The sheriff nodded at Dewayne, who touched Lee's arm and motioned for her to follow him. Rather than going back to the room where they had left Becka, Dewayne led her to yet another room. As they were going in, Lee heard a noise and glanced back in time to see a deputy leading Becka into the viewing room.

"They didn't want you both identifying them at the same time. It's just a precaution."

Lee nodded and waited until the door was closed before she

171

turned to Dewayne. "What's going on? Who was that woman in there with us?"

He waved her to a chair before he sat down across from her. "She's with the FBI," he replied. "Jefferson Depew died early this morning."

Lee shook her head. "His poor family. What are they going to do?" She stopped and frowned. "Wait a minute. Those two were the shoplifters. Why is someone from the FBI interested in them?"

Dewayne took a deep breath and slowly released it. "Early this morning, we went back out to your place with the dogs."

Lee knew he meant bloodhounds. They were occasionally used when a hiker or camper got lost in the forest.

"It didn't take them long to pick up a scent and we caught those two about six miles from your place in an old cabin."

"Was it the one back by Wildwood Creek?" she asked. She had used the old place as a model for a couple of her paintings.

"Yeah, that's the one. We sort of caught them by surprise." He glanced away and she could pretty well guess how the couple had been found. "Anyway," he went on, "we found a rifle and shells that matched the caliber of the ones we've been finding all over the county. I'm sure that once the ballistic results are back, they'll find it's the same gun. When they brought them in, Sheriff Rogers thought the girl would crack under questioning." He grinned. "It was the guy who broke down, started bawling and spilled his guts."

"So my place was just a random accident?" Lee asked.

He shook his head. "No. According to the guy, you pissed his girlfriend off when you spoiled their party yesterday at the gallery. So they made a few inquiries around town and as you can imagine it didn't take them long to find out where you lived. He said they never intended to hurt you. They just wanted to shake you up a little."

"Well, they sure as hell succeeded in that," Lee replied as she continued to think about Jefferson Depew's family. "What about Jefferson? Was it an accident?"

172

He shrugged. "The guy said it was. He admitted he had been tracking the bear and he just shot the first thing he saw move."

"Why were they shooting the animals?"

"The animals provided them with moving target practice." Dewayne's voice filled with disgust. "They got bored shooting at stationary targets."

She shook her head. "That's it?"

"That's the only excuse he gave."

A cold chill ran through Lee's body.

"You don't have to worry about them anymore," he replied. "The FBI has been looking for them for a while. They think these two are responsible for robbing a liquor store over in Pulaski County last month. If they're the ones, they shot the owner, but he survived and is on his way here now to see if he can pick them out of a lineup. If he does, then they're out of our hair." He leaned back in his chair. "You may be called to testify, but again maybe not with the way the guy is confessing."

Lee thought about her home and wondered if she would ever again feel completely safe there.

CHAPTER TWENTY-SIX

After leaving the sheriff's office, Lee and Becka walked slowly toward the gallery and discussed what had occurred at the sheriff's office.

"I'm really sorry about Jefferson," Lee said.

"Thanks. He was a nice guy. I don't know what Joan is going to do without him. It'll hit his parents and Granny hard."

"I'll get a few things together and bring them by later this afternoon," Lee said. A death in the family was something locals took to heart. The Depew home would be crowded with people until after the funeral.

Becka stopped sharply. "Listen, I know this isn't the time or place, but I don't know when I'm going to be able to see you again alone."

Lee nodded.

"I wanted to tell you that last night…before…" She gazed up

at Lee. "I want to finish what we started."

"So do I," Lee admitted, "but we need to talk." She fell silent as a group of tourists rushed by. "I'm not very good at this. I'm not even sure if I'm capable of having a relationship that lasts longer than a few weeks."

"Can we plan on having dinner again as soon as—" She stopped. "Would you listen to me? Poor Joan is going through hell and all I can think about is when I'm going to see you again. I'm sorry. I don't mean to sound so cold-hearted."

"Why don't we just take things as they come?" Lee said. "I'm not going anywhere and hopefully neither are you." To her surprise Becka seemed to pale slightly. Lee glanced up to see Clarissa Jenkins headed their way. They waited for her.

"Lee, you poor thing, I heard what happened to you at the gallery and then your home. How are you doing?" Clarissa asked as she rushed up to them.

"I'm fine. Thanks for asking."

Clarissa's ever-flickering gaze assessed her clothes. "You're not working today?"

"I haven't had a chance to get home and get another costume. I'll be in my studio most of the time." In theory, Lee liked the effort the community put into maintaining the charade of a Victorian town, but there were times when it was a pain.

"Well, I just wanted to let you know that if you need help at the gallery, I can speak to the members of the committee and get someone over there to help you. After all, that's why we went to all that trouble to compile the volunteer list and train them."

Lee almost declined. The only training the volunteers had received had been on using a cash register, not that it really helped because nearly every business had a different setup. At the last minute, she decided to take the offer of help. Since the next few days were traditionally slow, the volunteers should be able to handle it. If not, she was only a few minutes away. "Thank you. If I could have a couple of people to work until Monday, it would really help. I have an ad in today's paper, so hopefully it won't take Gladys and me too long to hire someone."

"Don't you worry," Clarissa replied. "I'll get you two or three dependable people." Clarissa kept glancing at Becka.

It suddenly hit Lee that they probably hadn't met. "I'm so sorry," she said. "I swear I don't know where my head is." She introduced them. "Becka is living out at the old Peterson place."

Clarissa smiled brightly. "Oh, yes. I'd heard someone had moved in there. It's so nice to meet you." She shook Becka's hand. "Are you working somewhere here in town?"

Lee stepped in before Becka had time to speak. "Clarissa, I'm so sorry to be rude, but we need to leave. Becka was just on her way out to the Depews to deliver some things."

"Oh, mercy, yes. I heard about poor Jefferson. Whatever will Joan do? We simply must do something to help her." Clarissa's charitable soul kicked into overdrive. She gave them a vague wave as she rushed off muttering to herself.

They continued toward the gallery in silence. When they finally arrived, Becka handed Lee her car keys.

"The truck doors aren't locked," Lee said. "You'll find a spare key beneath the passenger side floor mat." She slipped Becka's keys into her pocket. "I really appreciate your loaning me your car." She wondered how long it would take her wrist to heal enough to bear the pressure of shifting her truck.

"I'm sorry we didn't have the foresight to park it in the lot rather than on the street in front of Gladys and Dewayne's house. Will you be stuck here all day?"

"Don't worry about that. If I have to leave, I can always sneak out of town through a back street. It's really just Main Street that they're concerned the most about."

"Will you be all right about staying at your place?" Becka asked.

Lee sensed her reluctance to leave and it gave her a warm feeling inside. "Sure. Now that they've caught those two, I'll be fine."

"You'll call me if you need anything?"

Lee smiled. "You can bet on that."

Becka nodded and slowly walked away.

When Lee stepped into the gallery, she wasn't surprised to see only one lone shopper viewing the displays and a man at the register. She glanced around and smiled when she saw at least four members of Betty's sewing club. They were scattered around the room, each with a feather duster. Lee had a weird moment of insight and for a fleeting second she saw the room as a visitor might. The décor and clothing worn by the workers did give her a feeling of having stepped back in time. She pretended to browse through a bin of prints until Betty finished ringing up the customer. Once the man had left, she moved over to speak to Betty.

"How are you doing?" Betty asked. "I heard about what happened out at your place. I tried to call, but you're cell phone must have been turned off."

Lee tried to remember if she'd heard her phone ring last night, then remembered turning the ring volume down at the hospital. She nodded to the women moving around the gallery. "I see you've called out reinforcements."

"It has been very slow today. All I've sold is a few postcards and one print." Betty nodded toward her friends. "I asked them to come over. You can never be too careful these days." Betty made a visual circuit of the room. "Of course, they are here to sit with me, and they certainly don't expect you to pay them. With things being so slow, we aren't actually doing much work anyway. We sew when there are no customers."

"I appreciate the help."

Betty nodded. "I heard Sheriff Rogers had caught those two young hoodlums. I certainly hope he gives them what they have coming."

Betty obviously hadn't heard the entire story. "I don't think we'll be seeing either of them around here again," Lee said and filled Betty in on what had been happening. They discussed the matter until another customer strolled in. Since Lee hadn't worn her Victorian period clothing, she couldn't work on the gallery floor without being in violation of the holiday ordinance. She left Betty in charge and went back to her studio. She still needed to call the insurance company. As she stepped into her studio, she stopped sharply and slapped herself on the forehead with her good hand. "My God," she mumbled. "I've become a full-fledged gossip."

Lee spent the rest of the morning dealing with the insurance company and making arrangements for having the glass in her home windows replaced. By the time she had finished she was exhausted and her wrist was hurting again. She found a bottle of aspirin in her desk and took two. They might not work as well as the pain reliever had, but she wasn't up to another trip to la-la land. Clarissa Jenkins called to let her know that she had four volunteers lined up to come in and help at the gallery. Lee arranged for them to work in pairs. Before she left her desk, she used her left hand and carefully printed two checks. Her signature was a bit shaky, but by now everyone over at the bank would know what had happened. She doubted they would question the validity of the signature. One check she left in her desk to give to Betty at the end of the week; the other was a donation to the sewing club. Since they had come over to help their friend, Betty, it would be considered rude for Lee to offer to pay them, but a cash donation to the sewing club would be acceptable. She was careful to date the check for the previous day. They would know the truth, but appearances were everything.

When she stepped back out into the gallery, there were no customers. Betty and her friends were sitting in a circle beside the checkout counter. They each held an embroidery ring and were hard at work. As they drew their needles in and out of the material, Lee was reminded of the violin section of a symphony— each bow moving in synch. She stood off to the side and watched them for a few minutes before interrupting. "You ladies do such beautiful work," she said as she stepped closer. As she studied their stunning embroidery, it occurred to her that their sewing was as much an art form as her paintings. Stitches were their brushstrokes and brightly hued skeins of thread their paint. "Ladies, how would you feel about framing some of your pieces and selling them here?" she asked.

They looked up at her as if she had lost her mind. "No one would buy something like this in a frame," Sadie Lewis replied. "On a dishtowel or table runner maybe." At eighty-something, she was one of the oldest members of the group, which automatically gave her a lot of influence.

Lee didn't agree but knew better than to be so rude as to say so. She decided to try a different approach. "Ms. Sadie, most of the people who come out here are from the city. They love seeing the things that we take for granted. I think that's why they buy this." She waved her hand toward a wall of paintings that reflected the local environment. "That's why they drive all the way out here when they could easily shop at a hundred different stores in their own area. Here they're able to shake off the city for a few hours." She picked up a beautifully detailed embroidered image of a cardinal that had been lying beside Betty's chair. "Imagine how much joy visitors get from coming out here where they can relax for a few hours. Some of them will even notice things like this very bird. Sure, there are plenty of cardinals in Little Rock, but who has the time to actually stop and look at them? Here not only do they see the real bird, but they come into the gallery and see this beautiful reminder that they can take home and hang on their wall. It'll be there for them to look at every evening when they come home."

Sadie peered through her thick glasses and shook her head. "Lee Dresher, I'm surprised your eyes aren't brown with all that bullcrap you just shoveled out." She rocked rapidly as she resumed her stitching. "But I suppose the group could discuss the matter and get back to you. After all, a little extra pocket money never hurt anyone." She squinted at Lee. "I guess you'll be asking for a commission out of our profits."

Lee struggled not to show her surprise. "I'm in business to make money, but considering how your group came out to help me, I think that rather than the usual thirty percent commission, I could settle for, say, twenty percent."

"If we decide to let you sell our work." She pointed with her needle, "And I said if. Then we'll give you fifteen percent and not a penny more."

"That's a hard bargain, Ms. Sadie." Lee pretended to consider the matter. "I'll accept those terms, if—" she paused just long enough to make them all look up— "you can convince the members of your sewing group to provide the gallery with at least five pieces a month." She pulled the donation check from her pocket. "Ms. Sadie, since you're here, would you mind if I gave this to you? I meant to mail it in, but with everything that happened yesterday and today, it completely slipped my mind."

Sadie took the check and peered at it closely before giving a heavy sigh. "We do appreciate you wanting to join our club, Lee, but you know the club's bylaws state that we only accept members over the age of fifty-five." She shoved the check into her sewing basket. "But we'll be happy to apply this amount to your future membership."

Lee barely managed to keep a straight face as she thanked the group and retreated to her studio.

CHAPTER TWENTY-SEVEN

Lee drove out of town by using back streets. She stopped by the grocery store and bought some things to take out to the Depew family. Then she started home to change into something more suitable for the occasion.

It felt strange to drive a car after having driven the truck for so many years, and she held her breath more than once as she eased her way down the road that led to her house. She had never noticed before how badly rutted the road was.

When she finally pulled up to her house, she realized that the remote control for the garage door was in her truck. She parked in the driveway and examined the front of her house where a large sheet of plywood covered the broken windows. The repair made her think of an old man who had lived in Christmas when she first arrived. He had worn an eye patch that frightened Sara.

She got out of the car slowly and made her way to the front

door. Never before had she been hesitant to enter her home. After standing with the key in hand for several heartbeats, she took a deep breath. This was her home. She had worked too hard on it to let a couple of warped misfits drive her out. She squared her shoulders and unlocked the door. There was no longer broken glass beneath the living room window. She knew Dewayne and Clint were responsible for sweeping up the mess. That knowledge made her feel safer somehow. After going into the kitchen and finding the mess had been cleared away there also, she made her way upstairs. The glass was gone, but here there was a memory that would take a lot longer to get rid of. She stared at the spot by the file cabinet where she and Becka had waited, not knowing whether the gunman would come inside or not. Then that awful moment when the glass exploded and Becka fell. Lee rubbed her left hand across her face before looking around the room. Of all the rooms in the house, this had been her favorite. This was where she came when she needed to find a sense of peace. Somehow, she would find a way to make it that way again, she promised herself as she hurried down the hallway to her bedroom. She needed to change clothes and go to the Depews' home.

When she arrived at Lincoln and Zelda Depew's home, the long driveway up to their house was lined with vehicles. She parked Becka's car on the roadway with the other latecomers. On her last trip here, she had noticed that most people had brought food, but almost no one had brought drinks. This time rather than bringing a ham, she had brought a case each of water and soft drinks, a large canister of coffee and two boxes of tea bags. Unable to carry much because of the cast, she grabbed the bag with the coffee and tea. As she started up the driveway, she experienced a sense of déjà vu. She and Grant, along with his two sons, had played this same scene just a few days earlier.

She hated this part but took a deep breath and prepared herself. She nodded to each of them in turn. "I'm sorry for your loss."

"We thank you," Grant replied. He took the bag from her.

"I brought some drinks," she said to the boys, "if you guys wouldn't mind carrying them in for me." They rushed off. "I'm in Becka's car," she called after them. She held up her wrist. "She was nice enough to switch vehicles with me for a few days until I can manage the gear shift again."

"We heard about what happened out at your place," Grant said. "If there's anything me and the boys can help you with, just let us know."

They started walking toward the house. "Thanks. I appreciate the offer. How are your parents and Joan doing?"

"Mom and Pop are hanging in there." He shook his head. "Joan is struggling."

From conversations Lee and Gladys had shared previously, she knew the national forest rangers had decent benefits, but she didn't know if they would cover all the hospital expenses. Even if they did, there were still the funeral expenses, and the baby was due in a few months. She knew she would have to tread lightly on the next subject, but someone would have to do it eventually. She cleared her throat. "Grant, I don't mean any disrespect in asking, but will Joan be all right...financially? I could arrange—"

He held up a hand to stop her. "That's right neighborly of you, but it has already been taken care of. Joan and the babies will be fine."

"Babies?"

He smiled sadly. "They hadn't told anyone yet, but Joan's having twins."

Lee hid her surprise. With this new bit of information, she couldn't help but wonder how they would make it.

When she entered the house, she quickly scanned the crowd for any sign of Becka. The depth of her disappointment in not seeing Becka surprised her. As she consoled the stoic-faced Lincoln and hugged Zelda Depew, she couldn't help but wonder how a parent could ever get over losing a child. The mere thought of losing Sara caused her stomach to cramp up into a tight knot. Joan sat in a tattered blue velvet armchair that looked as if its better days had long since passed. She sat with her hand placed protectively over her bulging abdomen. Her vacant stare reminded Lee of photos she had seen of disaster victims. Her movements and responses were so mechanical that Lee doubted she even knew who she was talking to.

Annabelle stood in the far corner, but there were too many people to negotiate through to get there politely, so Lee simply waved. Annabelle shyly returned the wave and ducked her head.

Lee continued greeting Jefferson's family members before she moved on to the kitchen in hopes of finding Becka. Granny was sitting at the table alone. As Lee approached, the older woman raised her head. In her face shone the pride and spirit of the thousands of men and women who struggled and died to tame the land they called home. Lee rarely did portraits with either her camera or brush, but as she stared into the face of Ida Jane Peterson Depew, she ached to capture every story that was so deeply imprinted on the woman's face. A face etched with a roadmap of her life that had begun in the rugged, poverty-stricken hills of Tennessee and that would probably end here in the remote mountains of Arkansas.

"Lee?"

"Yes, ma'am. It's me, Granny Depew." Lee leaned down to hug her. "I'm sorry about Jefferson," she whispered. She had made it through all the relatives out front without breaking down, but trying to console Granny made her eyes tear up. She struggled to control herself.

"He lived a good life," Granny said. "He never had an unkind word for anyone. He loved his family. I think he was happy." She exhaled loudly as if she were exhausted. "I don't know why the Lord couldn't have been satisfied with taking my tired old bones and leaving him, but I guess He'll let me know soon enough what He wants from me. Do you believe in God?"

The question caught Lee completely off guard. Her family had never been a religious one and she normally wasn't comfortable participating in conversations dealing with such.

Lee sat down in the chair beside her. "I don't have much use for organized religion." She thought about the times she had given a silent word of thanks to a patron saint. "When I capture an excellent photograph or a painting comes out much better than I had hoped for, I often express my thanks to one or another patron saint. I don't know if I do it because I truly believe they helped me, or because I'm afraid of taking on the full responsibility of having created the art myself, because if I did it myself, then there's only me to blame if the next attempt isn't as good." She realized she was rambling and tried to condense her answer. "I think we have to believe there's something greater out there looking after us. Otherwise, life would be too frightening."

Granny nodded slowly. "I sometimes forget how scary it was to be young." She rubbed her fingertips over the linen tablecloth. "When you get to be my age, there's not much left that scares you anymore."

Lee didn't know how to respond, so she simply placed a hand on Granny's arm.

"Speaking of which, I hear that you've had a pretty scary week." Granny seemed to shake off some of her sadness.

"Yes, ma'am, it was. I stopped by my place on the way over here. I hate to admit it, but it was a little unsettling to go back inside the house."

"That can happen. What you need to do is to make a point of remembering the good times you've had there. Invite people you care about over and make a bunch of new good memories. My papa always used to say that a house carries the soul of the people who live in it. That's why an empty house goes down so quickly. Have you ever noticed that?" She didn't wait for Lee to respond. "That's why I was so happy that Becka took over the old place. She has a good heart. Any house she lives in will thrive." Granny took her hand and squeezed it. "You're the same way, but I think you're an older soul than Becka. You're more grounded and sure of yourself."

Lee wouldn't argue because it was discourteous, but Granny had missed her mark on that call.

"You don't believe me."

"How do you do that?" Lee asked, not realizing until too late that she had confirmed the older woman's suspicions.

Granny chuckled. "I'm a wise old sage."

"Your pulse rate either went up or your hand got sweaty."

They both looked up at the sound of Becka's voice. Lee couldn't stop the smile that sprang to her face.

Becka nodded to Lee's hand. "You might want to remove your hand from hers. I'm telling you, this old woman is a major con artist." She leaned down and kissed Granny's cheek. Becka lowered her voice slightly as she spoke. "I'm sorry it took me so long to get back. Things were a little more complicated than I thought they would be."

"Is it taken care of?"

Becka hesitated a moment before replying. "No, ma'am. I'm going to have to go back."

"When do you have to leave?"

"Monday." Becka's voice was so low Lee nearly missed it. She had tried not to intrude on what was obviously meant to be a private conversation, but she couldn't help but overhear it. She eased her hand from Granny's. She didn't want anyone to know what she was feeling at that moment.

CHAPTER TWENTY-EIGHT

A new wave of visitors saved Lee from having to make an awkward retreat. While Becka was occupied with greeting them, Lee said a quick good-bye to Granny and slipped out through the back door. She knew it was inexcusably rude to leave without saying good-bye, but she couldn't face anyone right now. Becka was leaving and hadn't even bothered to tell her. All that talk a few hours ago about wanting to get together and pick things up where they had left off. It had all been a line of bull.

When she reached the road where she had left Becka's car parked, she saw her trusty old truck sitting a bit farther down. Grant's sons, Hank and George, were unloading boxes from the back onto a kid's red wagon. Lee made a fast decision. Becka had been using the spare key. The original key was on the key ring in her pocket. She walked to her truck and handed Becka's car keys to Hank. They had removed all the boxes except for two. She waited for them to finish.

Hank pointed to the cast on her hand. "Ma'am, are you sure you can drive with that?"

She nodded. "I'll be fine."

He looked as though he wanted to argue, but for once country manners worked in her favor. Instead, he nodded and they left with the wagon.

Lee waited until they were down the road some before she attempted to move the truck. She was relieved to find that it actually wasn't that painful. The cast held the wrist stiff and all those years of excellent maintenance allowed the truck to shift without much effort. Her cell phone started ringing less than ten minutes later. She ignored it. Right now, she didn't feel like talking to anyone. When she arrived home, she parked her truck in the garage, and then went to get her camera gear.

The pack proved to be a little difficult, but she soon had it on. She turned her cell phone off and dropped it into her vest pocket without looking to see who had called. It was the wrong time of day to be going to the blind, but she didn't care. With her hand injured and her studio darkened with the plywood, the blind was the one place she knew she could go and find some peace. As she walked down the path, it felt like it had been weeks rather than a few days since she had last been there.

When she finally arrived, she took her usual precautions of checking for unwanted reptilian guests before climbing inside and closing out the world behind her. Even with the entranceway and makeshift windows closed, the midday sun kept the blind from being as dark as it normally was when she was there. Rather than setting up her camera, she removed her pack and sat on the old rickety chair. Only then did she attempt to face the questions that Becka's whispered announcement had given birth to in the Depew's kitchen. If Becka had known she was leaving, why had she said those things about starting over? Why hadn't she said she was thinking about leaving? Lee rubbed her forehead when she realized what an idiot she had been. Becka had told her several times that she didn't intend to stay, but Lee had been too wrapped up in her lust to hear it. How many times had Becka said, "If I decide to stay?" Even Granny Depew had said they were trying to convince Becka to buy the old Peterson place and fix it up.

Lee propped her elbow on her knee and cradled her head. Why had she not noticed that sooner? She knew the answer and chose not to dwell on it. She felt a rising sense of loneliness start to bloom. She straightened up and pushed the feeling away. This was precisely the reason she didn't get involved with anyone. It hurt too much when they left and they always left. She sat on the ground and started assembling her camera. It wasn't that difficult to attach the lens with her left hand, neither was screwing on the cable release. The tricky part was getting the camera's quick release mechanism coupled to the corresponding piece on the tripod. By the time she had everything set up she was sweating and her wrist was burning. She zipped her vest part way up and used it as a makeshift sling by slipping her injured wrist inside.

Then she settled down to wait. There was a distant twittering of birds and occasionally she'd see a flash of color as one flew past, but nothing caught her attention. Birds and animals tended to feed early in the morning and just before dusk, so she wasn't expecting to see much in the way of activity until much later in the day. She was pleased to note that the dappled shade would help diffuse the harsh sunlight. As she gazed out at the clearing, she started a mental calendar of things she needed to do both at home and the gallery. She kept building the list with every nit-picky chore she could imagine until it reached gargantuan proportions. Simply trying to remember the items on the list would be enough to keep her mind too occupied to think of Becka. Once she had completed that list, she started another one of things she wanted to photograph or paint. Two hours later, she was exhausted, but her brain was now thinking about work. All thoughts of lust had been driven into the nether regions of her awareness. She told herself that from now on she would keep those thoughts safely locked away.

Her marathon of list making had tired her out. She pulled

the pack toward her to start packing up. As she reached up for the camera, she saw a doe standing in the meadow. It wasn't the magnificent buck she had been hoping for, but the soft dappled sunlight combined with the sprinkling of fall color made a nice background. She snapped several shots before simply sitting and watching the deer graze on the lush green grass. Would the buck ever return? Maybe it was time she just moved on and painted the animal from memory. The doe she was watching was beautiful. Why not use her as a substitute for the buck? She pushed the thought from her mind and turned her attention back to observing the doe.

Even after the doe left, she continued to sit in the blind. She had nowhere to rush off to. As sundown approached, the temperatures began to drop quickly. She broke down her equipment and headed home.

For dinner, she opened a jar of Clarissa Jenkins' vegetable soup that she had purchased at a fair. At the last minute, she added a grilled cheese sandwich to the menu and made the couple of trips needed to haul her meal to the den where she parked herself in front of the television. She flipped through the channels until she found a so-called documentary on UFOs. She didn't believe in them so it didn't scare her to watch shows about them, there were no blood-and-guts involved to ruin her meal and best of all there wasn't even a hint of sex. After ten minutes of watching pie plates spinning on strings, Lee became convinced of three things—one, a heck of a lot of people were way too gullible; two, Clarissa Jenkins should never make vegetable soup and three, neither UFOs nor bad soup were enough to make her stop thinking about sex. She turned the television off and put the rest of her grilled cheese and the soup down the garbage disposal. Then she grabbed her favorite jelly glass and the nearly half-full bottle of room temperature Merlot on the counter. She took the wine back to the den and finished it as she flipped aimlessly through the channels. When the wine ran out, she turned the television off and took the empty bottle and glass back to the kitchen. She nearly dropped her glass when the doorbell buzzed as she was putting it into the dishwasher.

Along with the flash of fear the sudden noise had triggered there was also a flare of anger. Even without opening the door, she knew it would be Becka. In a childish moment, she considered not answering the door, and then chided herself. All that big talk she'd been handing herself didn't mean a thing if she couldn't face Becka James and tell her to move on down the road. She yanked the door open and was all poised to unload a wagonload of anger when she came face to face with Melinda Thayer.

For a long instant, they stood staring at each other. Finally, Lee managed to find her voice.

"Melinda, what do you need?"

Maybe it was the slow way in which Melinda eyed her from head to foot, or the half bottle of wine on a nearly empty stomach, or it could've simply been because Lee was hornier than a rabbit in springtime. Whatever the reason, she found herself pulling Melinda into the house and clamping her in a lip-lock that nearly loosened the fillings in her teeth. Within minutes, they were rolling around on the floor with the real dust bunnies.

The episode ended almost as quickly as it had begun. They both lay on the floor with pieces of clothing strewn around them or hanging half off their bodies.

Regret set in long before Lee ever caught her breath. What had she been thinking? She pulled her bra down and reached for her shirt. The sleeves were turned wrong side out and one button had disappeared. Her slacks were in a tangled heap around her ankles. She didn't look at Melinda as she gathered her own clothes. After they were once more dressed, Melinda stood by the door. She seemed to be as shaken by the encounter as Lee was. She cleared her throat twice before speaking. "Um...I just came by to—" She blew a heavy sigh. "Damn, this is really awkward now."

Lee looked at her for the first time and nearly burst into laughter. Melinda's hair poked out at odd angles all around her head.

Melinda tried again. "Lee, I'm sorry, but I came out here to tell you that I'm moving to LA." She looked so distraught that Lee couldn't be angry, but she also couldn't think of anything to say.

"I went by the gallery and picked up my unsold sketches." Suddenly she started toward the door. "When I get settled, I'll drop you a card with my new address. You can mail me a check for whatever you owe me." She practically ran from the house.

Lee didn't move for several minutes. When she did, it was to lock the door. After encasing the cast in a protective layer of plastic wrap, she stood beneath the hot spray of the shower until her body turned bright pink. It took nearly a half bottle of body wash before she started to feel clean again. When she finally stepped out of the shower, she dried herself vigorously before she pulled on an old pair of sweatpants and a T-shirt. Then she began to clean the house with a vengeance that was normally reserved for a visit from her mother. It was after two in the morning when she finally dropped into bed completely exhausted, but at least Melinda Thayer's scent was no longer on her or in her house.

CHAPTER TWENTY-NINE

On Friday morning, Lee sat at the kitchen table, drinking her coffee and planning her day. Today was Halloween. She made a notation to remind herself to buy candy to pass out at the gallery. In all the commotion of the past few days, she hadn't given the holiday much thought. She had just gotten off the phone with Gladys, who was feeling better now that she was able to get up and move around a bit. She hoped to be able to return to work the following week. Gladys also told her that Ollie Waters still hadn't regained consciousness and the FBI had taken the two who had shot up her house into custody.

Lee stared at the photo envelope containing two canisters of film that sat on the table ready to be mailed to a lab in Little Rock. She had gone to the blind. There had been a lot of activity around the stream, but still no sign of the buck. She had almost resigned herself to either changing the focal point of the image or else starting over completely. It wouldn't be the first time she had obliterated a partially completed painting with a coat of gesso.

Her thoughts strayed to the gallery. There had been no interest shown in the ad she had placed. She should have run it before all the bustle of the holiday season kicked in. Neither of the two applications she had received were acceptable. Becka had mentioned that Annabelle was interested in the job. Lee really didn't know anything about her, but she seemed a little on the shy side. That didn't bode well for her customer-service skills, but to be fair, at the time they had been talking, Granny Depew had been forcing Annabelle to show off a painting she had done when she was a child. She might be less inhibited in a workplace environment. Becka had said she worked at Wal-Mart.

Her thoughts jumped to Sara and her upcoming visit. She again wondered why Brandon was coming, and what had prompted her parents to decide to take a vacation during the holidays. She knew she should probably have called her parents and Sara to let them know what had been happening, but since it wasn't likely they would hear anything about it, she decided to wait until they came before mentioning it. Otherwise, they would all worry for no reason. The doorbell interrupted her thoughts.

Despite going to bed exhausted from her cleaning frenzy, she had not slept well. She got up slowly and made her way into the living room. "Keep your hands to yourself and your pants up," she told herself before opening the door. She wasn't surprised to find Becka standing there, but she was taken aback by how exhausted she looked.

"May I come in?" Becka asked.

Lee stepped back and let her in.

"Why did you leave so quickly yesterday?" Becka asked as she came inside.

The last thing Lee was in the mood for was a confrontation. "Can we please skip this conversation? I don't see where it could possibly change anything for the better." Lee didn't want Becka to leave, but they needed to keep to a safer topic. She chose a quick fix. "There's a fresh pot of coffee, if you'd like some."

Becka obviously wasn't ready to let go quite so easily. "If you're mad at me, I think I at least have the right to know why."

"Becka, please drop it while we're still friends."

Becka gave a surprised sound. "What's going on? Did I completely misunderstand what's been happening between us?"

Lee held her tongue, determined that she was not going to let herself be drawn into an argument.

"That's just great." Becka's words were sharp with anger. "Now, you're going to pull the strong, silent type routine. It's easy to see why you have problems with relationships."

Lee's anger flared. "You want noise? I'll give you noise." All of the stress of the last few days poured out like hot lava. "Did you think you could simply breeze in here, dangle a few carrots of attention under my nose and I'd hop in bed with you? Then you could jump into your fancy car and drive off to who knows where."

"What are you talking about?"

The genuine look of surprise on Becka's face almost fooled Lee, but she caught herself in time before she fell for a smooth line. "I heard you tell Granny Depew that you were leaving on Monday."

A slight flush tinted Becka's face. "That's why you left? You got mad because—" she stopped and rubbed the back of her neck.

"What's the matter?" Lee prodded. "Now you have nothing left to say?"

The fight seemed to have drained from Becka. "No, I have plenty to say." She paused before she glanced at Lee. "I just can't do it now."

Lee couldn't believe her audacity. "Isn't that convenient for you?"

"I didn't come over here to argue. I just thought—never mind." She turned to leave.

Lee felt an overwhelming need to stop Becka from walking out the door, but at the same time she was angry and hurt that Becka had made plans to leave and hadn't told her. After the other night, she had thought that maybe there was a chance for something between them. She pushed the thought away. There was no need to punish herself with thoughts of maybe.

Becka stopped. "I'm sorry about coming over and upsetting you. I was on my way home from the hospital and thought—" She shook her head. "I apologize. I shouldn't have stopped by." She started out the door.

"Why were you at the hospital?" Lee asked, automatically thinking of Granny Depew.

"Joan started going into labor last night around eleven. We took her over to the hospital. Lincoln and Zelda were exhausted so I stayed there with her."

"I thought she wasn't due for a couple months yet."

"She's due in six weeks. For a while the doctors weren't sure they'd be able to stop the labor, but they finally got her stabilized around six this morning."

"She and the babies are okay?"

"Yes. They want to keep her at the hospital for a couple of days for observation, and then she'll be on complete bed rest until she delivers." Becka rubbed her neck again. "Jefferson's funeral is scheduled for tomorrow, so it's really going to be rough on her."

"She won't try to go, will she?"

"No. I think she realizes how dangerous it is for the babies. It won't be easy for her, though. I feel so bad. Joan is going through so much and I can't do anything to help."

The sudden droop of Becka's shoulders drained all of the fight from Lee as well. "Why don't you come in have some coffee? I'll fix you something to eat."

"Why would you want to fix me breakfast if you're mad at me?"

"I'm sorry. I was being childish. I know it's silly, but I was hurt that you were leaving without telling me." Lee shrugged as she stared down at the floor where only a few hours ago she and Melinda had rolled around with the dust bunnies. "I'm not mad at you. I'm upset at myself for doing something really stupid. I simply took it out on you."

Becka took a tentative step toward her. "I do care for you,

but there is so much going on in my life right now." She glanced away and then back. "I came to Christmas because I needed time and space to make some decisions about my life. I thought that if I got away from everything I could find a solution. I want to do the right thing." She seemed to be speaking to herself. "It would be easy except doing what I want will adversely affect the lives of several people." She gave Lee a pleading look. "These are people who have supported me, and I care about what happens to them."

She didn't know how to respond, but she did understand everything Becka was saying. Owning the gallery gave her some perspective. She wouldn't be the only person affected if it closed. Did Becka own a business somewhere, or was she referring to a more personal commitment? "You said you weren't with anyone, right?"

"Relationship-wise I'm completely free." She glanced away again. "I don't mean to sound all double-oh-seven on you, but this really isn't something I can talk about yet."

"When you leave on Monday—are you coming back?"

The silence that followed told Lee more than she wanted to know. She looked away.

"I want to," Becka said as she reached out and touched Lee's arm.

A thousand questions raced through Lee's mind, but she muzzled her curiosity and turned toward the kitchen. "Come on in. I'll fix you something to eat."

"I'm not hungry, but I will take a cup of coffee."

Lee started toward the kitchen.

"I never got a chance to tell you so the other night, but I really like your home. I love all the colors from the woven tapestries, blankets and rugs."

Lee stopped and glanced around the living room with its high wood-beamed ceiling. The furniture was cedar and had been crafted by a local artisan. She loved the rich colors in the wood. The blanket on the back of the sofa was a gift from her parents. They had bought it in Peru. Two of the rugs were also the work of a local artisan. The rest she had picked up from various vacations she and Sara had taken. Over the years, she had grown so accustomed to the room that she rarely noticed it anymore.

"I prefer to buy things directly from the artist." She grinned. "Can't imagine why." She pointed to the tapestry that covered the large wall over the fireplace. It was composed of a series of brightly hued geometric designs. "Sara wanted to go to Mexico for her eighteenth birthday. We flew into Mexico City. I had the not-so-brilliant idea of renting a car and traveling around for the two weeks we were there." She glanced at Becka. "My plan was that I would drive through the cities and Sara could handle the smaller towns. That was a huge mistake on my part. I just thought traffic in Houston was bad. In Mexico City the traffic was so bad it scared me even to ride in it much less drive, but Sara, it didn't faze her. The poor thing drove the entire two weeks. Anyway, we went to Oaxaca and I went crazy with all their beautiful work." She started toward the kitchen again. "Sara is so much more practical than I am. She kept trying to warn me that I was buying too much stuff but, of course, I didn't listen. After all, everything fit into the car just fine."

"I suppose it was a different story on the plane," Becka said as she sat down at the kitchen table.

Lee poured another cup of coffee and placed it in front of her. "I'll save myself the embarrassment of telling how much I had to pay for the additional baggage, and that was after I had tossed all my clothes so that I could use that suitcase."

"Was it worth it in the long run?"

"Gosh, yes. I love that piece. I have another one hanging in my bedroom that's a quaint Mexican street scene. It's the first thing I see every morning. The colors are so vibrant that they make me want to grab a paintbrush and start working even before I have my first cup of coffee."

"I'd love to see it sometime."

There was a touch of suggestion in Becka's voice that gave Lee's stomach that feeling of driving over a hilltop too fast. She tried to think of something to say.

Becka saved her. "I saw some of your photographs at the gallery. They're very good."

"Thanks. I actually started out working as a photographer." She gave Becka a short history of her background.

"So painting is your second career?"

"No. Painting is my life. The gallery would be my second career, and I'm trying my best to get rid of that." She stopped. "I should say I'm trying to get rid of most of the responsibility of running the gallery. For the most part, I love talking to the people who come in, especially those who wander in during the off-season. Now, everything is so hectic, most people barely have time to say hi when they come in. I hate dealing with the administrative part of it, the accounts, taxes and all that stuff."

"Is that why you went into partnership with Gladys?"

Lee rubbed her forehead. "Why does it always surprise me? I know how the gossip mill works—heck. I've even found myself becoming a part of it—but still sometimes it floors me at how quickly it works." She sipped her coffee. "Yes, that was part of the reason. Gladys was already doing a large portion of the paperwork. The other thing is that it was simply the right thing to do. She loves the gallery as much as I do and she works just as hard. She deserved more than a salary and a yearly bonus."

"Most people would think you're being overly generous."

"Those people should start their own business and mind it." She smiled to take the sting out of the words, in case Becka was one of those people.

"I think you have a big heart," Becka said, "and there should be more people like you."

Lee shook her head, embarrassed by Becka's words. "Don't mistake my self-centeredness for generosity. My motives are geared toward my own self-interest. I want more time to paint. The fastest way for me to get that was to find a partner and hire another employee who can take care of all those things I hate."

"If you say so, I won't argue. I'll withhold final judgment until I get to know you better." Becka was watching her closely.

"I'd like to get to know you much better." She reached over and placed a hand on Lee's arm. "The last time I was here we were interrupted. Why don't we stop wasting time? Take me to see that beautiful tapestry that hangs in your bedroom."

CHAPTER THIRTY

Lee took a deep breath and told herself to think before she jumped into something she might regret later. She had rushed into marriage and lived to regret it. She was not proud of her hasty move with Melinda yesterday. She didn't want to make the same mistake with Becka. It didn't take a genius to know what would happen once they went into the bedroom. Becka was leaving on Monday and by her own admission didn't know if she would be returning. More than anything Lee wanted to lead Becka into the bedroom and make love to her, but she feared she'd regret it later.

"I guess I was mistaken." Becka stood. "I should be going."

"It's not that I don't want to," Lee said.

"Then what's the problem?"

"I don't want to start something that I suspect has no future. You're leaving and I don't think you're coming back."

"What if I weren't leaving?"

A spark of hope flared in Lee's chest. She looked up at her and the tiny flame sputtered out. "But you are."

Becka hesitated. "If I can get my life in order and move back here to live—"

"Then I'll be more than happy to show you my tapestry."

"If things go as I hope they will, I'll be back in less than two weeks."

"If not?"

"It'll be a long time. Maybe never."

Lee was too stunned to speak and simply nodded.

Becka turned to leave.

Lee tried to resist, but there was some weakness in her and her resolve crumbled. "Don't leave."

Becka stopped and looked back for a long second. "I don't want to be tomorrow's regret."

Lee sat at the table and listened to Becka's footsteps fade across the living room floor. When the door opened and softly closed the house suddenly felt very empty. She stayed at the table and waited. The log walls were much too thick for her to hear the car crank or leave. After several minutes of silence, she got up from the table and cleared away their coffee cups. Then she went to change so that she could go in to the gallery. There would be plenty of work there to keep her too busy to think.

Kellie Thompson and Deanna Velker, the two volunteers Clarissa Jenkins had sent over, seemed surprised when Lee entered. Both were married to men who worked for the forest service.

"How's business today?" Lee asked, already suspecting the worst, judging from the empty parking lot.

"There has only been one man in early this morning, but he bought one of your paintings."

Normally that would have been enough to make Lee's day, but today the news did little to cheer her. "I'll be here the rest of the day and I doubt business will pick up much. So if you two want to go on home it's all right."

"If you don't mind," Deanna said, "we'll stay."

"Yeah, otherwise Clarissa will have us cleaning her storeroom," Kellie piped in.

Deanna quickly added, "That woman gets more things accomplished from October to December each year with volunteer help than she accomplishes the rest of the year."

Lee tried to smile. She had heard how Clarissa liked to keep the volunteers busy. "That's fine. I'll be in the studio if you need me."

"Will you need anyone for tomorrow morning?" Kellie asked.

"No. I'll close the gallery for the funeral. If I decide to open later, I can handle it for the afternoon." Though tomorrow was Saturday, most of the nonessential businesses would close so that the owners and employees could attend Jefferson's funeral that had been scheduled for ten.

"How's your hand?" Deanna asked. "We heard about the shoplifters and the shooting out at your place."

"My hand is fine. It's just a sprain. The cast will be off in a few days."

"It's a good thing you weren't alone," Kellie added.

Lee realized for the first time that the gossip mill must have been having a blast with that little tidbit. She'd never stopped to consider that some people might interpret Becka's being there at that time of night as something other than what it was. She thought about explaining what had really happened but didn't have the energy. In the end, people were going to think whatever they wanted to. She merely mumbled an agreement and went to her studio. Once she had closed the door, she leaned against it. With her hand in a cast, she couldn't paint. She looked around the room for something that would keep her busy. Her gaze settled on the four file cabinets against the back wall. They held the gallery's records, old catalogs and a host of things that Lee had long since forgotten about. Gladys had started hounding her to clean them out two years ago. Instead, Lee had purchased an additional cabinet, but it was full by now. Before she got started, she went to the grocery store and bought a jumbo carton of garbage bags and an assortment of Halloween candy. If she was going to do this, she intended to do it right.

Back in the gallery, she left the candy with the volunteers to pass out. Once back in her studio, she moved the paper shredder next to the file cabinets and started on the oldest files first. When the volunteers left at eight, she locked the door behind them and went back to work. It was nearly eleven before she had the contents of the first cabinet reduced to a mere half a drawer. She hauled the bags one at a time to the trash bin out back. It was slow going since she could only use one hand. By the time she had finished she was exhausted. She swept up the mess she had made before calling it a night and going home.

The house seemed darker and colder than usual. The glass company wasn't due out until Monday to replace her broken windows. When she stepped into her bedroom, she flipped on the bedside lamp. Her gaze fell on the tapestry. She couldn't help but wonder if Becka would ever see it. After a shower in which the plastic wrapped cast seemed more bothersome than usual, she crawled into bed. She tossed and turned for a while and gave up trying to sleep. Instead, she turned on the television and searched through the channels for the most boring thing she could find in hopes it would put her to sleep. She finally found an infomercial that promised to make her a millionaire. All she had to do was buy their amazing book that gave her the seven easy steps to follow. The last thing she remembered hearing was the announcer promising to send her two books for the price of one if she would just order in the next ten minutes.

When Lee opened her eyes the following morning, she found herself staring at the same infomercial. It was as if it had stopped and waited for her to wake up. She still had only ten minutes to place her order and receive the second book free. She turned the television off and went to make coffee.

While the coffee brewed, she grabbed the plastic container

that she kept birdseed in and started out back to fill the feeders and put fresh water in the birdbaths. As she opened the door, she was hit by a blast of cold air. The temperatures had dropped considerably since she'd gotten home the previous night. She hurried back inside, grabbed a jacket from the hall closet and pulled it on. She loved the cooler temperatures. After the first frost, the fall colors would really start to pop. She glanced over to the trees where she had seen Ollie Waters standing a few days ago. Rather than focus on the negative memory she chose to think about how within a week or two, the woods behind her house would glow with brilliant hues of red, orange and yellow.

When she had finished with the feeders and birdbaths, she went back inside and washed up before she fixed herself a bowl of Cheerios. She tried not to think about seeing Becka at the funeral. It was inevitable that they would see each other. Courtesy dictated that Lee stop by the Depew home after the funeral and stay for a while.

When she had finished eating, she took her coffee and headed for the balcony off her studio. On the way, she grabbed a spare blanket to ward off the cooler temperatures. She had gone to the balcony with the intention of watching the birds flock to the feeder, but instead she sat there and thought about Becka.

On Saturday morning the parking lot to the First Baptist Church was packed for the funeral. Lee nodded to several people as she made her way inside. There was already a line of people waiting to approach the coffin and another one to speak to the family. She got in line to speak to the family. As the line moved slowly forward, she searched the pews, but Becka wasn't there. Lee was both relieved and bothered by the fact that she wouldn't have to face Becka. As she gave her condolences to the family members, she noticed that Joan and Granny Depew weren't there either.

Lee returned to the rear of the church to sit as far away from the coffin as she could politely get. The older she got the more she hated attending funerals. After finding a seat, she settled down to wait for the service to begin. Her thoughts quickly turned to Becka. Had she left early? Or perhaps she had stayed with Joan or Granny Depew. Lee wondered if she could possibly skip going to visit the family after the graveside services. Would anyone notice if she wasn't there? Of course they would. Everyone noticed rudeness.

A few minutes later, Dewayne and Gladys came in. Gladys was walking, but she was moving slowly. When Dewayne saw Lee, he started toward her. Gladys seemed to be protesting, but if so, he wasn't listening. He helped her down on the pew beside Lee before he leaned over and said, "Will you please try and talk some sense into her?" He disappeared before she could respond.

When they had spoken the previous morning, Gladys had mentioned that Dewayne was going to be a pallbearer at the funeral, but she hadn't indicated that she would be there. "I didn't know you were coming," Lee said in a hushed tone. "Is that why he's upset?"

"Yes. He thought I should stay home and rest, but I'm sick and tired of resting. I wasn't planning on coming today, but when I woke up this morning I was feeling so much better. I couldn't in good conscience not come."

Lee didn't bother to argue. She knew Gladys well enough to know that once she'd made up her mind it was useless to try to change it.

"Why are you sitting way back here in the sinner's section?" Gladys asked quietly.

"It's where I belong."

When Gladys gave her a questioning look, Lee whispered. "I'll explain later."

The preacher's appearance brought a halt to the respectful whispers. Lee tried to focus on what he said, but she couldn't stop thinking about Becka. She replayed the kiss they had shared that night the front window had been shot out. If they hadn't been interrupted, would she have stopped Becka? She nearly rolled her eyes at the ludicrous thought. Of course she wouldn't have stopped. She tensed when a new thought struck her. What if, in her attempt to curb her tendency to rush into situations, she had overdone it and waited too long? What if Becka never returned? *I should have made love to her yesterday morning.* She squirmed at the thought.

Gladys prodded her with an elbow and gave her a questioning look.

Lee felt her cheeks begin to glow and forced her attention back to the service.

CHAPTER THIRTY-ONE

After the church service, Lee walked slowly outside with Gladys. "You seem to be doing much better," Lee said after they made their way down the steps.

"I'm a little slow, but I get there eventually. Can I ride over to the cemetery with you? Dewayne will be going over with the other pallbearers."

"Sure." Lee's cell rang. She saw Dewayne's name in the display.

"I hate to ask at the last minute, but can you drive Gladys home?" Dewayne asked.

She stepped away a short distance before replying. "Sure, but I don't think that's what she wants."

"I know, but the doctor told her not to stand for long periods of time and you know how stubborn she is."

"All right, but she's not going to be happy."

"I know and I'm really sorry." There was some background noise. "I have to go."

Lee stood staring at the phone for a moment before going back to where Gladys waited by the car.

"Was that Dewayne?" Gladys asked before Lee even had a chance to say anything.

"Yes."

Gladys shook her head. "You don't have to drive me home. You can go on to the cemetery. I'll wait for him here."

For her to give in so easily Lee knew her back must be hurting badly. "Actually, driving you home would sort of be doing me a favor," Lee confessed. When Gladys didn't say anything she continued, "I know it's terrible of me, but I didn't want to go to the cemetery or to the house afterward."

Gladys pulled a set of keys from her purse and handed them to Lee. "I can't climb up into your truck. So you'll have to drive our car."

"How will Dewayne get home?"

Gladys made a small dismissive noise. "The same way I am. He can bum a ride with a friend."

Lee frowned. "Well, how am I going to get back over here for my truck?"

"When Dewayne gets home he can drive you back over here."

Lee helped her in the car before going around to the opposite side. Lee eased the car through the crowd until she reached the street.

"So what's going on?" Gladys demanded as soon as they were out of the crowd.

Lee thought about trying to bluff her way out but knew it would be useless to even try with Gladys. She wanted to tell her about everything that had been going on but couldn't bring herself to talk about her feelings for Becka. How could she tell anyone, when she wasn't even sure herself? Instead, she told her about the spontaneous tryst with Melinda, and then she released a maelstrom of smaller matters that were wearing on her nerves.

She told her about the frustration with not seeing the buck again and not being able to finish the painting, or any painting, thanks to the cast on her wrist. She talked about how much the damage to her house had upset her, and how she was afraid it would never be the same again. She even told her about Brandon and her parents coming for Thanksgiving dinner. By the time she had poured it all out, they were approaching Dewayne and Gladys's house.

Gladys made a small clucking noise. "Girl, I think we'd better wait until we get inside the house before we continue on with this conversation. This is going to take a slice of cheesecake and maybe even a little chocolate sauce for me to get through all that misery."

As soon as they were inside, Gladys eased herself down into a straight-backed chair at the kitchen table while Lee collected plates, forks and a knife.

Once they were settled and both happily munching on the creamy cheesecake, Gladys finally began to respond. "What are you going to do about this mess with Melinda?"

Lee swallowed. "Nothing. Thankfully, I won't have to since she's gone. She picked up her things at the gallery before she even came out to talk to me. She told me she would send me her new address and I could forward the check to her. So, I don't have to worry about seeing her, because she left already."

Gladys shook her head. "No, she hasn't. Or at least she hadn't left as of around nine thirty this morning. Dewayne and I drove by her house on the way over to the church. She was in her front yard pruning that big old rosebush that's growing along the fence."

The cheesecake stuck in Lee's throat. She coughed. "My God, you don't think she decided to stay here." The thought of running into Melinda at the grocery store or on the street made her cringe.

Gladys shrugged. "Maybe she's hoping for another slow dance with you." She started to chuckle until she looked up and saw Lee scowling at her. "I don't know what she has planned, but you need to get this right in your head. If she is staying, you can't dodge her forever. Even if she leaves, you can't walk around regretting it for the rest of your life."

"Why not? I do regret it."

"I can't believe you. Sometimes you remind me of a prissy old maid."

The comment hurt Lee's feelings.

"Don't look at me like that," Gladys said. "You know I love you like a sister, but why are you beating yourself up over a little roll in the hay, or the floor, in your case? You're both consenting adults. I don't see what the big deal is."

"The big deal is I don't like Melinda in that way," Lee said, struggling to keep from raising her voice.

"So you don't love her. The important question should be did you enjoy it? Did she?"

Lee felt herself blushing.

"Ah," Gladys said and pointed at her with her fork. "Look at you go all red. So, at least one of you enjoyed it." She went back to work on the cake. "I think you ought to go over to the gallery, tally up what you owe her and take the check over to her."

Lee nearly dropped her fork. "Are you crazy? She'll think I'm there for another round."

Gladys looked up. "I take it you're not interested in a second go-round. Although with the mood you're in, I don't think it would hurt you any."

Lee glared at her.

"There's no need for those eye-daggers. A simple no would suffice."

"No," Lee replied forcefully.

"If she makes a move for you, just tell her you're not interested. Tell her the other time was a mistake, but now that you've gotten your rocks off—"

"Gladys!"

"All right. I'm sorry. I forgot who I was talking to there for a moment." She set her empty plate aside. "Truthfully, she's probably no more interested in another round with you than you

211

are with her."

"What do you mean by that?" Lee couldn't keep the indignation out of her voice.

"Relax. I didn't mean anything. It's just that Melinda Thayer never struck me as the roll-around-on-the-floor type."

Lee put her plate down in a huff. "Oh, yeah? Exactly what type do you think she is?"

"Oh, I don't know. A nice dinner with good wine, soft music, candlelight—"

"That's what Becka likes." Lee clamped a hand over her mouth.

Gladys held out her plate. "I'm going to need a little bit more sugar."

Lee gathered their plates and went to the counter to get Gladys another slice of cheesecake. She'd had enough sugar for a while. She took her time and tried to think of a way to avoid telling Gladys all that had and hadn't happened between her and Becka.

"I know you're stalling," Gladys said.

Lee kept her head turned away and made a face.

"You can stall all day, but eventually I'll hear the whole story."

Defeated, Lee grabbed her own plate and added a slice of cheesecake. If she got lucky maybe she would die of a sugar overdose and not have to tell Gladys everything.

CHAPTER THIRTY-TWO

Gladys waited patiently as Lee ran through a recap of the entire list of her recent woes and troubles. She would occasionally comment or offer suggestions, but she never pushed Lee to discuss Becka. By the time Lee had finished with her litany, Gladys had finished most of the second slice of cheescake. She was moving a piece of the crust around with her fork. Gladys didn't push until it became obvious that Lee had run out of things to talk about.

"We've danced all around the room to avoid the subject, so are you ready to tell me what's really bothering you?"

Lee gave Gladys a wry look. "You think you know me so well, don't you?"

Gladys raised her eyebrows.

"All right, so maybe you do." Lee took a deep breath to gather time to organize her thoughts. "I'm not sure I know where to start."

"The beginning would probably be nice, but please try to start at some point after the Immaculate Conception."

"I guess it actually started the first day I saw her in the clearing. There was something so…so distressing about the way she was crying—as though she were completely alone in the world. I found myself thinking about her for days."

"I don't see anything unusual about you thinking about her. Anybody would."

Lee nodded. "I agree, but somewhere along the way I stopped thinking about her crying and started thinking about her. Then when she appeared at the gallery, I found myself wanting to get to know her."

"She's not interested?"

Lee leaned her elbow on the chair arm and rested her head on her hand. "No. She's definitely interested. I'm the one who's balking."

Gladys released a long-suffering sigh. "I'm sorry, but I'm confused. You're interested in her. She's interested in you. So what's the problem? After that little escapade with Melinda I know you remember what to do."

Lee sat upright and tried to ignore Gladys's sarcasm. "I don't want to jump into something that I'll regret later. I rushed into marriage with Brandon and look what happened. I came out here on vacation and a month later, I was making arrangements to move. I went to Mexico and bought more—"

Gladys held up both hands and waved them. "Whoa. Stop right there. First, I don't know where you're getting this idea that you're impulsive. You and Brandon had been dating for quite a while. True, when you had that episode with what's-her-name, you sped things up a bit, but you would probably have married him eventually anyway." She looked at Lee for confirmation. When Lee nodded, she continued, "Without that period of Brandon in your life, you would never have had Sara."

Again, Lee nodded.

"Your decision to move here may have been made rather quickly, but that's a matter of knowing when something is right

214

for you, not impulse. As for Mexico—" She waved her hand in exasperation. "Girl, the economies of the world would collapse without impulsive buys. You love what you bought. You don't buy and then hide it away in boxes. So, don't sweat the little stuff."

Lee pondered the comment. "I'd never thought about it that way."

Gladys leaned forward slowly and removed the small pillow that was behind her. "If you don't mind my saying so, I think you're looking for excuses." She placed the pillow on her lap.

Lee's brows pulled together.

"Don't start looking all mean at me." Gladys eased back in her chair. "You came in here looking for my opinion and I'm going to give it."

Lee wanted to make a catty remark about not being able to stop Gladys from giving her opinion, but she thought better of it.

"When I saw you two together the other day, I knew then that something was there." Gladys shook her head. "I have to tell you that I was pretty disappointed in you when I saw that both of those bedrooms back there had been used."

Lee's face burned. "I couldn't have made…done anything here in your house."

"Excuses," Gladys hissed. "You keep making them. I think you're scared."

"I am not."

"Yes, you are."

"No, I'm not." Lee nearly stomped her foot.

"You're about to pout and stomp your foot," Gladys said as she pointed her finger to Lee's foot.

Lee laughed. "I really do hate you."

"No, you don't. You love me, because you know I'll never lie to you, even when you want me to."

"All right, great sage of Arkansas. What do I do now?"

"You'll probably go home and hide in that old blind of yours. Becka will leave and whether she comes back or not, you'll never know what might have been." Gladys's voice softened slightly.

215

"Sometimes you just have to take a chance. It's possible she'll leave and break your heart. You have to ask yourself what will hurt the most when you look back on this in ten years—knowing that you tried and it didn't work out, or that you never did anything and will never know what might have been?"

"She's leaving on Monday."

"That gives you the rest of today and all day tomorrow to show her what she'll be missing." Gladys grinned.

Lee nodded and smiled until a new thought hit her. "What'll I do if I decide it's not right?"

Without warning, Gladys threw the pillow at her. "Why don't we just sit here and worry about one of those big old meteorites falling out of the sky and landing on our heads?" She made a shooing motion with her hand. "You can take the car back out to the church. Lock the keys inside it. He has his set."

Lee hopped up and handed the pillow back to Gladys before giving her a quick kiss on the cheek.

"Don't worry about the gallery," Gladys called as Lee headed toward the door. "I'm sick and tired of sitting around here anyway."

Lee stopped and turned back toward her. "Are you sure you're able to go in?"

"What difference will it make where I sit? My butt gets just as tired here as it will there. I'll let Clarissa's volunteers do any lifting."

"I guess you know better than anyone else about how you feel."

Gladys nodded. "Amen to that. Now go on and I don't want to see you again until Monday."

Lee saluted and grabbed the keys.

After a quick stop by the gallery, Lee drove toward her first destination. Gladys was right. It was time to clear the air. She tried to think of something to say as she drove, but everything seemed trite.

Melinda was painting the wooden gate when Lee stopped in front of her house. Lee saw the look of surprise in her eyes when she recognized her visitor.

"Hi," Lee said as she stepped out of the car and started toward her. Country music wailed from a radio on the porch. "I heard you were still around, so I thought I'd bring your check over." She pulled it from her pocket and handed it to her.

"Hi." Melinda's hands were spattered with paint. She took the check by the corner and slipped it into her shirt pocket. She looked as if she wanted to run. For the first time, Lee realized that perhaps Melinda wasn't as confident as she pretended to be. Somehow, that gave her more courage.

"I wanted to say I'm sorry about what happened out at the house. I don't know why I…" She groped for a word.

Melinda put the brush down and wiped her hands on a paint-smeared rag. "I'll admit you shocked me," she said with a small smile, "but please don't say you're sorry." She motioned toward the fence. "I meant it when I said I'm leaving. I just wanted to spruce the place up a bit before I left." She stared at her hands as she continued to wipe the paint from them. "I've had such a crush on you—"

"Please don't say that," Lee interrupted. "I feel bad enough as it is."

"Don't. You ignoring me made me reevaluate a few things. My ex called and wanted to try again. I kept putting her off because of my feelings for you."

Lee covered her eyes with her hand for moment. "God, you came out to the house to tell me you were leaving to go back to your ex and then I acted the way I did."

"Sort of ironic, isn't it? If you had acted a day earlier, I would have told Rita no."

"That would have been a mistake," Lee said.

"I know that now, but at the time all I could think about was jumping on you." She looked up and grinned. "You're pretty hot, you know. The way you just—"

Lee's hand shot out. "Stop. Just stop. Promise me if we should ever bump into each other, you won't ever mention that episode again."

Melinda nodded. "I promise."

"Thanks." Lee glanced toward the car. "I guess I should get going. I hope things go well for you and Rita."

"Thanks. So are you actively pursuing Becka James or just looking?"

Lee stopped sharply. "Was I that obvious?"

Melinda nodded. "I'm afraid so."

"I don't know what I'm going to do about that."

Melinda stuffed the rag back into her pocket. "I sure wish I could remember where I've met her."

"I thought that was one of your pickup lines."

"Please. I'm more original than that."

Lee waved. "I have to go. Good luck."

When she drove away from Melinda's house, she felt as though a weight had been lifted from her shoulders. As usual, Gladys had been right. She hoped she was as right about Becka. As she made her way out of town through the side streets, her confidence began to fade. What if Becka wasn't interested now? What if she didn't return to the old Peterson place tonight? After all, she would probably be helping out at the Depew home. Lee rubbed her forehead. Becka had buried a family member today, albeit a distant one, but still they seemed close enough. How could she just show up and throw herself at Becka?

By the time she finally pulled into the church parking lot, Lee had worked herself into a frenzy of doubt. This simply wasn't going to work. In all their talking, she and Gladys hadn't taken Jefferson's funeral into consideration. She glanced guiltily at the church before locking the keys inside the car and going to her truck. As she drove away, she wondered what she was going to tell Gladys on Monday morning.

CHAPTER THIRTY-THREE

When Lee arrived home, she changed clothes and went in search of her pruning saw. She needed to trim some of the limbs inside the blind. The chill in the air prompted her to find a heavier coat to wear under her photography vest. The extra material felt too bulky, so rather than wear the coat, she tied it to her backpack and wore the lighter jacket that she usually used.

As she made her way toward the blind, she tried not to think about how disgusted Gladys was going to be with her. Some things just weren't meant to be, she told herself. She forced her thoughts away from Becka and started making plans for Thanksgiving dinner. If her parents arrived before Thanksgiving Day, she wouldn't have to worry about anything other than having the pantry fully stocked. Her mother would take over the cooking, which was perfectly all right with her. She made a mental note to call her dad when she got home and get him to make a firm commitment on when they would be arriving. Then she could start talking to her mother about what she needed for the meal. She also needed to get a firm commitment from Sara as to when Brandon would be arriving and leaving.

By the time she arrived at the clearing, she was feeling better about her decision. She did her usual inspection of the blind before crawling inside with the pruners. At first, she was concerned that the effort of working the tool would hurt her wrist, but there wasn't even a slight twinge when she made the first tentative cut. Her wrist felt fine. The secret to the blind's effectiveness was to keep it looking as natural as possible on the outside while making it as comfortable as she could inside. As she trimmed and rewove the vines, she found herself humming. It was the first day of November. The first month of the holiday season was over. Until the previous two days, business at the gallery had been better than expected. Business would pick up again after Halloween. It always did. Someone suitable would apply for the position at the gallery. She simply had to be patient and remember that things moved slower here. Her house would soon be back to normal. Gladys was coming back to work and the cast would be removed from her wrist in a few days. In no time, all this stuff would be behind her and her life would once more fall back into its normal comfortable routine.

"What are you doing?"

Lee gave a small squeal of fright and nearly fell when Becka's head suddenly popped through the blind's doorway. "You scared the crap out of me," Lee snapped.

"I'm sorry. I heard all this rustling and thought it was a bear until I heard you humming." She looked around. "What is this?"

Lee wiped the back of her hand across her forehead. The tight weave of the blind served to make it warmer. That, combined with the physical exertion and the jacket, had caused her to work up a sweat. "It's my photography blind."

"May I come in?"

"Sure." Lee stepped to the side and hooked the pruners over

a limb.

Becka eased her way in and looked around. "It's much bigger than I thought." She turned. "So, you hide in here and photograph animals."

Lee nodded and leaned down. She carefully pushed her hand through leaves. "I set up the camera on a tripod and then slip the lens through slots like this."

Becka smiled. "This is ingenious." She knelt down and peeked through the leaves where Lee had placed her hand a moment before. "You can sit here and not—" She stopped.

"What's wrong? Is something out there?" Lee's first thought was of the buck.

"How often do you come here?" There was a different tone in Becka's voice.

Lee suddenly realized that by looking out where she had, Becka had a clear view of the rocks along the stream. The same rocks she had sat on and cried. She didn't know whether it would be kinder to pretend as though she hadn't seen Becka or to confess now. Her indecision took the choice from her.

"You were in here that morning, weren't you?" Becka asked softly.

Lee crossed her legs and sat down Indian-style. "Yes. I know I should have said something, but you took me by surprise and then it was too late." She shrugged. "I couldn't just step out and say hello, and I knew you'd hear me if I tried to leave. I thought I was doing the right thing."

Becka sat down also. "You must have thought I was a lunatic."

"No. I wondered what tragedy could have happened to break the heart of such a beautiful woman."

Becka shook her head. "Don't say that."

"Why not? It's true."

Becka picked up a twig and rolled it between her fingers.

When she didn't say anything, Lee decided to change the subject. "I thought you'd be at the Depews' house."

"I was there this morning. Joan was released from the

hospital, so I picked her up and took her over there. After the services, people started pouring in. It got to be too much so I went on home." She hesitated a moment. "Joan and Annabelle are thinking about moving into the old place."

A cold hand of dread gripped Lee's stomach. "So you aren't coming back?"

Becka met her gaze. "I honestly don't know." She looked down. "We're just trying to help Joan. She and Jefferson were renting that little house they lived in and she simply can't afford it anymore. Annabelle has been talking about moving for several months now. I'm not sure she will, though. She lives with her mom still and, frankly, I think she's afraid to try to strike out on her own. If she did, this would work out perfectly for both of them. The house is more than big enough for each of them to have their own space. Annabelle could be there to help Joan with the babies and they can share expenses."

"What happens if you decide to come back?"

Becka tilted her head slightly and smiled. "Lee, that's not the only empty house in town."

Lee flushed. "I know that."

"You'll be happy to know," Becka continued, "that I had the electricity turned on and a crew is coming in on Monday to start fixing the old place up. Uncle Walter's kids don't want to move back here, but they don't want to sell the place either, so we worked out a deal that will allow Annabelle and Joan to live there."

"I'm glad. It's a beautiful home and deserves to be taken care of."

"I should have turned the electricity on sooner. It was silly of me to live like that." Becka glanced at Lee again. "You must have thought I was a basket case."

"At first, it may have crossed my mind to wonder if you were one of those back-to-nature types, but we all have our little quirks."

Becka pushed herself up. "I should go so you can get back to work."

Lee stood and took Becka into her arms. "Don't go yet. I want to give you something first." Without waiting, she gently kissed Becka's full lips. When there was no protest, the kiss grew more intense. Arms slipped around Lee's neck and nothing had ever seemed more right. There was none of the frantic urgency she'd felt with Melinda. Instead, a simple choreography of soft touches and whispered words passed between them. As passions intensified, articles of clothing dropped to the ground. Lee's world narrowed into a pulsing tunnel of desire. She wanted to please and be pleased—to feel warm breasts in her hand, hardened nipples between her fingers and then her lips. She marveled at the softness of skin beneath her hand as it glided over Becka's body. Their discarded clothes made a thin barrier of protection from the ground, but neither of them seemed to notice anything other than the feel of their naked bodies pressed together. Lee stared down into Becka's eyes as their bodies molded together and settled into a synchronized rocking motion. As their passions intensified, so did their movements. When Lee was sure she couldn't wait much longer, she slipped her good hand between them and skillfully stroked Becka's wetness until the peaceful clearing filled with their cries of pleasure. Afterward, neither of them moved for a long moment, but Lee soon felt her need building.

"Do that again," Becka whispered, providing the small spark needed for Lee's passion to fully ignite.

She kissed Becka and started the slow rocking motion again. This time rather that slipping her hand between them, she slowly inched her way down Becka's body and let her tongue carry Becka over the edge.

Darkness dropped over the forest. With it came the chilly night air, but it didn't cool their need. Lee removed the coat tied to her backpack and covered them. They talked and made love deep into the night.

When the morning sun painted its first subtle rays of light, Lee opened her eyes and eased herself to her elbow. She found it nearly impossible to believe she could feel such happiness. As she stared down into Becka's sleeping face she felt a bittersweet pain deep inside and for the first time in her life, she truly understood what the lyrics to all those sappy love songs meant. She fought back tears brought on by the multitude of emotions surging through her. This sense of rightness and emotional homecoming was what she had been blindly searching for all those years.

Beyond the woven limbs of the shelter, birds began to sing their assorted melodies, waking the world to a new day. Lee knew she would forever think of their melody as Becka's song.

CHAPTER THIRTY-FOUR

Becka opened her eyes and smiled. "I should have known you were a morning person," she said sleepily as she ran her hand over Lee's cheek. "How long have you been awake?"

"Just a few minutes." Lee traced a fingertip along Becka's chin. "I like watching you sleep. I used to watch Sara sleep when she was a newborn." She stretched out alongside Becka. "I was terrified she'd stop breathing if I wasn't watching."

Becka squeezed her hand. "I promise I won't stop breathing while you're not watching." She sat up and looked around. "I never mentioned it, but I was pretty embarrassed when you came over to the house and had to use that bucket of water to flush the commode. Now here I am with you and you don't even have a bucket."

Lee squirmed. "I sure wish you hadn't mentioned that. I was doing fine until you spoke up."

"Sorry."

"I guess it's time to see just how good your pioneering skills are." Lee reached for her pack.

"What are you doing?"

Lee held up a plastic bag holding a roll of toilet paper. "We won't have it quite as rustic as the pioneers."

Becka's eyes widened. "I can't pee behind a tree."

Lee started gathering her clothes. "Then you'd better start walking fast, because it's quite a hike to my house and even farther to your place."

"How far away is your house?"

"About a mile," Lee said as she pulled on her jeans and top.

"I can't wait that long."

The look on Becka's face made Lee laugh. "Then you'd better find yourself a tree." Lee scooted out of the blind. "Just make sure you don't squat over any poison ivy."

Becka scrambled after her, wriggling into her clothes as she went. "Wait a minute," she hissed. "I wouldn't know poison ivy if it bit me on the ass."

"I thought you grew up in the country." Lee grabbed her hands and led her away from the blind.

"I did, but it was civilized country."

"What the heck is civilized country?"

"Well, for one thing we didn't have poison ivy growing around us," Becka said as she looked at each plant skeptically. "Or maybe we did and I just never knew it."

Lee chose a large pine tree where the pine needles had smothered back most of the undergrowth. She pulled off a stretch of toilet paper before handing the roll to Becka. "You take this side of the tree, and I'll use the other."

A few seconds later, Lee heard a sharp hiss and then a deep sigh of relief. "I sure hope no one else has a blind out here," she said and clamped her lips together to keep from laughing out loud as she heard Becka's curse followed by a hurried rustle of clothing.

After burying the toilet paper beneath the loose soil, they

raced back toward the blind, laughing like schoolgirls when they stopped at the stream to wash their hands.

With her good hand, Lee splashed her face with the icy water. "Gosh, that's cold." She shivered. "Let's go back to the house and I'll make breakfast."

"Yum. Waffles would be good."

Lee shook her head. "My cooking abilities are limited to bare survival skills."

"Why does that not surprise me?"

"I suppose you know how to make waffles?" Lee asked as they walked back toward the blind hand in hand.

"I can make any kind of waffles you want," Becka bragged.

"Good. I like blueberry. I happen to have a jar of canned blueberries that I bought at the fair and a waffle iron that someone gave me." She thought for a moment. "I think I even know where it's hidden."

Becka squinted up at her. "Why do I get the feeling you just put one over on me?"

Lee stopped and pulled Becka to her and kissed her. "I want to make love to you again," she said as she teased Becka's earlobe with her tongue. "How hungry are you?"

Becka pulled Lee closer to her and rocked her hips against her. "I'm starving for what you're offering." They stumbled back to the blind and started discarding clothes.

They eventually made their way back to the house. Pieces of crushed leaves and smears of dirt covered their clothes. After they showered, Lee found a pair of Sara's sweatpants and a pullover for Becka to change into and tossed their dirty clothes into the washer while Becka made waffles.

After breakfast, they took their coffee to the studio balcony. As they passed through the studio, they didn't talk about the frightening few minutes when they had last been there together. Instead, they sat on the balcony, held hands and simply enjoyed each other's company. When the chilly wind finally drove them back inside, Becka looked over Lee's paintings and admired her work. As they moved around the room, their touches grew more urgent.

"I believe you have a tapestry you promised to show me," Becka said.

Lee led her down the hallway to her bedroom. They barely made it into the room before clothes started dropping. It would be a while before Becka noticed the tapestry.

There were times throughout the day as they lounged on Lee's bed when she would be painfully aware of how quickly time was slipping away. She told herself to focus on the present and to not waste the precious few hours they had left worrying about what might happen. There seemed to be an unspoken understanding between them that neither would ask questions. For this one day, they would live in the moment. As the day gave way to night, they both seemed content to simply lie on the bed and hold each other. That's how they fell asleep.

When Lee's eyes opened, the sun was already up. She glanced at the clock.

"What time is it?" Becka asked sleepily.

"It's a little after eight."

The way Becka suddenly snuggled her head against Lee's chest and wrapped her arms around her tightly told Lee they didn't have much time. Her stomach felt as though she had swallowed lead weights.

"What time do you have to leave for the gallery?"

Lee ran her hand over Becka's hair. "Gladys and Betty will be there, so I don't have to go." She desperately wanted to ask when Becka had to leave, but at the same time she didn't want to know.

Becka pulled back and gazed at her. "I want you to make me a promise."

Not sure she could trust her voice, Lee nodded.

"No matter what happens, I don't want you to be sad."

Lee blinked back tears.

Becka reached up and cupped Lee's face in her hands. "Please don't cry. If you do I'll never be able to walk away."

"So stay."

"I wish I could, but I've put this off long enough."

"Is there anything I can do to help?"

Becka smiled softly. "You've already done more than you'll ever know."

"Are you coming back?"

Becka hesitated. "If I don't, it won't be because I don't want to."

"Why can't you tell me what's going on? Maybe I could help you."

Becka sat up and leaned over on one arm. "This won't make much sense now, but I need to know that what's between us is real." She seemed to be searching for words. "I want you to know me as I am. I want you to know Becka James."

Lee frowned. "You make it sound like you're someone else as well."

Becka leaned down and kissed Lee before she sat up and swung her feet off the bed. "I'm sorry, but I need to leave." The clothes that Lee had washed for her were lying on a chair across the room. She picked them up and began to dress.

Lee wanted to reach out and stop her. "I'll fix some breakfast." She started to get up.

Becka came over and stopped her. "Please don't get up. I want to remember you lying here, not standing in the doorway watching me leave."

"You can't walk all the way home. I'll drive you."

Becka shook her head. "No. I called Annabelle last night while you were sleeping. She's going to pick me up in a few minutes." She quickly dressed.

Lee had never felt so helpless in her life, not even when she was trying to get away from the shooter.

As soon as Becka was dressed, she came back and sat on the side of the bed. "I know this is hard to understand, but I can't call you or contact you after I leave." She took Lee's hand. "If things go as I hope they will, I'll be back in two weeks."

"If not?"

Becka shook her head. There was a deep sadness in her eyes that Lee had not seen before. "Let's not think about that." She stared into Lee's eyes for a long moment. "There are so many things I want to say to you." She kissed her suddenly before rushing out of the room.

Lee listened to her footsteps running down the stairs. As soon as the front door opened, Lee jumped out of bed and ran to the front window that looked down over her front yard. Becka was running toward the road. Lee watched until Becka reached the end of the driveway. When she stopped to look back, Lee stepped away from the window. She would keep part of her promise.

She pulled on her robe and went to the kitchen to make coffee, but as she stood in front of the sink filling the carafe, she suddenly poured it out and headed back upstairs. She couldn't stand being in the house alone. After a quick shower, she put on one of the Victorian era suits. There was plenty of work at the gallery to keep her busy and help get her through the next two weeks. She didn't want to think about what she would do if Becka didn't return after those two weeks.

CHAPTER THIRTY-FIVE

Two weeks. Fourteen days. Three hundred and thirty-six hours. Twenty thousand one hundred and sixty minutes. One million two hundred and nine thousand, six hundred seconds.

Lee pushed the calculator away and stared at the wall. When she had arrived at the gallery, Gladys and Betty were sitting at the counter chatting. Lee made an excuse about needing to prepare a print order and escaped to her studio. She had seen the questioning look in Gladys's eyes.

Lee started to sort through the papers in the second file cabinet. She appreciated the fact that Gladys waited over an hour before she came back to the studio.

"I take it things didn't go as planned," Gladys said as she closed the door and took a seat in the desk chair.

"No. It went exactly as planned," Lee replied. "We had a wonderful day yesterday, and then she left this morning."

"Is she coming back?" Gladys asked.

Lee swiveled the stool she was sitting on around to face her. "She didn't know." She told Gladys what Becka had said, being careful to leave out the more intimate details.

Gladys tapped her fingernails on the desk. "What do you suppose she meant when she said she wanted you to know the real Becka James?"

"I don't know. Maybe it's not her real name. Or she isn't the same person with everybody." Lee slammed the cabinet drawer shut. "Hell, maybe she just wanted to get away."

"Come on," Gladys chided. "Did she ever give you the impression that she was only after fun and games?"

"No."

"If it's meant to be, she'll be back."

"Next you'll be dishing out that old adage about if you love something you let it go," Lee scoffed.

"You do," Gladys said. "But, I also adhere to the belief that if it doesn't come back, you hunt it down and wallop the crap out of it." She stood slowly. "Don't worry. I think she'll be back."

"For once, I hope you're right."

"When are you going to learn that I'm always right?" She pointed to the file cabinet. "Now, get back to work. I intend to milk this lovesick puppy stage you're going through to the fullest. As soon as you finish those file cabinets, you need to get started on the storeroom."

"Your compassion overwhelms me."

"If you want compassion find yourself a priest. Now get back to your shredding." She stopped at the door. "Why don't you come by the house for supper? Dewayne is off today and is barbecuing ribs."

Lee nodded, again not trusting her voice. She had a feeling that despite her friend's bluster, she'd be seeing a lot of Gladys and Dewayne over the next two weeks.

True to her word, Gladys kept Lee busy over the next few days. Lee kept working on the jobs she'd been putting off forever, even after Dr. Lyman removed the cast. For the first time in many years, she felt no desire to work on a painting. Once the storeroom was cleared out, Gladys convinced Lee it needed to be painted. She was on a ladder painting the ceiling the day Gladys strolled in with Ollie Waters.

Gladys gave her one of those I don't know what he wants looks.

Lee had heard that he'd been released from the hospital a few days earlier, but she hadn't seen him around. She stepped down from the ladder.

"I 'spect you got a few questions as to why I was snoopin' about your place," he said without preamble.

"I assumed you were back there hunting," she replied.

"Nope. That weren't it at all. You see, I'd seen that there gal and her fellar when they busted into her daddy's huntin' place."

"I didn't realize it was his daughter." She motioned to the pot. "Would you like a cup of coffee?"

"Nope. Don't have the time. I'm on my way to Little Rock. One of 'em Federal guys is goin' pick me up. They want me to testify 'ginst 'em two." He scratched his chin, which was for once shaved. "You see, after I seen 'em bustin' into that cabin, I figured they were up to no good, so I started watchin' 'em. 'Course, I didn't know she was his daughter then. Sheriff told me that this mornin'." He shook his head. "I'd been follerin' and watchin' 'em, but I guess I ain't as young as I thought, 'cause I fell asleep." Tears glittered in his eyes. "That's when they shot Jefferson." He shook his head again. "I shoulda been there to stop 'em."

She wanted to ask him why he hadn't called the sheriff, but she knew that some of the folks of Ollie's generation, who had grown up in what was then isolated mountains, lived by a different set of rules. She remained silent as he continued.

"That mornin' when you seen me, I'd follered that fellar when he cut across your property back there." He shuffled his feet. "I know you ain't got no use for me and all, but I wasn't goin' to let him hurt you none."

Lee was touched by his admission. "Ollie, I thought you

didn't like me because I'm a lesbian."

His face turned crimson. "I ain't got no use for such myself, but I figure a fellar's entitled to float whichever way the wind blows him…or her," he added quickly.

Lee walked over to him. "In that case, I'd be more than happy to call you my friend." She extended her hand. "And thank you for looking out for me." She realized that must have been why he looked so haggard when she saw him at the Depews' house. He had been out following them.

His shook her hand quickly and tucked his head. "I'm right sorry I wasn't more careful of that there little gal. I misjudged her. She was the mean one." He shook his head. "Still don't seem possible that she got the drop on me like that." He looked up at her. "There I was a watchin' him and that little wildcat snuck up on me and shot me."

"Well, I'm glad her aim wasn't any better."

He chuckled. "Hell, her aim was fine." He reached into his coat pocket and pulled out a plastic bag that held a mangled pocket watch. "See that there?" He pointed at the center of the distorted mess. "The bullet hit that, ricocheted off and tore through my side. Otherwise, she would've hit me right in this old ticker." He punched the area over his heart. "But she wasn't as wily as I am, 'cause I got away from her."

Before Lee could respond, Gladys stuck her head in the door. "Ollie, there's a woman out front asking for you."

He winked at Lee. "I was hopin' they'd send that cute FBI gal over to pick me up." He turned to leave.

"Ollie, thanks again for your help."

He waved her off. "Weren't nothin'." He stopped short and glanced back. "If'n you wanna get a picture of that buck, though, you ought to spread out some corn down there. That's what that gal and fellar were doin'." He took off before she could say anything.

She thought about the day when she'd thought she heard something in the woods. Had it been Ollie? She hadn't gone back to the blind since Becka left. It held too many memories. She made a mental note to not go slipping off behind a tree to relieve herself anymore. Now that Ollie knew where the blind was there was nothing to prevent him from wandering over there again. Thoughts of Becka started creeping in again, so she grabbed the brush and went back to work.

Lee worked each day until she was too exhausted to think about Becka. It was only in the wee hours of the morning when she'd wake up and stare into the darkness that the loneliness would broadside her.

The house windows had been replaced and it was impossible to tell that anything had ever occurred with them. She tried to paint at both the house and gallery but couldn't get her mind to settle down enough to concentrate.

As the end of the second week drew near, Lee found herself growing more and more anxious. She had even driven out to the old Peterson place and had been surprised to find it empty. After a little snooping, she discovered that Joan had moved to Mena to live with her parents.

She supposed Annabelle had changed her mind also, or maybe she couldn't afford to move without Joan's financial help. She thought about calling Granny Depew on the pretext of seeing if Annabelle was still interested in the job, but she knew she couldn't call without asking about Becka and she had promised not to do that.

Later that same day, Clarissa Jenkins' niece Rachel McCormick came in to fill out an application and they hired her on the spot. She was a natural with people and fit in well at the gallery.

With Rachel available to help Gladys, Lee took off early on Friday and turned her attention to getting her house ready for her parents and Sara. She had finally gotten her father to commit to arriving on the Tuesday before Thanksgiving. Sara was due to arrive on the Sunday before Thanksgiving.

She spent the rest of Friday cleaning her house and sprucing up the yard. On Saturday, she went shopping for Sara's favorite foods. On Sunday, she paced the floor until she saw her daughter's lime-green Beetle pull into the driveway. Lee could hear Sara's music even before she stepped off the porch. Thankfully, it died when the engine did. She met Sara on the walkway and enveloped her in a hug.

"Mom," Sara mumbled, "you're choking me."

"Sorry." Lee stepped back and took Sara's bag. "I've missed you, kiddo."

Sara smiled up at her. "Have you missed me enough to let me stay?"

"You know you can stay as long as you like—"

"—as soon as I graduate." Sara rolled her eyes.

They went inside. "Are you hungry?" It was a silly question, because her daughter was always hungry. Lee looked at her skinny frame and wondered how she managed to stay so slim.

"I'm starved."

"There are cold cuts in the fridge. Make yourself a sandwich. I've got a pot roast in the oven for dinner."

She carried Sara's suitcase to her room at the back of the house. Sara flipped on the radio as soon as she stepped into the room. Lee knew from previous experience it would be on constantly until Sara left.

"So have you been bored here without me?" Sara asked as she went back into the kitchen and made an enormous sandwich.

"Not exactly." Lee had been intending to wait until her parents arrived and only tell the story of the past few weeks once, but she didn't want Sara hearing about it in town. She highlighted what had happened, being careful to gloss over the worst parts. Still, by the time she had finished, Sara's face had paled.

"Mom, why didn't you call me?"

Lee tried to make light of the situation. "Everything happened so quickly that there wasn't time for me to get concerned about anything," she replied casually. "Really, it was over before it even began."

"Some maniac shot out three of your windows and you weren't worried?" Before Lee could respond, Sara rushed on. "Who is this Becka woman and why was she here so late at night?" She gave Lee a little smile.

"Stop that," Lee warned. She went on to explain the problem with the medication and how she hadn't been able to drive.

Rather than push the sandwich away, as Lee would've done when upset, Sara started chowing down on it. "Granny is going to crap when she hears about this," she said when she'd finished it.

"Your grandmother will box your ears if she hears you calling her Granny. Where did that come from anyway? You've always called her Grams."

"Everyone around here calls their grandparents granny or grandpa."

Lee tried not to laugh, but she kept picturing her mother. She would have a conniption if Sara called her Granny. "Sweetie, you need to remember my parents aren't from around here, so it's probably best if you stick with Grams and Granddad."

"All right. I will." She grinned and added, "Maybe I'll try it once."

Lee loved her daughter's feisty spirit. "All right, but I'm warning you that you'd better not be within arm's reach of Mom when you do."

"You never did tell me who this Becka is," Sara said.

"She was just a woman who was staying over at the old Peterson place for a while. She's gone now."

"That makes you sad."

Lee looked up sharply. The compassion on Sara's face was her undoing. All this time she had managed to get through without the tears that were now flowing down her cheeks.

Sara jumped up and went over to hug her. "I'm sorry. I didn't mean to upset you." The concern in her voice touched Lee's heart.

"You didn't." She tried to stop the tears but once they had gotten started, it seemed as if there was no shutoff. When she finally got herself under control, she tried to laugh it off. "Don't look so worried. I think I'm going through early menopause."

"Mom, you're too young. You should go to a doctor."

She took Sara's hand. "Please, don't worry. I'm over it. I swear I'm all right."

Sara didn't look as if she believed her, but thankfully she let it drop.

CHAPTER THIRTY-SIX

Lee got up early, made coffee and gathered her photography gear. Becka had left three weeks ago. It was time to accept the fact that she wasn't going to come back. After filling a thermos with coffee, she left Sara a note, slipped on her pack and headed to the blind. A cold front had moved through on Saturday night and she was glad she had put on her thermal underwear. As she walked along the dimly lit path, she allowed the memories of Becka to drift back. She examined each remembrance carefully before mentally locking it away. This trip was a catharsis. After today, she would no longer permit herself to think about Becka returning. It was time to move on with her life.

Perhaps she was one of those people who were meant to go through life alone. "I'm not alone," she reminded herself. She had Sara and her parents. She had Gladys and Dewayne. She could accept the fact that there didn't appear to be anyone special out there for her. It wasn't an option she would have chosen, but that's the way it seemed to be. She would keep herself open to the possibility of another person in her life, but she refused to let being single stop her from living her life to the fullest.

She had already decided that she would surprise Sara with a trip to Paris. They could go in May after Sara's classes ended. She didn't want to plan the entire trip without Sara's input. Maybe she'd want to see London or some other European destination in addition to Paris. She and Gladys had already talked about hiring either one more full-time employee or two part-timers. That would allow them both to have a couple of days off during the week.

She was also contemplating a new project that would be extremely time consuming if it took off as she hoped it would. Her conversations with Granny Depew had planted the idea in her head and it had slowly been germinating. Christmas was a haven of artists, so why didn't it have an art school where people like Annabelle could come and build their skills? It wouldn't be anything fancy to begin with, but over time, it could be built into something to be proud of. All she had to do was to convince the other artists to volunteer their time. If the school was successful maybe it could eventually reach the point of being able to pay the instructors.

Her excitement grew as she walked and brainstormed about the new school. It wasn't until she reached the blind and stood outside it that her steps faltered and a stab of pain returned. She removed the flashlight and proceeded to do her regular snake check. A large spider crawled out into the beam of her flashlight. Once she was satisfied there were no snakes waiting for her, she slowly stepped inside. She staggered at the weight of the memories that poured over her. With her arms braced on the back of the old chair, she waited for the feelings to leave. The vivid images of Becka's body beneath her were hard to shake, but they finally settled into a more manageable ache. Only then did she sit down and take a deep breath. Rather that setting up the camera as she usually did, she dropped the backpack and simply sat and waited for the sun to climb above the horizon. She left the pack in the blind and went over to the rock by the stream where she had first seen Becka. She sat on the rock and crossed her arms, hugging herself. Then she closed her eyes and let Becka's face slowly come into focus.

"What happened that you couldn't return?" she asked softly. She concentrated and tried to reach across the miles to wherever Becka was. She knew it was impossible, but there were times when she felt like if she turned around suddenly she might find Becka waiting there. When Lee finally did open her eyes, she almost toppled off the rock in surprise. There, less than ten feet away stood the twelve-point buck. It seemed as though the animal stared at her for a good thirty seconds before it softly tossed its head and blew loudly. Then he casually turned and disappeared into the woods.

Lee stared after it for a long moment before she jumped to her feet and ran to the blind to grab her pack. She made the trip home in half the time it normally took her. She didn't even bother to change clothes before she grabbed her car keys and rushed out the door.

By the time Gladys arrived at eight, Lee had already sketched in the buck, applied two base coats and was starting to add the major highlights that would eventually mark out the animal's muscles. Hours of work still lay before her before the painting would be finished.

"Did you finally get a photo of him?" Gladys asked when she saw Lee working.

"No. I was sitting there, without my camera, and he practically walked right up to me." She kept painting as she talked. "I swear, Gladys, it was like he had no fear of me whatsoever. He was only about ten feet from me."

"You've spent so much time out there he probably thought you were just another woodland creature."

She continued talking, but Lee tuned her out. The painting demanded all of her attention.

When Lee finally moved back from the painting, her joints ached from being in one spot so long. She would now set the painting aside somewhere out of sight for several days. The time away from it would allow her to study it more objectively to determine whether something more was needed, or if it was truly finished. She slowly stood and stretched.

"You've rejoined the living."

She turned, surprised to hear Sara's voice. "When did you get here?" Her voice was hoarse from lack of use.

Sara lay the book she was reading aside and looked at her watch. "Around nine o'clock this morning. I rode my bike in. I need to get new tires for it."

Lee glanced at the clock on the wall. It was after eleven. The darkened windows told her it was night. "As in fourteen hours ago?" Lee asked, stunned that she had gotten so lost in the painting.

Sara came over to stand by her. "Mom, it was sort of eerie the way you just completely zoned out. You were like a machine."

Lee stared at the painting. She was far too modest ever to say so aloud, but she could already tell it was going to be one of her best works.

"I think you should stop now and let me drive you home."

Lee started to protest that she could drive herself, but she was exhausted. She simply nodded.

"Since Grams and Granddad are supposed to be here tomorrow, I told Gladys that I would come in and work for you. I thought you might like to spend the day with them," Sara said. "Plus, I knew you'd probably have to go grocery shopping with Grams."

"If I know Mom, she'll arrive with the rental car loaded with groceries." Her parents always flew into Little Rock and rented a car. She had offered to borrow Gladys's car and pick them up on the rare occasions when they came to visit, but they always declined. She suspected her father never wanted to be caught without available transportation in case he had to dash back to the store. "Thanks for offering to work tomorrow," she

242

added. "Gladys and I decided that we'll close earlier than usual on Wednesday, if it's slow." The gallery would close at five on Wednesday afternoon and not open again until Friday morning. Some of the stores remained open for Thanksgiving, but Lee never had. She took a step and winced.

"Are you okay?" Sara asked as she reached out to steady her mother.

"Nothing a long hot bath won't cure," Lee assured her.

Sara got her bike from the storeroom and wheeled it to the parking lot. Together they placed it in the back of Lee's truck.

"Are you sure you want to drive?" Lee asked.

"Yes. I don't want you falling asleep."

The walk helped ease the kinks out of Lee's joints, but she was glad for the opportunity to relax in the passenger seat.

After they were in the truck and headed toward the house, Sara mentioned that she had talked to her father that day.

"Has he changed his mind about coming?" Lee asked, hopeful.

"No. He's flying into Little Rock Wednesday afternoon and then driving out here Thursday morning."

Lee didn't say anything.

"Since it's a three-hour drive, I was wondering if—"

"No. He can't spend Wednesday night with us. We don't have room."

"He could sleep on the sofa or in the den."

"Sara, we talked about this before. I don't want Brandon spending the night with us."

"Why not?" Sara pouted. "I don't see what the big deal is. It's not like the house isn't big enough."

"For one thing, your grandmother would have a stroke." Lee tried to curb her impatience. There were times when Sara seemed so mature, then when she least expected it a shadow of the bratty teenager slipped out.

"She said she didn't care."

Lee looked at her sharply. "Are you telling me that you actually asked Mom if she would mind if Brandon stayed over?"

Something in her voice must have transmitted her displeasure, because Sara grew more hesitant.

"It's not like I called her just for that. We were just, you know, talking."

Lee received and reviewed Sara's cell phone bill each month. She knew how rarely she called her grandparents. In fact, it was something they had discussed before.

"Whatever," Lee said. "You can forget it. He's not spending the night at the house." She stared out the side window and wondered how hard he had pushed Sara to get him invited to dinner. Maybe he wanted to borrow money. If so, it must be a lot for him to drag her parents into it. "You said your father was publishing a book? When is it due out?" He had probably decided to self-publish and needed money.

"I told you, it's already out." Sara fumbled between the seats and handed a book to her.

Lee flipped on the overhead light so she could see. "Darien's Gold," she read aloud. "Is it a mystery?" She opened the front cover, intending to read the inside flap of the dust jacket.

"No. It's a romance. It's about a guy who discovers that true wealth is love."

Lee looked at her in astonishment. "Brandon wrote a romance!"

"What's wrong with that?" Sara asked defensively.

Lee backed off. She had never derided Brandon to Sara and she wouldn't start now. "There's nothing wrong with it. I'm just amazed, that's all."

"I think it's cool that he's an author."

Lee put the book down and switched off the light. "I didn't mean to upset you. It's just that for all those years he talked about writing the great American novel." She realized she still sounded catty. "I'm happy for him that he was finally published."

"Are you going to read his book?"

Lee had no desire to read the book, but Sara wouldn't understand that. "Of course I will, after the holidays."

"Can't you read it before he comes to visit?"

"No. You know how busy I am. Your grandparents are coming in tomorrow and business is picking up at the gallery again. I won't have time."

"He always supported your endeavors," Sara said, clearly peeved.

Lee kept silent. She was tired and it would be easy for her to take all of her frustrations out on Sara. She needed to let her emotions settle before she tried to explain.

Brandon had never been a bad husband, but she wouldn't have classified him as being emotionally supportive. He was too wrapped up in his own world, and when things weren't going his way, he tended to turn to alcohol. She had never told Sara that Brandon hadn't paid the court-mandated child support, or about his drinking problem. She wondered if she had made a mistake in gently misleading Sara about how he really was, but then, how did you tell a child her father was weak and self-centered?

They rode the rest of the way home in silence. When they pulled into the driveway, Lee released her seat belt and waited for Sara to turn off the engine before she spoke. "Sara, I need for you to try and understand a few things. Yes, your father and I parted under amiable circumstances, but we've not spoken in several years. Those years with him weren't times I care to remember for a variety of reasons. While it's not entirely his fault, those were quite honestly the worst years of my life. I was struggling to accept who I was. I was married and trying to get through college. Then you were born. I wasn't prepared to handle any of that. Your father was never a cruel man, but he was extremely focused on his own goals. I don't dislike him or resent him, but his presence in the house is going to be uncomfortable for me." She looked at her daughter. "Can you understand that?"

Sara played with her car keys. "I guess so. I just thought that maybe...this one time...we could all have dinner together." A glint of tears shone in her eyes.

It hurt Lee to see Sara so upset. "Sweetie, I'm sorry I couldn't give you a traditional home while you were growing up. I know it wasn't easy for you."

Sara shook her head. "No. I'm the one who should be sorry. You gave me a wonderful home." She looked up. "Mom, you should hear how some of my friends grew up. I know how easy I had it, and believe me, I do appreciate everything you did." She turned her attention back to the keys. "It's just that sometimes I wonder what it would have been like if you guys had stayed together."

Lee leaned her head against the seat and decided to try to lighten up the conversation. They could talk again later, but right now, she needed to get to bed before she passed out from exhaustion. "I can tell you that. I would have eventually gotten so fed up with him not working that I would have killed him. Rather than coming home from college to spend your holidays in this beautiful home located in the heart of God's country"— Sara giggled, so Lee continued— "you would be driving over to Gatesville, Texas, to visit your poor old mother at the women's prison."

"At least there you would've been able to find a girlfriend."

Lee sat up, shocked. "Sara Leanne Dresher, I can't believe you said that."

"Well, it's true. Gosh, sometimes I wonder if you're even a real lesbian."

Lee opened the door and stepped out. "What has happened to my sweet, lovable child? Where has the little angel, who brought me bouquets of wildflowers and fixed me frozen waffles for breakfast on my days off, gone?"

Sara peered at her over the hood of the truck. "I stopped gathering wildflowers after I accidentally picked up that grass snake, and I only served the waffles frozen because you wouldn't let me use the toaster oven."

As they walked to the house arm in arm, Lee suddenly had a vision of Becka leaning over her as they made love. She smiled. There might be many things in life that confused her, but the one thing she no longer doubted was that she was indeed a real lesbian.

CHAPTER THIRTY-SEVEN

The following morning, Lee lay in bed staring at the ceiling. She had so many things to do she didn't even know where to start. A soft tapping on the door made her sit up.

"I'm awake," she called out.

The door opened to reveal Sara with a large tray. She looked at Lee and grinned. "Since I was so mean to you last night, I thought I'd better try to make it up to you." She came into the room and placed the tray on the bed. "When I saw the waffle iron sitting on the counter, I decided to surprise you."

Lee looked at the two plates of waffles and bacon and two cups of coffee. "Those look like the real deal," she said, carefully scooting up until her back rested against the headboard. "Where did you learn to fix waffles?"

Sara placed the tray over Lee's lap before she crawled up on the bed beside her. Lee's heart filled with love as she watched her precious, mischievous child. She had grown up so quickly.

"You'd be surprised what they teach us in college now," Sara replied as she bit into her dry waffle.

"You know those taste a lot better with syrup." Lee poured a generous glug of a delicious-smelling maple syrup over her waffles.

"It's loaded with calories," Sara said, staring down at Lee's plate. "Right now you're about to ingest a bazillion calories. Besides, all I've done is eat since I got home."

Lee cut off a piece of a waffle and swirled it around in the puddle of syrup on her plate. "One of the great advantages of being happily single is that I never have to watch my waistline." She savored the rich flavors. "I can eat whatever I want." She crunched a slice of bacon.

Sara sipped her coffee as she looked around the bedroom. "This room looks almost the same as it did when I was a kid."

Lee continued eating her waffles and glanced at the walls. "I guess it could use a new coat of paint."

"Along with some new linens," Sara said as she ran a hand over the quilt.

"I love this quilt. It was one of the first things I bought after we moved here."

"The quilt is okay, but you should get some of those organic linen sheets. They're sexy."

Lee looked up from over her coffee cup. "How come you know so much about those sheets?"

"I bought a set."

Lee placed her cup back on the tray and held up her hand. "Please try to remember that I'm your mother, so use extreme care and judgment whenever you tell me anything that could in anyway drive me crazy."

"Mom." She drew the word out, clearly exasperated. "I'm twenty years old."

"Sara." Lee used the same exasperated tone as Sara had. "I don't care if you're a hundred and twenty. There are certain things that I know you're old enough to do, but I don't want to know you're doing them." She picked up her coffee cup again.

"Otherwise, I might have to ground you for life."

"Was Grams as bad as you are about sex?"

"Are you joking? I don't think my mom has ever even said the word sex. Sometimes I wonder how she managed to conceive two children." Lee pointed at Sara. "I should not have said that and don't you dare repeat it."

They ate in silence for a moment.

"Am I really that bad?" Lee asked.

Sara shook her head and swallowed. "You can be when we're just joking around, but I know you'd be cool if I really needed to talk to you."

Lee stared at her daughter. She didn't appear to be trying to tell her anything, but sometimes it was hard to tell. "Do we need to talk?"

"No. I'm fine. I know all I need to know about sex." She poked at the crumbs on her plate. She had that little grin that told Lee she was about to tease her. "You taught me great moral standards. Sex education taught me how to take care of myself. As for the actual deed—"

Lee covered her ears. "Stop right there. I don't want to know any more." The phone rang. She grabbed it as if it were a lifeline. It was her mother and Lee knew right away she wasn't happy. "What's wrong, Mom?"

"It's your father. As usual."

"What's wrong?" Sara whispered.

Lee shrugged and hit the speakerphone button. "What did he do?"

"He insists he's not coming to your house for Thanksgiving dinner."

Shocked, Lee blinked and looked at Sara, who also looked surprised. "Have I done something to offend him?" Lee asked when she finally recovered enough to speak. In the background, she heard her father's voice. He had apparently just walked into the room.

"If that's Lee you're calling, you make sure you tell her the entire story. Don't you try to drop this mess in my lap. Once she finds out—" There was a rustling sound and her father's voice became too muffled for her to hear.

"What was Dad saying?" she asked.

"I'm sorry we won't be coming after all. Give Sara my love." She disconnected before Lee could reply.

"Weird," Sara said as Lee turned off the phone. "What do you think? Are they arguing or something?"

Lee rubbed a finger over her chin. "I don't know. I don't think I've done anything that would upset him." She looked at Sara. "When was the last time you talked to him?"

Sara's eyes widened. "Don't blame me."

"I'm not blaming you. I only asked because I thought maybe he had said something to you that might give us a clue."

Sara relaxed. "I haven't talked to him in a while. I usually just talk to Grams."

"Did she seem upset the last time you spoke with her?"

"No. The only thing different that I noticed was that she talked about Dad a lot."

Lee frowned. "Was that after you told her he was coming here for dinner?"

Sara's brow creased as she thought for a moment. "I'm not sure, but I think she mentioned him first. I remember thinking it weird that she talked about him."

"So you don't normally talk about him?"

"No," Sara looked at her as if she'd lost her mind. "I never talk to them about Dad." She glanced at the clock. "I need to get going. I promised Gladys I'd help her change some displays."

"I had your dresses cleaned. They're hanging in the back of your closet." Lee finished the last of her waffle. She wasn't surprised her father hadn't wanted to be away from the store during the Thanksgiving holiday. It was strange that he had gone back on his word. Normally, once he committed to something he followed through. There was obviously something more going on. She wondered if she should call her mom later or wait. Eventually, her mom would tell her what had really happened. She decided to wait.

"I always feel like I'm playing dress up," Sara said as they placed the dishes back on the tray.

"Thanks for serving me breakfast in bed."

"You should really buy yourself some of those sheets, Mom. I'm telling you they are fabulous."

"Now you sound like Alan." Lee got out of bed.

"Mom." Sara shifted her weight from foot to foot. "Did you and Dad used to go to a little Italian restaurant named Luigi's?"

"Yes, but it wasn't Luigi's. It was something like Tuscan Hills or Tuscan Sun, something like that. Why?"

Sara just shook her head.

"Since I don't have to wait around for Mom and Dad, I guess I'll go on in to work," Lee said.

Sara stopped suddenly. "Oh my gosh." She looked frantically at her mother. "Mom, what are we going to do? If Grams isn't coming, who's going to cook dinner?"

Lee shrugged. "I guess it'll be like the old days. You, me and frozen dinners."

"Dad's coming."

"So? I'm sure he has eaten his share of frozen meals."

"Mom!"

"All right. I'll see what I can do. I guess I may as well, since I've already ordered the turkey."

"Do you know how to cook a turkey?"

"Sure I do," Lee teased. "You put it in the microwave for an hour to defrost it and then—" She never got to finish. Sara had already stormed out of the room.

By the time Lee took a shower and got dressed, Sara had left for the gallery. Lee went down to the kitchen and used a stepladder to access the small cabinet above the refrigerator. With a grunt, she pulled out the cookbook her mother had given her years ago.

She looked at the massive tome and grimaced. "There has to be a faster way." She shoved the heavy book back inside the cabinet.

Twenty minutes later, she had printouts of several recipes

lying on the kitchen table in front of her. She had been able to find and download everything she would ever need to know about a Thanksgiving dinner from the Internet. She went through the recipes and made a shopping list.

Confident that she was in complete control of the situation, she picked up her keys to go shopping. She decided to try the grocery store in Christmas first, and if they didn't have everything she needed then she would still have time to drive over to Mena where there was a larger supermarket.

As she drove out the driveway, she started thinking about her parents again. What could have happened to make them cancel their trip? Her father had seemed all right with not working over the holiday weekend when she last spoke to him. Maybe they were just having a little tiff between them. She didn't remember her parents arguing very often. Her father was so easy-going that he normally gave in to whatever her mother wanted as long as it didn't interfere with his work. She thought about giving her father a call but hesitated. If they were arguing, her interfering might make it worse. On a more selfish note, she didn't want to be caught between them.

She slowed the truck down slightly, as she always did now when she reached the road that led to the old Peterson place. On an impulse, she turned down the road. She had been avoiding it, because it made her think of Becka. When she approached the place, she almost didn't recognize it. Becka had mentioned that it was being fixed up for Annabelle and Joan, but since they had decided not to move in after all, she assumed the renovations were never completed.

The grand old house seemed to stand taller with its new brilliant coat of white paint with maroon trim. The trees had been pruned, and the yard had been mowed. Someone had repaired the plank fence that ran across the front of the yard and painted it white. The gate now sported sturdy-looking wrought iron hinges and a lock.

Lee turned around in the driveway and left. She wondered where Becka was and if she ever thought of their time together.

CHAPTER THIRTY-EIGHT

By seven o'clock on Thanksgiving morning Lee's home was filled with the smell of baking pies. She was chopping celery and onions when she glanced up to find Sara staring at her.

"What's wrong?" Lee asked.

"I smelled food. It woke me up." She looked around. "You're like...cooking...real food."

"Anything for my darling daughter," Lee said breezily.

Sara went over to the coffeepot and poured herself a cup.

Lee saw her peek into the trashcan beneath the sink. "What are you looking for?"

Sara grinned sheepishly. "The frozen-food boxes."

"Shame on you for not having more confidence than that in me. I told you I would cook and I am." She told herself she wasn't exactly lying. After all, she was cooking.

After finding a slim selection at the grocery store in Christmas,

Lee had driven to Mena. As she was standing in the baking aisle trying to make head or tails out of the unbelievably large selection of different types of flour, an older woman, Mrs. Perkins, asked her to get something off the top shelf for her. They struck up a conversation and within minutes, Mrs. Perkins was leading her through the store showing her what to buy.

"Who has time to cook from scratch?" Mrs. Perkins asked as she pointed out the best-tasting frozen pies, frozen cranberry sauce, canned gravies and such to Lee. "I don't like those instant potatoes, though," she went on, "but that's okay. Mashed potatoes are easy to make."

Lee nodded. She wasn't worried about the potatoes. She could actually make decent mashed potatoes.

"Remember, the secret to using frozen food is to toss in just enough fresh or canned ingredients to give everything a little crunch or make it look like it's made from scratch."

"What about bread?" Lee asked.

Mrs. Perkins led her over to the refrigerated section again. "These take a little work," she said, handing Lee a package, "but they're easy. When you get up Thursday morning, you just take the dough out of the bag and put it in a bowl. Set the bowl on top of your stove and let it set there for about an hour, then you punch the dough down with your fist and let it rise again." She peered up at Lee. "That'll take another hour or so, but then you just pull off pieces a little smaller than your fist and put it in a big bread pan and bake it until the rolls are pretty and brown." She patted Lee's arm. "Everyone will think you were up half the night making fresh rolls." She even told her how to take boxed cornbread dressing and add ingredients to it that would make it taste like it was made from scratch.

Lee had thanked her profusely and left the store with a treasure trove of ideas and cooking secrets.

On Thanksgiving Day, Lee had gotten up early in order to hide the evidence before Sara got up. The dressing was mixed with the precooked shredded chicken Mrs. Perkins had pointed out to her and was now sitting in the refrigerator ready to be cooked. She would pop the turkey into the oven after the pies came out in ten minutes. The canned gravy had been poured into bowls and refrigerated. Minutes before they were ready to eat, she would heat it and add the canned mushrooms along with chopped giblets that were now cooking in a pot on top of the stove. All of the evidence of her deceit had been incinerated in the burn barrel out back. No one but she and Mrs. Perkins would know the truth.

Sara lifted the cloth that covered the bowl on the stove.

"Be careful," Lee said calmly. "The dough needs to rise a bit more."

Sara stepped back and stared at her again. "This is scary. I feel like you've become one of those Stepford Wives or something." She shivered. "Do you need any help?"

Lee smiled sweetly. "No. I think I have everything under control. Why don't you go relax and watch the parade on television? You used to like to watch it."

"Please, I was seven years old then." Sara kept looking around the kitchen. "When did you learn to cook?"

Lee shrugged. "I don't know. I guess you could say it just sort of came to me." She wanted to change the subject. "What time is your father supposed to be here?"

"He called me last night to let me know his plane had landed in Little Rock. He said he'd get here between eleven and twelve." Sara took an apple from the bowl on the counter. "Did you hear anything else from Grams?"

"No. I meant to call her back, but I've been busy getting everything ready."

"Shouldn't the turkey be cooking now?" Sara bit into the apple.

"No. I'll put it in after the pies come out. Don't worry. I have everything under control. We'll be sitting down to eat promptly at one."

Sara glanced around again before heading back to her room and flipping her music on.

Lee nearly danced a jig. Everything was going perfectly.

She'd pull off a fantastic Thanksgiving dinner with hardly any fuss or knowledge and no one would be the wiser.

When the timer for the pies dinged, Lee had just finished chopping the vegetables. She set them aside and carefully removed the pies. As soon as she saw them, she smiled and sent a silent thank you to Mrs. Perkins. They looked beautiful and smelled heavenly. The nuts on the pecan pie were perfectly toasted and the pumpkin pie looked as beautiful as the ones her mom made. She set the pies on a back countertop and turned her attention to the turkey. The turkey and the potatoes were the only two things that she was actually making herself. She had been concerned about knowing when to remove the bird until Mrs. Perkins had pointed out that most of them now came with an indicator that told you when it was done. She had been ecstatic when she got home and discovered that the turkey she had bought a few days earlier actually had a little red button that popped out to let her know when it was thoroughly cooked. All she really had to do was baste it and make sure the wing tips didn't burn. Mrs. Perkins had told her to wrap the wing tips in aluminum foil until the final hour of cooking.

Things were moving along so well that she poured herself a cup of coffee and went out back to walk around a bit. The weather was perfect. It was warm enough to allow her to stay outside a little while, yet cool enough that a small fire in the fireplace would feel wonderful later on in the day.

She went back inside. The kitchen felt overly warm from the oven being on, so she opened the window over the sink before she gave everything a final check. Satisfied that the whole thing was moving along as planned, she went back to Sara's room. The door was open and she was playing Solitaire on her laptop. She was still dressed in the sweats she had been wearing earlier.

"I'm going to change clothes," Lee said. "Would you mind keeping an eye on things in the kitchen? Everything should be fine."

Sara followed her out. "I can't believe how calm you are. I thought you'd be a basket case today."

"It's just a matter of planning," Lee said lightly as she went to her room. She chose a pair of autumn brown slacks. Then she pulled on a matching turtleneck, with a lightweight, multihued V-neck sweater over it. She chose a pair of black boots with low heels. For accessories, she added a delicately woven gold chain, which Sara had given her for Christmas the previous year, and a bracelet with various colored glass beads that were shaped like leaves. She gave her hair one last pat and headed back toward the kitchen.

"You look nice," Sara said when she saw her.

"Thank you very much." Lee wondered if she should prompt Sara to change. At what point did mothers stop telling their children to change their clothes? Her mother had never stopped. That alone held Lee's tongue.

Sara pointed toward the stove. "I guess everything is fine. I mean, nothing blew up or anything."

Lee had to laugh. "You poor thing. You're going to be as bad as I am in a kitchen."

Sara's eyes widened. "There's no way...no way I could have pulled this off, and look at you. You're so calm."

Sara looked so innocent that Lee nearly broke down and divulged her secret, but the doorbell stopped her.

"That's Dad," Sara said excitedly as she ran toward the front door.

Lee took a deep breath. "Remember this is for Sara," she whispered. "He'll be gone in a few hours." After one more deep breath, she followed her daughter into the living room.

CHAPTER THIRTY-NINE

Time had been kind to Brandon Dresher. His once nondescript brown hair had given way to that distinguished salt-and-pepper look that some men pulled off so well. His beanpole body had finally matured and he looked nice in his stylish suit. He was carrying a cardboard box that he set by the door.

Lee found herself in the awkward situation of whether to shake his hand or give him a friendly hug. He smoothed it over by smiling brightly. "Lee, how are you? Thank you so much for allowing me to spend the day with Sara. I know it must have been a terrible inconvenience for you." He kissed her lightly on the cheek as if she were his sister.

Before she could speak, Sara piped up. "Wait until you see the fantastic meal she has prepared."

Lee took his topcoat. "Come on in and sit down."

He picked up the box. "I bought some wine last night." He

held up the box that contained at least six bottles of wine. "I wasn't sure how many would be here today, so I said what the heck."

"Take it into the kitchen," Lee said. "Sara, show him where the kitchen is, while I hang up his coat."

Lee took the coat to the hall closet. She couldn't help but notice that the garment was made from fine wool. She peeked at the label. Her brows raised in astonishment when she saw the Hickey-Freeman label. Her father had always worn the finest in men's suits and she had often seen this same label on his suits. Apparently, he was doing much better than she had thought.

She went back into the living room and sat on the sofa. After a moment, she jumped up and moved to the recliner beside the sofa where she normally sat. Why should she give him the best seat in the house? When Sara and Brandon returned, they were carrying an opened bottle of wine and three glasses.

"Now, before you scold us," he began, "I told Sara that if you didn't mind she could join us with a small glass of wine."

"I'll be twenty-one in nine months," Sara said.

"I know how old you are," Lee replied. "You can either have a glass now or with dinner, but not both." Lee didn't really care if Sara had an extra glass of wine, but it ticked her off that Brandon had assumed it was all right with her. She knew she was being petty, and was about to relent when Sara turned to leave.

"I'll wait for dinner," Sara replied, clearly disappointed. "I guess I'd better go shower and get dressed for dinner."

Lee watched her leave.

"You did an excellent job raising her," Brandon said after a moment.

"There are days when I wonder, but she's a great kid."

"Not such a kid anymore." He sighed. "Does she ever make you feel old?"

"Now, everything makes me feel old."

He poured two glasses of wine and handed one to her. "The clerk assured me this was an excellent Merlot."

Lee took the glass of warm wine and was broadsided by memories of Becka. She shook off the images that flashed through

259

her mind.

"How have you been?" Brandon asked.

"Good." She didn't want to talk about herself. "Congratulations on the book. I hear it's doing well."

He leaned forward. "Really? Who was talking about it?"

"Sara."

"Oh." He sat down on the end of the sofa a few feet from Lee. "It's doing quite well." He slowly turned the wineglass in his hand. "Have you read it?"

"No. It's the holidays. I barely have time to read my mail." She was expecting him to be disappointed, but he actually seemed relieved.

"None of your family was much interested in reading fiction."

His tone struck her as being a little too self-righteous. "Especially romances," she said and sipped her wine.

He seemed nervous as he glanced at her then scooted closer to the edge of the sofa and leaned toward her. "I suppose you're wondering why I came today."

"I thought you wanted to spend time with Sara." She shifted slightly to put more distance between them.

"Well, aside from that." He reached into his jacket pocket and removed a slip of paper. "I know I'm inexcusably late with this, but now that the book is doing well, I wanted to make things right between us."

Lee took the paper. It was a check for forty-five thousand dollars. "What's this?"

"It's the back child support I owe you."

For some unexplainable reason, the check made her angry. In fact, she was much angrier than she had been all those years ago when she hadn't been receiving it. She tossed it back at him. "I don't want that. Sara and I did fine and I certainly don't need it now."

He picked up the check that had fluttered to the floor. "I'm so sorry. I'm making a complete mess of this." He looked at the floor. "Lee, are you seeing anyone?"

The sudden switch in conversation threw her. "No." Had she not been taken by surprise by the unexpected subject change she might have lied or at the very least told him it was none of his business. Little by little, she was starting to remember the other side of Brandon, the side she hadn't liked.

He held out the check again. "I need to make things right between us. I know that money can't begin to compensate for all the love and energy you put into raising our daughter."

"Brandon, I didn't do it for the money." She leaned toward him. "Since you're so concerned about making things right, how did you manage to come up with this figure? Do you really believe that this would cover half the cost of raising a child? This wouldn't even begin to cover her college expenses. What's really going on? And please spare me anymore bull."

He sat back on the sofa. "I don't know how closely you've followed my life."

"I know you're still alive. Let's say that about sums it up."

"Why are you so angry at me?"

Lee rubbed her head. "I honestly don't know, but I can tell you it has happened since you decided on showing up here today. So I guess that has something to do with it."

"Could it be because you still care for me?"

Lee stared at him so dumbfounded she couldn't speak.

He apparently took her silence as a sign to continue. "You know I still care for you. It was you who wanted the divorce. I always thought you were the perfect wife. You're talented. Your family has an impeccable reputation. You're pretty." He stared at her. "Lee, I'd like to make you a proposition. I think it would do wonders for your career as an artist." He smiled brightly. "I'm living in Houston. Even though I spend a lot of time in New York, I reestablished my Texas residency years ago. Over the years I've made some powerful friends who are going to help me go places." He took a deep breath. "I'm going to run for the Houston city council. Then in a couple of years, I'll run for the state senate, and you are a politician's dream wife. I want you by my side when I run."

She flew out of the chair. "Are you out of your mind? Where in the hell do you get off coming into my home and—"

"What's going on?"

Lee turned to find Sara standing in the kitchen doorway. Sara was staring at her with the incredulous look of a child who had just caught her parents drowning her new kitten.

Lee rubbed her head again. "I'm sorry, but I need to check the turkey."

She stormed into the kitchen and leaned against the sink. The food didn't need her attention, but she did need a few minutes alone before she completely lost it and ended up having to bury Brandon's pummeled body in the backyard. She ran icy cold water over her hands and pressed them to her face. At least his desire to pay off his back child support made sense. She supposed a lesbian ex-wife might be a determent, or at the very least an embarrassment. What better way to fix it than to remarry her? He could rectify a divorce and convert a lesbian all in one fell swoop. She leaned over the sink and splashed her face again. As she did, she heard the doorbell.

"Now what?" she mumbled as she shut off the water and grabbed a paper towel to dry her face. She was about to walk back into the living room when she heard her mother's voice. She closed her eyes. As much as she loved her parents, she didn't think she could deal with her mother now. For one thing, her mother wouldn't be satisfied until she discovered how Lee had suddenly developed cooking skills. Lee glanced over at the five wine bottles sitting on the counter. Maybe she could get them all drunk before it was time to eat. If this dinner didn't mean so much to Sara, Lee would have simply walked out the back door and hid in the blind until tomorrow morning. She put the wine bottles in the refrigerator, even the Merlot. Before she was finished her mother, father, Brandon and Sara all crowded into the kitchen.

"Look who's here," Brandon called out. He acted as if nothing had happened between them.

Even as she crossed the room to greet her parents, she could see her father was fuming. She guessed whatever was going on between them hadn't been cleared up. This was going to be a long day.

"All right, everyone get out of my way and I'll have dinner on in no time," her mother said as she headed toward the stove and opened the oven door.

"Mom, I have everything under control," Lee replied. "We'll eat at one."

"Not unless you get this turkey to cooking we won't," her mom replied. "This oven isn't even on."

"Yes, it is." Lee struggled to control her irritation.

"I beg to differ." Her mom placed her hand flat on the roasting pan.

Lee jumped forward, expecting her mother to howl in pain. When it didn't happen, she leaned down and put a hand inside the oven. It was cold. "I don't understand." She looked at the temperature dial on the stove. "It's set for three hundred and twenty-five degrees, just like the instructions said." She noticed that the burner beneath the pot cooking the giblets was also off. A sick feeling hit her when she smelled the faint nasty scent of propane. In all the chaos of the past few weeks, she had forgotten to call Barry Masters to have him refill the propane tank. "Not today," she said as she turned the oven and burner off.

"Maybe the wind from the open window blew out the flame," her father said.

Lee prayed he was right, even though she knew it wasn't logical that the air from the window would have blown the oven out. She reached into her junk drawer for a box of matches and tried to light the burner manually, but nothing happened. She blew out the match and rubbed a hand over her face. "I'm sorry, but I seem to have run out of gas."

"Can't you call someone?" Sara asked quietly.

"No. The company is closed for the holiday." She knew she could call Barry's house and he would come out, but she didn't intend to drag him away from his holiday meal simply because she had been negligent.

"What are we going to do about dinner?" Sara was on the verge of tears.

"Give me a minute. I'll think of something," Lee said as she racked her brain. "Maybe we can cut the turkey up and barbecue it."

"Mom," Sara howled. "You promised today was going be perfect." She burst into tears and ran toward her room.

Lee started to go after her, but the doorbell rang.

Her parents and Brandon were locked in their own squabble.

Sara's bedroom door slammed and almost instantly, music boomed from behind the door.

As she turned to go answer the door, Lee grabbed her head. It was beginning to ache.

"Who is that?" her mother called after her. "I thought it was only going to be us."

Lee glanced back in time to see her mother look at Brandon. Suddenly all the pieces slipped into place. She stopped and turned to her mother. "You knew what he was going to do, didn't you?" When her mother looked guilty, Lee eyed her father. "That's why you didn't want to come."

He nodded. "I tried to tell her not to do it."

"It's for your own good," her mother said. "You're not getting any younger. This lesbian business obviously isn't working for you or you wouldn't still be alone. You need someone to take care of you." Her mother was clearly on a roll. "You can't hide out here in the boonies forever. It's time you started thinking about Sara's future."

Lee frowned. "What does any of this have to do with Sara's future?"

"Do you think it's easy for her to tell people that her mother is a lesbian?" Brandon asked.

"Helen, leave her alone." Her father's voice held that tone that indicated he had reached his limit. They were all talking at once, and the doorbell sounded again.

Lee spun on her heels and charged out of the kitchen. The

other three followed. When she opened the door, she nearly cried out in relief when she saw Becka standing there.

"I'm sorry I was a little longer than I anticipated," Becka said. "But I'm back." Her glance flickered past Lee. "I promise I'll explain everything to you. From now on my life will be an open book."

Lee stared at her. "How long are you planning on staying in Christmas?"

"I'll be around for as long as you want me."

Heedless of the ruckus behind her, Lee pulled Becka into her arms and kissed her.

When she finally stopped kissing her and simply held her tight, Becka whispered, "Do you know there are three really shocked-looking people standing behind you?"

"Yeah, but if you close your eyes maybe they'll go away."

CHAPTER FORTY

Lee's mother cleared her throat loudly. "Excuse me," she said.

Before Lee released Becka, she whispered, "Please don't run away when you meet my mother. She lives in Houston and rarely ever visits."

Becka whispered back, "Trust me. After what I've been through the last three weeks, your mother doesn't scare me in the least."

Lee took Becka's hand and led her inside where she made introductions.

"Your friend," her mother repeated. "I thought you didn't have a friend."

"I'm sort of a work in progress," Becka said with a smile. She turned to Lee. "Didn't Sara make it home? I've heard so much about her. I can't wait to meet her."

"I'm afraid my nearly grown daughter is in her room pouting," Lee said. "Unfortunately, you've arrived in the middle of one of those so-called awkward family moments." She was so happy to see Becka that she had forgotten about her anger.

"Maybe I should leave—"

"That's an excellent idea," Brandon said, stepping forward. "We really need to discuss some family business."

"Brandon,"—Lee's father moved closer to Lee—"I don't think you're a member of this family. If you wish to stay and have dinner with your daughter, I suggest you remember that you're a guest in my daughter's home."

Lee had a childish impulse to stick her tongue out at Brandon and sing nan-na-nan-na-boo-boo. No wonder Sara had never grown up, she chided herself.

Brandon straightened his jacket. "In lieu of what's happened, I don't see where there's any need for me to stay." He looked at Lee. "Considering there's no longer a dinner to be eaten." He looked around. "Where's my coat?"

Lee went into the hallway, took his coat from the closet and brought it to him. "You're not leaving without talking to Sara first."

"You can tell her I had to leave."

"No. You're going to go tell her." She suddenly thought of something else. "Brandon, I've changed my mind. Give me that check."

He frowned. "Why?"

"Because otherwise when the reporters start digging into your background and one eventually shows up on my doorstep, Sara won't ever have to learn that her father never paid child support." She held out her hand and he reluctantly handed it to her.

He walked out the front door without looking back.

Lee's father started after him, but Lee put a hand on his arm. "Let him go. I'll talk to her in a few minutes." She motioned to the sitting area. "Why don't we all sit down?"

Lee sat on the sofa next to Becka. Her parents took the chairs opposite.

"What are you going to do about dinner?" Her mom asked after a long silence.

"I don't know." Lee turned to Becka. "I forgot to call to have my propane tank refilled and, of course, with luck being what it is, the tank ran out today."

"We could take it over to the house," Becka said. "I have propane, but I won't have furniture until Monday." Suddenly she sat forward. "Does your fireplace work?"

Lee looked at her and realized what she was thinking. "Yes, but do you think it'll work?"

"Sure it will. It may take a while longer and it might not be as pretty as you're accustomed to, but it'll definitely work."

"What are you two planning?" her father asked.

Lee quickly told her parents about the roasted chicken and peach cobbler Becka had prepared using Dutch ovens.

"That'll never work with a turkey," her mother protested.

Lee's excitement drained. "I don't have a Dutch oven."

Becka grimaced. "I don't either. I gave mine to Granny Depew."

"I liked your idea of trying to barbecue it," her dad said.

"I think we should just head home," her mother replied.

"There's no way we could get a flight out today," he said. "Besides, I thought you'd promised Sara."

Lee jumped up. "Christ. I need to go talk to her." She looked down at Becka. "I'm sorry. I won't be long."

"Take your time. While you're talking to her, your parents and I will put our heads together and figure out a way to cook that turkey."

Lee wanted to kiss her again but went to talk to Sara.

When Lee knocked at Sara's door, she had to knock twice to be heard over the music. Sara finally opened the door, then flopped back down on the bed on her stomach and buried her face in her arm.

Lee lowered the volume on the music. The singer's voice was vaguely familiar, but she couldn't place the artist. She approached the bed. "Do you mind if I sit here for a moment?"

"It's your house."

Lee sat down. "Sara, I'm sorry about dinner. Things have been so hectic for me lately that I just forgot."

"I wanted it to be a perfect day."

"I know you did, and I wanted to give you a perfect day, but, sweetie, you're going to have to learn that things don't always happen just because we want them to. No matter how hard you try, your father and I are never going to get back together."

Sara rolled over with a bewildered look on her face. "I never said I wanted you and Dad to get back together."

"You mean you didn't know why he came here today?"

Sara sat up and gasped. "Dad came here to get back together with you?" She scrambled over to the bedside table and grabbed the book that lay there. "I should have known," she said as she flipped through the pages.

"What are you talking about?"

Sara stopped and looked at her. "Do you remember me asking you if you and Dad used to go to that place Luigi's?"

Lee nodded.

Sara closed the book and held it out. "Mom, I think Dad wrote about you in this book. He still loves you." Her eyes shone.

Lee started to tell Sara the truth about why Brandon had wanted to get back together, but she didn't have the heart to. "You know that's not possible for me. I could never live with Brandon again."

"I know that." She traced a pattern on the bedspread. "Dad's sort of self-centered, isn't he?"

Lee nodded slightly. "He definitely believes in taking care of number one first." She took a deep breath. "Sara, your father had to leave. He had to get back to—"

"Mom, it's okay. You don't have to make excuses for him. It's not like this is the first time he didn't follow through with a promise." She rocked forward on her knees and hugged her mother. "I'm sorry I was such a brat about dinner. I know you worked hard. Thanks for trying."

Lee held her. "There's someone here that I'd like you to meet."

Sara pulled back. "Is it your girlfriend?"

Lee smiled. "Well, things are still a little up in the air, but yes. I really like her."

"Is she the same woman who brought you home the other night?"

"Yes. Her name is Becka James and she's—"

"Beautiful, I'll bet," Sara teased.

"I think so." Lee stood. "Come on. I'll introduce you."

Sara jumped off the bed and rushed over to the mirror. "Wait. I can't look like an orphan when I meet her." She fussed with her hair.

"You look fine."

She draped an arm around Sara's shoulders as they went back into the living room. When they entered, Becka turned and stood.

Lee nearly stumbled when Sara stopped sharply.

"Oh my gosh," Sara whispered. The whisper quickly escalated into a shrill shriek. Sara began jumping up and down and screaming, "I don't believe it. I don't believe it."

Lee saw the look of disbelief wash over Becka's face before she shot an apologetic glance at Lee.

Sara suddenly grabbed Lee and squeezed her. "Why didn't you tell me you knew Amber James?"

"Who's Amber James?" Lee asked, completely confused.

"Just the hottest country music star in the whole freakin' universe," Sara squealed.

Maybe it was the headache, but it still didn't click with Lee. "Who is Amber James?" she asked again.

"That's what we were going to talk about later," Becka said. "I'm Amber James."

CHAPTER FORTY-ONE

The room became deathly silent.

"You mean you didn't know?" Sara asked in a hushed tone.

"No," Lee replied. "I didn't." She couldn't quite make up her mind as to whether she was mad or hurt or maybe a little of both. The fact that her daughter seemed to be more knowledgable about Becka than she did was not sitting well with her.

"Helen," her father said. "I think we should leave."

"Sit down, Richard." Her mother slipped to the edge of her seat.

Her father stood. "Helen, get up. Sara, you come with us and show us the way into town."

"Dad, you don't have to leave," Lee said.

"We're going to go see if perhaps there's a restaurant in town open. If so, we'll grab something and bring it back for dinner." Ignoring their protests, he ushered both of them out of the house.

As soon as the door closed, Lee went back into the kitchen, grabbed a large trash bag from the pantry and started dumping the half-cooked food into it.

"I know you're angry," Becka said from the doorway. "I did intend to tell you. I never dreamed anyone here would recognize me."

"I guess I should have mentioned earlier that my daughter is a huge music buff. She's particularly fond of country music for some ungodly reason."

"I take it you're not."

Lee placed the trash bag on the floor and sat down on a chair. "Becka." She stopped. "Or Amber, or whatever your name is, I'm tired. This was supposed to be a special day for my daughter. All she wanted was a simple Thanksgiving dinner with both of her parents in the same room." She shook her head and blinked back tears. "Was that too damn much to ask?"

Becka walked over and put a hand on Lee's shoulder. "No, it wasn't. It looks like you tried to give her that. Anyone could have forgotten to make that call."

"But it wasn't anyone. It was me. I was so busy trying to get everything else done that I spoiled the one thing she wanted. Well, Brandon didn't help."

"I suppose my sudden appearance didn't help any either."

Lee placed a hand on her forehead. "Actually, you probably prevented a huge family argument. If you hadn't gotten here when you did, I don't know what would have happened." She quickly filled Becka in on what had happened, then she stopped and peered up at her. "So why don't you have a seat here and tell me all about yourself before my daughter comes back."

Becka sat down. "There's not a lot to tell. I got tired of all the traveling and never being able to go outside without people running up to me. The final straw came when I woke up one morning to find a man shooting photos through my bedroom window. He had bribed my neighbor to let him climb one of their trees and crawled out on a limb near my bedroom. That didn't particularly shock me, but a short time later when the photos were published in one of the tabloids, there was a woman in bed with me. I'm not sure who she was since I'd never met her, but it caused a big ruckus." She looked at Lee. "Now, understand that everyone who works for me knows I'm a lesbian. I never tried to hide from any of them. Every label I've ever had was aware of it. They don't care, but they don't want the general public to know. So when the tabloid hit the stores, my record label went a little crazy. They started talking about a marriage of convenience, a lawsuit and a bunch of other crap. When I refused to have anything to do with it, they started talking about arranging an international tour that would keep me out of the country until all the fuss died down. I was already tired and I suppose that was just the last straw. I told them I wanted out, but they wouldn't release me from my contract. They threatened to sue. Honestly, I didn't care, until I realized that several other people would be hurt. People I cared for. So rather than face the problem, I simply ran away one night."

"Is that when you came here?" Lee asked.

"Yes. Since I hadn't been in the area since I was a child, I was certain that no one would come around looking for me. I was a little concerned that some of the older people here might recognize me, but then I realized that even if they did, they would never say anything."

Lee nodded. "Everyone minds their own business, especially the older folks. They would have kept quiet out of respect for your family, too."

"Exactly. My family knows who I am, of course, and I'm sure a few of the locals might have figured out who I am, but none of them ever said anything. I even had a minor scare in town when a tourist kept following me around. I guess the hair made her doubt it was me." She glanced up and blushed slightly. "I always wore a long, blond wig when I performed. It helped make me less recognizable when I went out."

"That's why you reacted the way you did when Melinda Thayer thought she knew you."

"Yes. People like you and her scared me most. I mean the outsiders who had moved in. I couldn't predict how you all would respond if you recognized me." She gazed at Lee and smiled. "I certainly never anticipated meeting anyone like you." She leaned forward and took Lee's hand. "I swear I never meant to hurt you."

"Why did you have to leave? If no one knew who you were, why not just stay here?"

"After I met you I realized I wanted my life back. That's why I went back and entered into negotiations to buy out my contract." She squeezed Lee's hand. "Financially, I'm considerably poorer than I was a few weeks ago, but at least I'm completely free."

"What are you going to do now?" Lee asked as her body began to respond to the warmth of Becka's hand on hers.

"I don't know yet, but whatever it is, I want you there beside me."

A small, scared portion of Lee's brain told her to run because this woman could break her heart, but at some point she had to take a chance or spend the rest of her life alone. Maybe now was the time to do so. "I think—no, I know, I'd like to be there beside you."

The phone rang.

Lee looked at it and shook her head. "That's probably my parents calling to tell me they've decided to drive all the way to Little Rock in search of a restaurant."

"I think it's sweet that your dad hustled everyone out so we'd have some time."

Lee picked up the phone. It was Gladys "What's this I'm hearing about you having a half-cooked turkey?"

"How did you hear about that?"

"Girl, I have my ways. Get yourself and that cute girlfriend of yours over here to my house right now. And bring any food that's salvageable with you. Dewayne invited some of the single guys from his crew and we have a houseful of hungry people."

"I'm not going to horn in on your holidays," Lee said.

"Oh, cut the dramatics and get your butt over here. By the

way, I'm holding your parents and daughter hostage, in case you two need a few more minutes alone." She laughed as she hung up the phone.

"That was Gladys," Lee said. "We've been instructed to bring all salvageable food and our butts to her house for dinner." She stood and offered a hand to Becka. "She said she'd keep the family busy if we needed a few extra minutes."

Becka stood and pressed her body against Lee. "Do we need a few minutes?"

"I'm afraid I might require several decades."

Becka tilted her head up. "Why don't you show me a quick sample of what I've got to look forward to?"

Lee kissed her and let her hands drift down Becka's hips. She pulled Becka tighter against her.

"What are you up to?" Becka asked.

Lee undid Becka's slacks and pushed them down until they hit the floor. "I was thinking about having a small Thanksgiving feast here before we leave."

CHAPTER FORTY-TWO

Dinner was in full swing by the time Lee and Becka finally arrived. Gladys met them to help them carry in the box of wine that Brandon had left and the pies that Lee had baked earlier that morning. Gladys quickly got them seated and their plates full.

Someone mentioned the Merlot was cold and Becka was soon passing on her extensive knowledge of wine. Conversation flowed freely as the guys from Dewayne's crew laughed and joked. Lee couldn't help but think about Joan Depew and Jefferson's parents. Their holiday table would have an empty place. She wondered where Ollie Waters was today and if there was anyone for him to share his holiday meal. As they continued to eat, Lee made a mental list of all that she had to be thankful for.

Becka seemed to sense her mood and pressed the side of her foot against Lee's. "Don't worry so much," she murmured. "Everything will be fine. Granny Depew said so," she added with a smile.

"If Granny Depew said so, then I have to believe it's true," Lee said. She lifted her glass. "Here's to Granny Depew."

The guy sitting next to her must have thought Lee was offering a toast, because he picked up his glass and said loudly. "Here's to Granny Depew."

After dinner, they all pitched in to help clear the table. To Lee's dismay, Sara volunteered to do the dishes. "I'll help her," Becka said. "Why don't you go talk to your mom? She seemed sort of down at dinner."

Lee had noticed it also. She looked across to where her mom was busy putting leftovers into plastic bowls. "All right, but don't let Sara finagle you into anything. She's a little con artist at heart." Lee picked up a bowl of green beans and a platter of rolls. "Should I put these rolls in a bowl or just wrap the plate?" she asked as she approached her mom.

"I usually just put a sheet of plastic wrap over them. You know how your father snacks all night." She snapped the lid onto a bowl and paused. "Lee, I'm sorry about this afternoon."

"I was sort of surprised to discover that you were in cahoots with Brandon," Lee admitted.

"He made it all sound so good when he called. It was like a marriage of convenience. You would still have your freedom to do as you want and at the same time you would have the security and respectability of marriage."

Lee lowered her voice. "Mom, you know that financially I'm set for life. My paintings alone would more than support me. I rarely touch any of the money that Dad gave me."

"But you need a husband."

"Why?" Lee asked, amazed that her mother felt that way.

"To look after you and take care of things, like the car and the plumbing. I don't know. I just think women need husbands."

Lee was tempted to say that her mother was just spoiled, but she kept her opinions to herself. "Things are different for me. I can take care of those things myself."

"You couldn't even keep your propane tank filled."

Lee's anger nearly got the best of her, but she knew that it was because her mom had hit a sore spot. Then she remembered what Becka had told her. "Mom, I didn't aim to bring this up, but maybe it would help if you knew what I'd been doing for the past few weeks." She told her everything that had happened with the animals killed by the shooter, Jefferson Depew being shot, her seeing Ollie Waters, the shoplifting incident, her windows being shot out, the law catching the two who were responsible and finally about Gladys's back and her own wrist. "So you see Mom, I've had a couple of other things on my mind. I simply forgot the propane."

"My God, Lee, why didn't you call your father?"

"Because I could handle it and did. Don't you see? I can take care of myself. I don't need a man."

"Don't you ever get lonesome?"

Lee dumped the green beans into a plastic bowl and snapped on the lid. "I suppose I do sometimes, but I am so busy that honestly I rarely thought about it until recently."

Her mother looked toward the kitchen where Becka and Sara were laughing as they filled the dishwasher. "Are you...I mean, is it serious with her?" She put a hand to her cheek. "I'm sorry, but I don't know if I should call her Becka or Amber."

"Her name is Becka. Amber was her mother's name. Her manager liked it better," Lee said, repeating what Becka had told her on the drive over.

"Well, is it serious with Becka?"

"I don't know. I mean, we've only known each other for a short while." Lee looked toward the kitchen again. "I think it is. I do know that I've never felt like this with anyone before."

Her mother nodded. "Won't she have to be gone a lot with her career?"

"No. She's retired from music."

"She's so young. What is she going to do?"

"I don't think she's decided yet."

"Lee, why did you insist on taking that check from Brandon?

You know he doesn't have nearly as much money as you do."

Lee bit back a smile. "I have plans for it." A thought suddenly hit her. "In fact, you might be able to help me."

"Help you?" Her mother's head came up. "How could I help you?"

"I want to open an art school here. Nothing fancy, but I want it to be an excellent school. I've seen and heard of so many people who wanted to paint or draw and never got the opportunity for one reason or another." She took her mother's hand. "Mom, I don't know how to thank you and Dad for all the things you gave me. I always took them for granted and I'm sorry."

Her mother was clearly flustered. "That was all your father's doing. He worked hard so you and John could have a good life."

"It wasn't just Dad. Yes, he went to the store every morning but without you at home and sometimes even at the store helping him out, he never could have achieved all he did."

"I've been trying to tell her that for years." Lee turned at the sound of her father's voice. He plucked a roll off the plate and tore it open. "She doesn't seem to remember how she used to do the books for the store when I first opened it or how many times she had to do without things because every penny we had was tied up in the store." He said to Lee, "You and John don't remember any of this because by the time you were old enough to remember the store had already taken off. I couldn't have done without your mother."

"Oh, Richard. You exaggerate so."

"No, I don't, Helen. You're just too stubborn to admit that you're a capable woman in your own right." He took a bite of the roll and ate it. "Sometimes, I think she likes to pretend she's helpless. It leads people to misjudge her abilities and that's how she became such a powerhouse in those women's groups she belongs to. They like to pretend they're nothing more than a social group, but I know for a fact that during the last state elections they were solely responsible for the defeat of a senator who thought he had a lot of clout."

Lee's mother made a dismissive noise. "That man was a

fool."

"He certainly was for misjudging the power your group wielded."

"Lee was telling me about a school she wants me to help her start."

"Really?"

With both of her parents' full attention, Lee gave them the vague details of what she hoped the art school would become. "I want to be able to keep tuitions as low as possible and maybe even eventually be able to offer a few scholarships." As she spoke, new ideas came to her. "There are so many wonderful artists here. I know I could convince at least some of them to teach one or two classes a year. We could start with a spring session and a fall session."

"That certainly sounds like something the gallery should get behind," Gladys said as she joined the conversation.

"Elena Barrera is a friend of mine and she's absolutely rabid about promoting the arts," Lee's mother said. "I'm sure she would love to hear your idea."

"You don't think she'd mind that I'm in a different state?" Lee asked.

"Oh heavens no. She'd fly to the moon if she thought there was art up there."

"I don't know any artist types," her father said, "but I do know people with money." He smiled. "I've been fairly successful in helping them spend it over the years, so I might be able to roll a few donations your way."

"I know lots of musicians who love to jump on these bandwagons," Becka said as she appeared beside Lee.

"And I know a lot of poor students who would love to get some of this free money you're all so generous with," Sara said.

Lee laughed and put an arm around her daughter. "At least I know I'll have plenty of help with this project." She turned to Gladys. "I guess we can take it to the city council meeting in January. Right now everyone is too busy to think of starting anything new."

"Wait until March," her mother said. "Everyone will be too tired in January and too cold in February. Come March, spring fever starts kicking in and everyone is ready to start something new."

"That's a great point, Mrs. Randle," Becka said.

"Since it looks like you're about to become a member of the family, please call me Helen or something less formal."

"Can I call you Granny Randle?" Sara piped in.

"Only if you want to be sold to the gypsies." Lee's mother snapped another lid on a bowl of leftovers.

Hours later, Lee and Becka lay snuggled in Lee's bed. "Sara is a smart kid." Becka said.

"She's too smart sometimes," Lee said. "I have to hustle to keep one step ahead of her."

"She thinks I should open a wine shop," Becka said. "You should have heard her popping out all the information on market studies and such. I'm embarrassed to admit that she lost me about halfway through her spiel."

"I'm glad to hear all that tuition money isn't going to waste."

"No. Not at all. She's a smart kid."

They were silent for a few minutes before Lee spoke. "I drove by the old Peterson place the other day and it really looks nice."

"You know, I bought the place. It's now the James place."

Lee smiled. "It'll always be called the old Peterson place. After all these years, a lot of people still refer to this as the old Crane homestead."

"Do you think anyone will ever refer to it as the Dresher homestead?" Becka asked.

"No, they'll just say, 'that place over there where that lesbian woman lived.'"

"My moving here is really going to mess things up. They won't know which lesbian they're talking about."

"No, as soon as word gets around as to who you are, you'll be 'that singer woman.'"

Becka snuggled closer to Lee. "Do you think it's possible that maybe someday this entire section might become known as the Dresher/James homestead?"

Lee smiled in the darkness. "I think that might be a strong possibility."

Publications from
Bella Books, Inc.
The best in contemporary lesbian fiction

P.O. Box 10543, Tallahassee, FL 32302
Phone: 800-729-4992
www.bellabooks.com

AFTERSHOCK: Book two of the Shaken series by KG MacGregor. Anna and Lily have survived earthquake and dating, but new challenges may prove their undoing.
ISBN: 978-1594931352 $13.95

BEAUTIFUL JOURNEY by Kenna White. Determined to do her part during the Battle for Britain, aviatrix Kit Anderson has no time for Emily Mills, who certainly has no time for her, either, not when their hearts are in the line of fire.
ISBN: 978-1594931284 $13.95

MIDNIGHT MELODIES by Megan Carter. Family disputes and small town tensions come between Erica Boyd and and her best chance at romance in years.
ISBN: 978-1-594931-37-6 $13.95

WHITE OFFERINGS by Ann Roberts. Realtor-turned-sleuth Ari Adams helps a friend find a stalker, only to begin receiving white offerings of her own. Book 2 in series.
ISBN: 978-1-594931-21-5 $13.95

HER SISTER'S KEEPER by Diana Rivers. A restless young Hadra is caught up in a daring raid on the Gray Place, but is captured and must stand trial for her crimes against the state. Book 6 in series.
ISBN: 978-1-594931-12-3 $13.95

LOSERS WEEPERS by Jessica Thomas. Alex Peres must sort out a possible kidnapping hoax and the death of a friend, and finds that the two cases have a surprising number of mutual suspects. Book 4 in series.
ISBN: 978-1-594931-27-7 $13.95

COMPULSION by Terri Breneman. Toni Barston's lucky break in a case turns into a nightmare when she becomes the target of a compulsive murderess. Book "C" in series.
ISBN: 978-1-594931-26-0 $13.95

THE KISS THAT COUNTED by Karin Kallmaker. CJ Roshe is used to hiding from her past, but meeting Karita Hanssen leaves her longing to finally tell someone her real name.
ISBN: 978-1-594931-31-4 $13.95

SECRETS SO DEEP by KG MacGregor. Glynn Wright's son holds a secret that is destroying him, but confronting it could mean the end of their family. Charlotte Blue is determined to save them both.
ISBN: 978-1-594931-25-3 $13.95

ROOMMATES by Jackie Calhoun. Two freshmen co-eds from two different worlds discover what it takes to choose love.
ISBN: 978-1-594931-23-9 $13.95

WHEN IT'S ALL RELATIVE by Therese Szymanski. Brett Higgins must confront her worst enemies: her family. Book 8 in series.
ISBN: 978-1-594931-09-3 $13.95

THE RAINBOW CEDAR by Gerri Hill. Jaye Burns' relationship is falling apart inspite of her efforts to keep it together. When Drew Montgomery offers the possibility of a new start, Jaye is torn between past and future.
ISBN-13: 978-1594931246 $13.95

TRAINING DAYS by Jane Frances. A passionate tryst on a long-distance train might be the undoing of Morgan's career—and her heart.
ISBN: 978-1594931-22-2 $13.95

CHRISTABEL by Karin Kallmaker. Dina Rowland must accept her magical heritage to save supermodel Christabel from the demon of their past who has found them in the present.
ISBN: 978-1-594931-34-5 $13.95

BEACH TOWN by Ann Roberts. Actress Kira Drake nurtures her dreams of stardom from the depths of the closet, which makes any hope of a future with Flynn impossible.
ISBN: 978-1-594931-32-1 $13.95

THE CANDIDATE by Tracey Richardson. Presidential candidate Jane Kincaid always expected to pay the toll the road to the White House would exact, but she didn't expect to have to choose between her heart and her political destiny.
ISBN: 978-1-594931-33-8 $13.95

WITHOUT WARNING: Book one in the Shaken series by KG MacGregor. A story of courageous survival that leads to steadfast love.
ISBN: 978-1-594931-20-8 $13.95